ALSO BY KASIE WEST

The Distance Between Us

Pivot Point

Split Second

On the Fence

The Fill-In Boyfriend

P.S. I Like You

By Your Side

Love, Life, and the List

Lucky in Love

Listen to Your Heart

Fame, Fate, and the First Kiss

Maybe This Time

Moment of Truth

Sunkissed

Kasie West

DELACORTE PRESS

Text copyright © 2021 by Kasie West
Jacket art copyright © 2021 by Anne Hard
Jacket lettering copyright © 2021 by Jill De Haan

All rights reserved. Published in the United States by Delacorte Press, an imprint of Random House Children's Books, a division of Penguin Random House LLC, New York.

Delacorte Press is a registered trademark and the colophon is a trademark of Penguin Random House LLC.

GetUnderlined.com

Educators and librarians, for a variety of teaching tools, visit us at RHTeachersLibrarians.com

Library of Congress Cataloging-in-Publication Data
Names: West, Kasie, author.
Title: Sunkissed / Kasie West.
Description: First edition. | New York : Delacorte Press, [2021] | Audience: Ages 12 and up. | Summary: Betrayed by her best friend and dragged off to a remote family camp, seventeen-year-old Avery's dreams of a perfect summer seem over until a whirlwind romance leads to an unexpected journey of self-discovery.
Identifiers: LCCN 2020031481 (print) | LCCN 2020031482 (ebook) | ISBN 978-0-593-17626-9 (hardcover) | ISBN 978-0-593-17627-6 (library binding) | ISBN 978-0-593-17628-3 (ebook)
Subjects: CYAC: Family life—Fiction. | Camps—Fiction. | Love—Fiction.
Classification: LCC PZ7.W51837 Sun 2021 (print) | LCC PZ7.W51837 (ebook) | DDC [Fic] —dc23

The text of this book is set in 11.2-Columbus MT Pro.
Interior design by Cathy Bobak

Printed in the United States of America
10 9 8 7 6 5 4 3 2 1
First Edition

To my big sister, Heather Garza. I've always looked up to you (even though you're the shortest in the family). Love you!

Chapter 1

I TOOK A BREATH AND CLOSED MY EYES, LETTING THE SUN-drenched glass warm me as I leaned my head against the car window. This was going to be a perfect summer. If I said it enough times, it would come true. After everything that had happened this week, I needed a good summer. The one before my senior year was mine to claim, Dad had said months ago. I was ready to claim it.

Up front, my parents had turned the radio to barely audible but I could just make out a Taylor Swift song. My AirPods had lost their charge ten minutes ago, rendering the remainder of my perfectly curated road trip playlist—*Stuck in the Backseat with You*—useless. As I felt myself drifting toward sleep, my sister's voice rang out louder than necessary from beside me.

"Hey, viewers. Happy summer! We're on hour four of our car ride and so ready to be done. Say hi to my older sister, Avery!"

Lauren had her elbows propped on the pillows between us and was holding up her phone, the camera facing me. Behind her phone, she gave a silent plea that said, *Give me something, anything, aside from*

1

your normal boring face. Since boring was the face I was born with, I held up a peace sign, which apparently was good enough, because she flipped the recording back to her. "This year, the parents are taking us to the middle of the forest. Are you ready to join us?" She pointed the camera out the car window, the tall pine trees zooming by in a hazy blur.

The middle of the forest wasn't exactly how I'd describe the four-star family camp we'd be spending the summer at, but exaggeration is the key to any good social media video. I shook my AirPod case as if that would make them charge faster. I needed some noise-canceling, head-clearing music.

"Did you girls pack your swimsuits?" Mom asked, even though there was nothing we could do about it now, four hours from home, if we hadn't.

Lauren dropped her hand. "Mom, I was recording."

"Oh, sorry," Mom whispered.

"Well, I'm not anymore."

"I hear there's a huge Slip 'N Slide at this camp," Dad said, as if this was the most exciting thing a seventeen- and a fifteen-year-old could hear. "Supersized for super kids." He laughed at his own joke, and I couldn't help but laugh too.

Lauren gave me the *Really?* look, then said, "There's real water, too, though, right?"

"Real water?" Mom asked.

"A lake or something?"

"Yes, there's a lake *and* a pool," Dad responded as he took a curve too fast, pushing me against the door.

"I don't know why we couldn't just go to the camp we went to a couple years ago," Lauren complained. "It was closer and the roads weren't so windy."

"Because this year is our epic adventure," Dad said. "Next summer Avery will be so busy prepping for college she'll boycott a family vacation."

"So true," I said, and smiled when my mom turned around to make sure she shouldn't be offended. When she saw my face, she gave my leg a little slap.

Both my parents had summers off. Mom was a professor at UCLA and Dad taught sixth grade and coached middle-school basketball. So most summers for as long as I could remember, we went on an "adventure." Sometimes it was a cabin on the lake or a KOA near the beach. And most of the time, it really was an adventure. Sometimes even a good one.

My phone vibrated against my thigh on the seat next to me, and I immediately tensed. I didn't want to look. I didn't want to read more excuses. I was trying to start my perfect summer. It buzzed again. I sucked in a breath and looked at the screen. As I expected, it was from my best friend, Shay.

I'm sorry. I can't go the whole summer knowing you're mad at me. It was an accident.

I wasn't sure how one *accidentally* kissed their best friend's exboyfriend. Trent and I had only been broken up for a couple weeks! I had even thought we might get back together. Now I wondered if Shay was the real reason we'd broken up in the first place. They obviously liked each other. I felt stupid for thinking Trent and I had just hit a rough spot and would work it out.

Another message popped up.

It was a big mistake. We were both just talking about how you were leaving for the whole summer and how much we were going to miss you! Please forgive me.

I put the phone, screen down, on the seat, as if the messages would go away if I couldn't see them.

"Hello, everyone!" Lauren said again into her camera. "Time for our summer trek into a wooded forest. Trees and lakes and excitement. Hope you're all ready to join me. Say hi, Avery."

The recording was on me again. I could feel my eyes stinging from the texts. I clenched my teeth and willed myself to control the tears. Finally, I faced Lauren and puffed my cheeks out like a blowfish, a creature with a defense mechanism I could appreciate.

She lowered her phone and raised her eyebrows. "Can I post that?"

I honestly didn't care what her fifty followers thought of me. Well, actually I did . . . and I hated myself for that. But she was giving me that pleading look again.

I sighed. "Post away."

"Thank you!" Her eyes were back on her phone, watching the clip.

I turned my attention to the very-much-still-there texts on my phone.

Shay had been my best friend since the summer before third grade, when she declared me such through a fence. She'd moved into the house behind us, and we'd met one day when her ball flew over the fence and directly into my head. I'd given her ball back, and after that we talked every day through a crack for weeks before we convinced our parents to let us actually hang out. And that's

4

how it had felt when she told me what happened with Trent: like a ball to the head all over again—unexpected and embarrassing—except without the happy ending.

My dad took another curve too fast.

"Ugggh," Lauren said, grabbing her stomach. "I'm going to be sick."

I scooted closer to my window. The last thing I needed was a lapful of vomit.

Mom smacked Dad's arm. "Slow down." Then she turned in her seat. "Do you need a plastic bag?"

"Didn't you take Dramamine?" I asked.

"Yes, *Avery*, I took Dramamine. But obviously it's not helping."

"I was just asking," I said.

"You weren't just asking. You were trying to say I had done something wrong."

My sister and I weren't exactly best friends, which was why she had no idea about my crappy week or the unanswered texts waiting on my phone. Nobody knew. "I'm sorry. That's not what I meant."

I caught my dad's eye in the rearview mirror and he mouthed, *"Fire and Ice."*

For the past couple years, Dad had taken to calling my sister and me Fire and Ice. We were opposites in nearly every way. Lauren was dramatic and over the top; I was chill and go with the flow. Lauren's looks begged to be noticed. She was tall and strong and had bright blond hair and big *blue* eyes. She always seemed happy, even when she was being a total grump. I, on the other hand, was one of those people who blended in. I had plain brown hair and a normal build. My smile was nice but nothing that drew stares. I did like my eyes. They were hazel, and I could say a lot with my eyes. Even though we were opposites, I didn't love the nickname (who wanted to be compared to ice?) but I loved my dad and I knew he thought it was cute and funny, so I did what any chill person would do—ignored it.

"Pull over! Pull over!" Lauren screeched, unbuckling her seat belt.

Mom riffled around by her feet and Dad jerked the car to the right and stopped on the dirt shoulder. Mom held a plastic bag in the air just as my sister flung open the door, jumped out, and threw up all over the side of the road with loud, heaving retches. She was dramatic with everything she did, even barfing. She moaned, bracing her hands against her knees, waiting for another round.

Mom turned to Dad. "Not sure why you're in such a hurry."

"I'm just driving."

"You know she gets sick when you take the curves like that."

I looked down at my phone, still trying to decide how to respond.

It's great! I typed. *Now we can compare notes and buy him extra ChapStick.* I immediately erased the text. Now was not the time for a dumb joke. *It's fine,* I typed this time. *We'll be fine.*

My finger hovered over the SEND button. *Fine* wasn't how I felt. I felt betrayed and angry and confused and alone. I felt like I'd lost my best friend and my boyfriend in the same week. I wanted to give her the silent treatment for a while. But I hated feeling like this. I didn't want to lose her. The sooner I forgave her, the sooner we could get past this.

The muffled sound of my sister's voice drew my attention. With her back pressed against the window, she recorded another video. I couldn't hear what she was saying, but it was probably something about throwing up. I didn't understand her videos at all.

I squeezed my eyes shut and pushed SEND.

"Everything okay?" Mom asked. "You're not feeling sick, too, are you? You look a little pale."

"What?"

Mom studied my face.

"No, I'm fine." Was that my favorite word today?

The side door flew open and Lauren's phone appeared first. "There's no service," she said, sliding in.

"Huh," Mom responded, handing Lauren a water bottle. "Well, we are in the wooded mountains."

"There's going to be service at the camp, though, right?" she asked, pulling the door shut and buckling her seat belt.

"A summer without cell service wouldn't be the end of the world," Dad said.

"What?" Lauren gasped. "What do you mean? What does that mean?" Each question got increasingly louder.

"It said right on the website I sent both of you months ago," Mom said. "No Wi-Fi. A chance to disengage from the world."

"You think we actually read that?" Lauren responded.

Mom shrugged. "Maybe you will next time."

As my sister's words finally sank in, my chest tightened and my eyes slid to my phone. Sure enough, there was a red triangle next to my text. It hadn't sent. Maybe I should've been happy that the lack of cell service was fulfilling my fleeting wish of giving Shay the silent treatment, but instead I felt worse.

"I have a channel to maintain!" Lauren whined. "My viewers

are counting on me! I promised a summer of updates! This is completely and totally unfair. You have to warn us about stuff like this."

"Maybe this is the best thing for both of you," Mom said, exchanging a look with Dad.

I slid my half-charged AirPods into my ears and turned on my only downloaded playlist—*Emos Need Love Too*. Most of my song catalogue was stored online. So much for my perfect summer.

Chapter 2

DESPITE THE FACT THAT BEAR MEADOW CAMP APPARENTLY resided in the last century, it was quite beautiful. Nestled in the pine trees sat a huge multistory lodge, a warm beacon of yellow light in the darkness. And behind it, the sky was a confetti of white stars. I could get used to a summer of this view.

Dad pulled into a parking space in front of the lodge. "Here we are. Everyone grab your things and let's get checked in."

My sister, for once, was speechless as she stared out the window at the building in front of us. It didn't last long. "A place like that has to have Wi-Fi . . . right?" she asked me under her breath.

"Or at least a suggestion box," I said.

"What?"

I pretended to write on a little note. "Please add Wi-Fi. Thank you."

She blew air between her lips and climbed out of the car.

I pushed my door open and stepped out as well, joining my parents. The air had the sharp, tangy scent of pine needles and a crisp chill had me wondering if I should dig through my suitcase for a hoodie.

"It's cold here," Lauren said from the other side of the car. "Is it going to be this cold the whole summer?"

"Just after the sun goes down," Dad said. "Isn't this so exciting, girls?" He gave me a side hug.

"Think of the potential!" Lauren said in a deep voice, quoting what Dad always said at the beginning of every summer trip. Sometimes I wondered if my dad was more excited about what a trip could be than what it actually ended up being.

"Exactly," he responded. "Our last summer together before everything changes."

"Are you getting a new family?" I asked, pulling out a joke before he made this too serious. I still had a whole year left of high school before college. Plus, if everything went as planned, I'd be going to UCLA and would probably live at home. Exactly how much did he think would change? I had a feeling nothing would and I wasn't sure if I should be relieved or disappointed about that thought.

"Maybe I can trade you all in here for younger models." He popped open the trunk.

Mom shot him a look as she clutched her pillow to her chest.

"I didn't mean you," he said. "I meant the kids because they're growing up and leaving us."

"Yeah, yeah, nice save," Mom said.

We unloaded the car and trudged up the paved path to the tall wooden doors of the lodge. My backpack was full of summer homework for my fall honors classes, and my suitcase was at max capacity because two months away required a lot of clothes. Dad held open the door and we all made our way inside.

The lobby was just as beautiful as the outside had been. A large oak tree sprung from the middle of the circular room, its branches reaching toward the skylight above. Everything else was wood—the floors, the desks, even the ceiling, almost as if we had walked into a tree.

Music drifted from a hall on the opposite end of the room.

Lauren sank to the bench that circled the tree as my dad went to the check-in desk, where a girl who didn't look much older than me sat ready to help. A big letter *D* adorned her green polo shirt. Was that her name or her initial?

"Hello! Welcome to Bear Meadow," she said in an overly friendly voice. "Last name, please."

I let my heavy backpack slide off my shoulder and onto the ground next to Lauren, abandoning my suitcase there as well.

"Young," Dad said.

"Welcome, Youngs." D typed something into her computer and then opened a tri-fold pamphlet in front of my parents. "We're here at the lodge. This is where the action happens. Movies on Friday nights." She pointed to the hall where the music was coming from. "Bingo nights on Wednesdays."

"I think I could get into bingo," Dad said.

D gave him a wide smile. "We also have dance lessons and crafts. Basically, something happens every day in this building."

"That's great!" Mom said, waggling her eyebrows at us. Lauren rolled her eyes.

"On the lawn area behind the lodge there's Grass Games—

11

badminton, volleyball, and such—then we have our tennis courts and pool."

"We heard you have a supersized Slip 'N Slide," I said, and my dad gave me an appreciative smile.

"We certainly do. The biggest one in California!" D responded with enthusiasm. She pointed at the map again. "The dining hall is in the middle of the cabins. That's where you'll have your meals."

"*All* of them?" Lauren asked.

D looked at the computer. "Your package includes two meals a day. We have a small general store, where we carry milk and cereal and such for that third meal."

While D showed my parents the road that led to our cabin, the lodge doors opened and a family of five came in. Two of the kids immediately began chasing each other around the tree, which at the moment also included Lauren and me, screaming about a bigfoot hunt. The woman went straight to the coffee station and poured herself a cup.

"Boys, stop running!" the man called out in a sharp tone, then went to stand in line behind my parents.

Lauren opened the front pocket of her backpack and dug around. "Movie nights, crafts, Slip 'N Slides?" she said at a volume only I could hear. "Is this a little kid camp?" At this, she pointedly stared at the kids who had not, in fact, stopped running. "I'm sensing no age-appropriate boys for us."

This thought did not disappoint me in the least. I had sworn off guys exactly three days ago. The guy drama I was in the middle of had left a bad taste in my mouth. The taste I worried would linger all summer now that I had no contact with the outside world.

Lauren freed a long cord from her bag with a breath of relief. "Oh good. I thought I forgot this."

"Good thing you can keep your overpriced flashlight charged."

"I haven't lost hope for Wi-Fi. And even if there isn't any, I can still record and do a compilation video at the end of summer. I'll figure something out," she said, like she was still talking herself down.

I wondered if I'd figure something out, a way to talk to Shay and get this taste out of my mouth, this weight off my chest.

The music from the hall caught my attention again and I moved to see where it was coming from. I had only taken a few steps before one of the boys running around the tree and the woman with her full cup of coffee collided, sending the cup flying. I watched as it tumbled through the air in seemingly slow motion. Its contents arced across the space between us, then drenched the entire front of my white shirt. The cup landed, drumming three short beats on the floor, before it skidded across the dark wood and came to a stop against my gray Converse. I didn't feel the heat of the liquid at first but then the burning sensation spread across my stomach. I sucked in air and pulled my shirt away from my skin.

"Oh my goodness!" D called from behind me.

"Boys!" the man said again.

The woman, now empty-handed, stared at me and then at the cup by my foot as if this was somehow my fault. "I'm sorry," I heard myself saying.

My mom had magically found a roll of paper towels somewhere and began mopping up the floor. My dad was helping Lauren move our luggage away from the expanding puddle on the floor. I wasn't sure how any coffee had made it on the floor, when it felt like an entire pot's worth was on my shirt. "You okay, Avery?" Dad asked.

By this time D was at my side. "The bathroom is this way. Follow me." And without a word, I did. We walked through the lobby to the hall where I'd heard the music. It was louder now—was it a movie? A radio?—but as we passed the doors where it was obviously coming from, I couldn't see inside. D continued to the end of the hall.

Once safely inside the bathroom, I took off my shirt, throwing it onto the counter, and studied my skin. It was red but not burned. D grabbed a paper towel off a stack on the counter, ran it under cold water, then handed it to me. I pressed the wet towel against my stomach.

"Should I get the nurse?" she asked.

"What? No." I already felt stupid enough. "I'm good."

"Are you sure?"

"I take really hot showers. Apparently, I've conditioned my skin for this specific scenario."

She didn't laugh, just picked up my shirt. "I'll have this laundered and delivered to your cabin." She backed out of the bathroom and the door swung shut.

I took a deep breath and slowly peeled the paper towel away from my stomach for another look. The redness was already subsiding. I dropped the towel in a gold-trimmed trash bin and faced the door.

I probably should've realized before this moment that I was standing there in my bra, my shirt in the possession of an eager-to-please (or probably more like a please-don't-sue-us) employee, and I

14

was trapped. I let out a low groan and turned a circle. The bathroom was nice—the stalls individual rooms with full doors, the counters shiny granite, and the fixtures polished brass. There was even art on the walls. But it didn't have the one thing I needed—a stack of extra shirts lying around.

Just as I was trying to think of a way to fashion one out of paper towels, the door opened again and D reappeared.

I took a breath of relief. "Could you ask my—"

Before I could finish the sentence, she held out a blue T-shirt. "Here you go."

"Or you could bring me exactly what I need."

She smiled. "Do you need anything else?"

"Coffee?"

She hesitated for a moment.

"It was a joke."

"Oh . . ." She gave the worst courtesy laugh ever and left.

I unfolded the shirt and held it up. Across the back was the Bear Meadow Camp logo—a friendly bear in front of three pine trees—and on the front, the word STAFF.

"Thank goodness for please-don't-sue-us employees," I mumbled, and pulled it over my head.

I leaned against the counter for a moment and looked in the mirror above the sink. My brown hair hung limp around my shoulders and my hazel eyes were tired. Was it too late to go home?

I let out a sharp breath. I knew home wasn't an option, but a bed was a good second choice, one that only existed outside of this bathroom. I ran my fingers through my hair, wiped a bit of mascara from beneath my eyes, and exited the bathroom.

This time as I passed the doors where I'd heard the music earlier, I stopped and peered inside.

The room was a small theater with stadium-style seats facing the stage. At the moment, the seats were dark and empty. But the stage was lit and a three-person band, surrounded by instruments, stood talking among themselves. I wondered what events here required a live band. Bingo night?

"Are you lost?" a voice said, startling me.

To my right, behind the last row of red velvet chairs, was another guy, squatting by a guitar case, closing the lid. He had long, wavy hair and intense blue eyes that seemed to stare right through me.

I almost took a step back. "You scared me."

He stood, and even though he was an average size, there was something about his posture or confident gaze or knowing head tilt that commanded the space. "You new here?" His question didn't sound rude, but it wasn't friendly either.

"Yes, just got here." A clash of cymbals echoed through the theater and I looked over to see the drummer, a big Polynesian guy, standing up.

"Sorry!" he called out, and then did a drumroll on his snare and laughed.

"Are you . . . Is this . . . a band?" I asked the guy near me.

His eyebrows shot up.

"I mean, obviously it is, but why?"

A half-smile finally crept onto his face, lighting up his eyes and making him seem more approachable. If a half-smile could do all that, I found myself wondering what his full smile was capable of.

"Mostly for, you know . . . the music," he said.

I rolled my eyes but also smiled. "The music? How unoriginal. I'd do it for the groupies . . . or the drugs."

"I've known for years that I'm a total sellout," he shot back.

My smile widened. I couldn't help it. He was the first person tonight who seemed to actually get my dumb jokes. "So where can this music be heard?"

"We play at dinner."

"Live dinner music? How fancy."

"Nothing but the best for our entitled guests."

I blinked, not sure if he intended that as a dig or not. No, we'd just been joking. It was a joke. "Well, if music isn't a human right, it should be."

"Agreed." He lifted his guitar case.

"Brooks! You coming?" another bandmate yelled out. The three of them were heading toward the black curtain at the back of the stage.

Brooks held up his hand to them, his eyes still on me. "Yeah!" His hand dropped to his side. "And you are?" he asked, seeming to imply that his name being called had counted as an introduction.

I sort of agreed. "Avery."

"Avery. We have band practice most nights after dinner. Next time come a little earlier and tell me what you think." And then the full smile I'd been waiting for took over his face. And I was right, it was magic.

I gave a small nod.

He walked several steps past me, up the aisle, then turned. "Is Janelle showing you around?"

"Um . . . no." I threw a thumb over my shoulder. "D."

"Well, then, welcome to Bear Meadow, where your paycheck will be small and your patience even smaller."

"What?" was my first confused response. And then, just as fast, I remembered the shirt I wore. The staff shirt. He thought I worked here.

I opened my mouth to correct him but found myself saying, "Thank you," instead. *Why* would I say that? Two reasons came to mind immediately. One, I hated making people feel stupid, and two, he still had on that magic smile.

He half jogged to the stage, joining the other guys. I tugged on the bottom of the shirt. Dumb shirt.

"There you are," Lauren said from behind me. "Everyone is waiting on you. What are you even doing?" She looked past me to the now completely empty theater.

"Nothing. I'm coming."

Back in the lobby, the coffee-spilling mom and her family were up at the counter listening to D explain the camp amenities. My parents were at the entrance with our luggage.

"Everything okay?" Dad asked as I joined them.

"All good," I said.

"You should go beat that lady up," Lauren said, narrowing her eyes toward the check-in desk.

I shook my head. "I think I stepped into the kid's way or something." It was the only thing I could think of—that the kid had been trying to avoid me. Why else would the woman have acted like it was my fault? "But maybe I'll go find that suggestion box." I pretended to write on a paper. "More Wi-Fi, less hot liquids."

Lauren let out a big impatient sigh.

Dad winked at me. "Fire and Ice."

"Right," I said. *Just let it roll off, Avery. Let everything roll right off.*

Mom held out several card keys. "Let's go see our home for the next couple months."

Chapter 3

"HAVE A FABULOUS DAY!" THE GIRL SAID AS SHE USED A pair of tongs to put a whole-wheat roll on my plate. It was dinnertime and we were in the big dining hall—buffet-style eating in what looked a lot like a school cafeteria. Unlike the big lodge and our family cabin, which seemed newly built, the dining hall was probably a relic from the camp's past—paneled ceiling, fluorescent lighting, oak-trimmed doorways. But they'd done a good job hiding all that with nice tables and chairs and big framed art of the lake and surrounding forests.

After settling into our cabin the night before, we'd woken up this morning and spent the day exploring camp—the general store, the sports courts, the lake, the lodge—my dad pointing out all the activities we could try over the summer. And even though the only thing we'd ended up doing that day was a family game of badminton, I was ready to spend the rest of the night back in the cabin reading or something.

"Will you say that again for my video?" Lauren said, holding up her phone, as if it really wasn't a question at all but a demand.

"Excuse me?" the girl asked. Her name tag said TIA.

"The 'have a fabulous day' thing. While you're putting a roll on my plate." She lifted her plate so it was in the shot.

"Lauren, not everyone wants to be an extra in your film." I sympathized with the helpless look on Tia's face.

Lauren waved her hand in my direction. "It's not a film. I have a channel. It's really just pieces of my life. This will be part of an end-of-summer mash-up. Please?"

"Sure!" Tia said, suddenly unleashing a dazzling smile.

Guess she didn't need my help. It's not like anyone would see it anyway. Who wanted to watch pieces of our boring life? I moved to the next station and filled a plate with lettuce and tomatoes, then drenched it in ranch. Several families sat around the dining hall, each at their own circular table. My parents waved me over to where they were already eating.

I slid into the seat across from my mom. The phone in my pocket dug into my hip, so I took it out and set it on the table next to my plate.

"It's my music," I said when Mom looked at the phone like it was pointless to carry around. "I won't listen to it now, of course." I liked music when I was walking around. A soundtrack for life.

"You don't need it anyway. They have live music during dinner." She craned her head around.

My heart seemed to stop. I couldn't believe I had forgotten—

Brooks and his band performed at dinner. I sank a little lower in my chair, my lie from the night before replaying in my mind.

Just as it registered that I couldn't hear any music, Mom turned back around and said, "They must be on break or something. They were playing when Dad and I first got here."

In the corner of the cafeteria was a makeshift stage with the abandoned instruments. It was mostly blocked from my view by my mom.

"They announced a ten-minute break a little while ago," Dad said.

Ten minutes. I could eat in less than ten minutes. Because avoiding Brooks seemed like the mature way to solve this problem I'd created. I sighed. Like avoiding Shay before we left had been? No, I'd clear things up, but not now, in the middle of the dining hall. Especially because my explanation would sound something like: *Well, you were smiling, so you can see how I couldn't correct you about me working here.*

"I added another item to my birthday list," Lauren said as she plopped her plate on the table and her body in the seat next to me. "A handheld phone stabilizer. It will help with my videos."

"Your birthday is not for five months," Dad said.

"I know. I'm giving you all plenty of time."

I knew my parents, especially my dad, thought her hobby was just that, a hobby. But they mostly kept quiet about it while redirecting her attention to other things.

Mom pointed to a laminated schedule that sat in the middle of the table. "If either of you are interested, there's a motivational speaker down at the lower amphitheater tonight," she said, in a perfect example of redirection.

"What are they motivating us to do?" I asked.

Lauren spread her arms wide. "Live a productive life without internet."

"Knit socks and bake banana bread?" I asked with a smirk.

Mom rolled her eyes. "Really? Is that what you think pre-internet life was like?"

"You probably also mapped stars and wrote poetry," I said.

Dad raised his fork. "I actually did take an astronomy class one semester in college." He flipped the schedule around to face him. "I wouldn't be surprised if they offered some stargazing here. . . . Aha!" He stabbed his fork into the middle of the page, his eyes lighting up. "All your wishes come true."

I smiled, looking between Dad's fork and his goofy expression. The stars the night before had been pretty amazing. It *would* be fun to learn more than the basic constellations.

I shoveled a couple bites of salad into my mouth, then stood.

"You done already?" Dad asked.

I swallowed. "Yes, that badminton earlier really took it out of me." I lifted my phone off the table.

Lauren scoffed at the lame excuse. Microphone feedback rang out and I dropped back into my seat as quickly as possible. That had *not* been ten minutes. Not even five.

"You don't have to stay," Dad said as if I'd changed my mind because of his question.

"It's fine, I'll leave when you guys do."

Lauren narrowed her eyes at me suspiciously, but continued to eat.

Brooks's voice came over the microphone. "We're back, and, just a

23

reminder, we take requests. The song list is on the back of the sched-ule on each table." Was he the lead singer?

"Hello," Lauren said, her eyes glued to the stage, which, un-like me, she could obviously see clearly. I ducked a little more and reached for the schedule at the same time Lauren did. I let her have it first.

"Hello, what?" Mom asked.

Lauren scanned the song list, then handed it to me. "Hello, cute band in the middle of the woods. Sign me up. Avery, check them out. Let's go request something."

I looked down the list, which contained mainly oldies—the Beach Boys, Elvis, the Beatles, and more. None of which were the punk rock vibe I'd heard the night before in passing. I peeked around Mom and watched as someone who wasn't Brooks began singing a Billy Joel song. He had a nice voice—smooth with just the right amount of rasp.

Dad, now staring at the band too, said, "They are way too old for you to be fraternizing with."

"How do you know how old they are?" Lauren asked.

I wasn't sure how old the others were, but Brooks hadn't seemed that old. Around my age maybe. Lauren was fifteen, though, so I could see why my dad was laying down the law.

"Plus," Mom said, "they work here. This isn't some dating camp. There are plenty of guests visiting that you can hook up with throughout the summer."

Lauren almost spit her mouthful of water all over the table.

I shook my head and whispered, "Mom, *hook up* means *have sex with*."

Now it was Mom's turn to be shocked. "That's not what I meant!"

"When did the meaning of that change?" Dad asked.

Lauren laughed, then stared longingly at her phone. "I wish I had been recording this whole conversation."

"Any good songs on there?" Dad asked, nodding at the list I held.

I passed it over and then wished I hadn't when Mom scooted her chair closer to Dad's, leaving me completely exposed. I sat still, knowing movement would only draw attention. None of the band members were looking at me. The singer, a wiry white guy with floppy brown hair, held the microphone stand with both hands as he sang. His body hardly moved. The buff Polynesian guy behind the drums looked like he'd rather be anywhere else. The bleached-blond guy on bass kept looking at the wall, where, following his gaze, I noticed a clock. And the commanding presence of Brooks I'd noted the night before was only half as commanding. He seemed as though he wanted to blend into the paint on the wall as he stood there strumming his guitar with zero energy.

I was surprised, but then noted the dining hall was loud with talking and clattering dishes and laughter, nobody paying much attention to the band. That would be a hard audience to perform to. As if he sensed me looking, Brooks's eyes caught mine.

Crap.

I gave him a little smile and a small wave. As he took in the table and my family, his brows went down. Maybe he didn't recognize me. Or maybe he was trying to fit me into the story he'd previously thought was true. He didn't return my smile, just looked away.

Over the next half hour, as my parents and Lauren carried on a conversation I pretended to be part of but didn't follow at all, I tried to catch his eye. I wanted to mouth *"Sorry"* or something. But he didn't look my way again.

Was he mad? Why would he be? We didn't know each other. It was just a silly misunderstanding. I'd clear it up. He'd caught me off guard the night before. That's all I had to say and then it would be over.

So when my parents announced they were done and stood to leave, Lauren standing as well, I said, "I'm going to check out the dessert bar."

"Okay, see you back at the cabin," Dad said.

Lauren pointed to the stage and said something to my mom as they walked away. My mom only shook her head.

I listened to three more slow-paced, low-energy songs before Brooks leaned into a mic and said, "That's a wrap. Thanks for being a good audience. We'll see you tomorrow."

I clapped, but when nobody else joined me, I let my hands fall back to the table. Then I watched as Brooks and the guys gathered up their instruments and walked through a door off the side of the stage. I stood, looked over my shoulder, and followed. I caught up with them on the back side of the building, where they were loading the drums and guitars onto a flat trailer attached to a golf cart. I stopped by the back door.

"We should put a tip jar on the edge of the stage," the drummer was saying. "Supplement our income, yeah? Tell me that's not the best idea you've ever heard." He held out a fake jar. "We take hundreds, people. Or fifties. Those work too." At this he laughed loudly.

The bass player slapped at his neck, the action making me aware of the bugs I could see dancing around in the last streaks of light from the setting sun.

Brooks shook his head. "They don't even clap for us, Kai. You think they'd cough up money?"

"Come on, have some imagination."

Brooks plucked a drumstick from the front pocket of Kai's shirt and pretended to stab him in the gut with it.

"Ugh!" Kai grabbed his stomach and stumbled forward. "Ian, Levi, save me." He reached out for the two guys who stood there as unimpressed by this performance as they were with their own earlier onstage.

"How many more drum pieces inside?" Brooks asked.

"Just one of the cymbals and the snare," Kai responded, recovered from his fake injury. "Oh, and the pedal."

Brooks turned back toward the door, toward me, and stopped cold when he saw me. After that initial reaction, he was in motion again. "You like to linger in doorways?" he asked as he swept past me and back inside. The friendly manner we had ended on the night before was completely gone.

I followed him. "No, I mean, I'm sorry."

The cafeteria was emptying out and employees were wiping down surfaces and putting away food. Brooks hopped up onstage and grabbed the two drum pieces by their stands. As he stared at the pedal still on the ground, it was obvious he was trying to figure out a way to pick it up too. I stepped onto the stage and scooped it off the floor.

"You're sorry for what?" he asked, heading back the way we'd come.

"I'm sorry that you assumed I worked here and—"

"*Assumed?*" he asked. "You were wearing a staff shirt and when I said 'Welcome to Bear Meadow,' you said thank you."

I groaned. "I know."

"Well, I hope you won," he said.

We'd stepped outside again and I stopped on the gravel path just short of the guys and the golf cart. "Won?"

He turned to face me. "Whatever bet you had going with your friend. Trick an employee or mock an employee or sneak into the lodge after hours and steal some stupid T-shirt for whatever night-time prank you wanted to play. I know your type and I'm over it."

"My type?"

He stood there with a drum in each hand like a weird version of Lady Justice with her scales in one hand and her sword in the other. "Yes," he said, obviously not needing any more evidence in his case. "Your type—entitled, rich snob."

I sucked in a sharp breath and tightly gripped the pedal in my hands. I wanted to chuck it at him. Say something equally rude back. But as it often did when faced with conflict, my brain went blank. He didn't need a response; he finished his walk to the trailer.

It took me a second to realize the lead singer with his floppy brown hair and kind eyes was now standing in front of me, reaching for the pedal. It was obvious he'd heard everything and felt sorry for me. I thrust the pedal forward and he took it without a word; then they all drove away, the cymbals in the trailer clanking together over each bump.

That's when I let out an angry breath. How dare he. One tiny misunderstanding and I was suddenly a snob? All the things I should've said when Brooks was standing in front of me now flooded my brain. "Useless brain," I muttered.

I turned down the nearest path and started walking.

Chapter 4

"EXCUSE ME," I CALLED OUT TO A GIRL WITH A NAME badge on.

She turned. Her tag said MARICELA. She had black hair and golden brown skin. She wore a pair a jean shorts darkened with the wet imprint of her bathing suit underneath. She must have been a lifeguard. "Hi, can I help you?" she asked with a big smile.

"I'm totally lost." I had taken the path off the dining hall that I thought led to my cabin, but after twenty minutes of wandering past trees that all started to look exactly the same, I knew I had gone the wrong way. It may have been the gray of dusk now, but soon it would be pitch-black, and I had nothing but my cell phone flashlight.

Maricela squinted at me. "Oh hey, you're Brooks's friend, right? I saw you helping him with the drums in the dining hall."

"Ha!" I reacted without meaning to.

"Is that a no?" she asked.

"Pretty sure Brooks hates me, and I'm pretty sure I'm answering for the sins of past guests."

She smiled as if she knew exactly what I meant. "Well, this is his third summer here. He's seen a lot and I've only heard a handful of the stories."

"Yeah, well, I don't judge all boys based on my jerk ex-boyfriend, so . . ." I trailed off, realizing that wasn't exactly true. I'd sworn off all guys after finding out what Trent and Shay had done.

"Jerk ex-boyfriend?" she asked. "Do tell."

I rolled my head as the same wave of pain I'd felt when Shay told me about the betrayal washed over me again. "Just home drama I don't want to think about right now." I sighed. "And now I have this drama with Brooks." I closed my eyes. "I hate drama."

She pursed her lips to the side, studying me for a moment, and then nodded as if deciding something. "Come on, I can help you resolve at least one of those. You two just need to talk. Brooks really is a nice guy and I'm an excellent mediator."

"You want me to march into Brooks's cabin and demand he talk to me?"

She laughed. "No. We have this staff campfire thing we do at nights. You'll like it."

I wanted to say no because I didn't feel like dealing with Brooks. But I was going to see him all summer. Just the thought of him standing up there every night at dinner, half-heartedly strumming his guitar while judging me, had me saying, "Okay."

She led me down the path and up a hill. "What's your name, by the way?" she asked after a couple of minutes.

"Avery."

"Nice to meet you. I'm Maricela."

"Yeah." I pointed to her name tag.

She laughed. "Oh right. I always forget about this thing." She took it off and tucked it in her pocket.

"How many summers have you worked here?"

"Last year was my first."

"So you're not jaded yet?" I asked.

"I was born jaded," she said with a single laugh.

We came to an EMPLOYEES ONLY sign halfway up the path, and I hesitated.

She patted it and gave me a wicked smile. "Just don't let Janelle catch you up here and you'll be fine." We kept walking.

"Who's Janelle?"

"She owns the place. But she sticks to the main lodge and her fancy house up on the hill. She doesn't slum it at the prehistoric employee cabins."

I relaxed until she added, "Oh, and D. Don't let her see you either. She'd probably tattle on you. But she works the front desk until nine."

I slowed down. "Maybe I should just . . ."

She hooked her arm in mine. "No, no, we're almost there."

We passed several rows of older cabins—dark wood siding, water-stained windows—until we reached a clearing behind them. A large fire burned high in a brick-encircled pit, and at least twenty people, probably more, sat around in mismatched camping chairs.

Maricela pointed to a stack of pizza boxes on a picnic table. "Want some?"

"No, that's okay. I just ate."

She flipped open the lid of a box and took a slice.

"You all don't eat in the dining hall?" I asked.

"Most of the time," she said. "But sometimes we just want really good food." She nodded to the picnic bench in front of the table.

I sat down and she joined me.

"Who has bug spray?" Maricela called out, slapping at her ankle.

A girl across the way tossed a bottle to her and she began spraying it all over her exposed legs like a misty shower of strong-smelling chemicals. I held mine out and she layered a coat on me, too, then passed the bottle back.

I looked around as she ate, and that's when I saw Brooks on the far side of the fire, holding an acoustic guitar in his hands but not playing. Kai was next to him, tossing a shoe back and forth across the fire to someone on the other side.

"He's such a goof," Maricela said.

"Kai?" I asked.

"Yes." She had a smile on her face.

"You like him?"

Her brows went down. "No, not at all. Janelle has pretty strict rules. Rule one, we can't date guests. Rule two, we can't date co-workers."

"That sucks."

"They're good rules, trust me."

"That sounds like someone who has broken one of those rules before."

She cleared her throat and smirked. "Who, me?"

I had only known Maricela for two point two seconds but I

already liked her a lot. Maybe she really could help me resolve things with Brooks. My gaze went back out to the group. "Is everyone who works here under twenty or something?"

"Well, it *is* a summer job. Not many adults are interested in summer-only work, so yeah, most. But we have a groundskeeper, he's ancient, and Janelle is in her fifties. The office manager is older, the cook, the paycheck lady . . ."

The distinct sound of someone fingerpicking a guitar rang out. I went silent, along with everyone else, as we listened. The only noise was the chirping of crickets and the crystal-clear notes of perfect guitar playing. I tried to place the song but couldn't. An original, then? The melody took my breath away. Brooks's dinner playing had been so dispassionate that I hadn't thought anything about his skills. But now I realized he was talented. And as I watched him play, the serene look on his face, the ease of his fingers on the strings, I knew this was his passion, his life. I could listen to him play like this forever.

My trance was broken when, reminiscent of dinner, he met my eyes and his serene expression immediately darkened. His fingers flubbed a chord, a sour note ringing out, and he flinched but then got back on track. His strong reaction to the mere sight of me reminded me how dumb he was being.

Even though he was still playing, the talking picked back up and soon there was a low buzz of voices all around. Kai got up and walked over to us.

"Did you eat all the pizza, Mari?" he asked.

"Yes, all five boxes."

His smile, which I was realizing was pretty much a permanent fixture on his face, lit up his eyes. "I thought so."

"Have you met Avery, Kai?"

"If listening to my best friend tell someone off is meeting them, then yes, yes I have. Hey, Avery." He reached between us and retrieved two slices of pizza, which he folded in half to eat.

"Hi," I said. "You carry those around everywhere?" I nodded toward the drumsticks still in his pocket.

He patted them. "Only so people will know how impressed they're supposed to be."

I smiled. "By the time you got to the Beach Boys at dinner, I was sufficiently impressed."

He put his hand over his heart, obviously sensing my sarcasm. "Hey, if we didn't have to play a Janelle-approved set list, we'd all be happier. Believe me."

Maricela nudged me with her elbow. "Now's your chance," she said, nodding toward Brooks. "Go."

I knew what she meant. With Kai gone, there was an empty chair next to Brooks. "I thought you were mediating."

"I just said that to get you here." She laughed when my mouth dropped open.

"Thanks a lot."

"You're a big girl."

I didn't feel like one at all. I felt like a child in time-out or something. But I stood anyway and walked over to Brooks, who was still playing the guitar. Before I thought about it too much, I lowered myself into the chair next to him.

"You following me now?" he asked.

"You're really good," I said, when what I really wanted to say was *Why were you such a jerk earlier?*

He seemed just as surprised by the compliment as I was that I gave it. "Thanks," he said, and then as if he didn't want to reward me with the sound anymore, he stopped playing and set his guitar off to the side.

"Are you friends with Mari?" he asked, a piece of glowing debris from the fire floating above his head before disappearing into the black night.

"We just met."

"I'm sure she told you that you're not supposed to be up here. We can't hang out with guests off the clock."

"She brought me here."

He sighed. "Nice."

"Yes, she is," I said, even though I knew that's not what he meant.

He shifted and it was obvious he was about to stand, take his guitar, and leave, so I blurted out, "I wasn't in the middle of some prank yesterday. This lady spilled an entire cup of hot coffee on me when we were checking in and D gave me the shirt so I wouldn't get second-degree burns."

It was so subtle I almost didn't notice, but his expression softened the tiniest degree. He was silent for a long moment, then said, straight-faced, "What did you do to make this lady so mad?"

I bit my lip as though trying to remember the exact details. "Let's see . . . I think I called her an entitled, rich snob."

I was rewarded with a smile. "Then you probably deserved it," he said. I had a feeling that was the closest thing I was going to get to an apology.

"I definitely did. She should've thrown the heavy bass drum pedal she was holding at me too."

He chuckled. "Probably."

I nodded toward his guitar. "What song were you playing earlier?"

" 'Someday.' "

"The Strokes?" I asked, surprised.

"You know them?"

"Yeah. But that didn't sound like 'Someday.' "

"I changed it up a bit, slowed it down, tweaked a couple chord progressions."

I nodded and then something occurred to me. Talking about songs reminded me of all my playlists trapped in space. I pulled my phone out of my pocket, holding my breath.

"What are you doing?" he asked.

"I thought you might have secret employee internet up here." But there were no bars. I would have no additional songs to listen to. I would have no new messages. I tried not to let the disappointment settle in.

"Nope. No secret internet." Brooks held out his hand.

"What?" I asked, confused.

"Let me see your phone."

"Are you going to throw it into the fire?"

"Does that happen to you often?"

My lips twitched but I held back a smile. "Well, no, I just don't know how extreme you all are about the camp media restrictions."

"I'll suggest that option at the next staff meeting." He continued to hold out his hand, and for whatever reason—maybe because it was mostly useless to me right now anyway—I gave it to him.

With my phone in his possession, I tried to think of every app I had ever downloaded. There were all my social media ones, of course, but then I had games, and a friend finder and an e-reader, and others I couldn't remember. It felt like he was seeing everything I ever valued all in one place, and I was sure that my life summed up in apps was very unimpressive.

He opened my music app and scrolled through a few playlists. I was distracted for a moment watching someone add a log to the dying fire. Sparks flew and the smoke thickened.

"You have a playlist called *Now I Don't Hate You?*" Brooks asked.

I looked back at him. "You don't? You should. It might help you with anger management."

"Funny."

"What's on *your* phone?" I asked, still feeling stupid that mine held nothing of real interest.

"I'll show you in three months when I get out of this place." He handed back my phone and his eyes were on the fire again.

I let my gaze drift there as well. The flames danced and leaned in the breeze. "How do you do it?"

"Do what?"

"Shut yourself away with no contact to the outside world for three months? Don't you worry that people back home will . . ." Forget about you? Move on? Think you didn't answer their apology text because you never want to speak to them again?

"Will what?" he asked.

I shrugged, the fire heating up my cheeks.

38

His voice was low when he said, "Need more than you can give?" His tense expression let me know without a shadow of a doubt that he'd left behind some drama too.

"Yeah," I said in nearly a whisper.

"You just try not to think about it." His gaze went from the fire to me and it was just as intense as the first night I met him. "But why are you worried? You'll be home in, what, a week? Two?"

"No, we're here for two months."

"Two months?" His eyes narrowed. "Two *months*?" he asked again.

"Do most people not stay that long?"

"No, they don't." His words were short, almost angry, and just like that his walls were back up.

What had I said? That we were staying a long time? He didn't want me here that long? Or did this new information confirm all his theories about me? I wanted to yell, *We don't normally do anything this big. Last year we slept in a tent for three weeks.* But I wasn't going to yell that at him because it shouldn't have mattered. I stood abruptly. As I rounded the fire and passed Maricela, I said, "Guess we needed a mediator after all."

Chapter 5

"WHERE WERE YOU LAST NIGHT?" LAUREN ASKED THROUGH a mouthful of toothpaste when I joined her the next morning in the bathroom we shared. We shared a bathroom at home, too, so it didn't feel much different. Well, aside from the rustic cabin decor. The wall behind the mirror and the shower were tiled with rough stones, and the sink looked like it was carved into a large polished rock.

The rest of the cabin, a cozy two-bedroom with a living room and kitchen, matched the bathroom style with reclaimed wood and stone dominating the space. There was also a cute potbelly stove and several antler-inspired light fixtures. It was exactly how I would expect a cabin in the woods to look if an interior designer was in charge of making something look like a cabin in the woods.

I picked up my toothbrush from the counter and added a bead of green gel. "I was just walking around."

"How come our whole room smells like campfire, then?"

"I don't know. Because there are campfires here." I wasn't a good liar, but I also didn't think my sister needed to know about my "employees only" trespassing session, especially with my parents within earshot. I could hear my mom banging around in the kitchen.

"Well, your little walk got you out of the motivational speaker I was dragged to after dinner."

"And? What did he motivate you to do?"

"He motivated me to avoid all future motivational speakers."

I laughed.

"That was funny, right?" she said. "Mom didn't find it funny."

"Yes. It was funny." Brooks hadn't found me funny the night before either. He was too busy putting me in a box. "What apps are on your phone?"

"On my phone?" she asked, but before waiting for my answer, she tucked the head of her toothbrush in the side of her cheek and picked up her phone. "My video editing stuff, of course, and I have this song-splicing one that's really cool." She turned her phone toward me like I would know exactly what app she was talking about. I didn't. "Do you have this picture design one on yours?"

"No."

"You should get it. Hmm . . . what else? Games, I guess, and social media. Why?"

"I was just wondering what apps people have."

"Wouldn't it depend on their interests?" she said.

"True." My interests. Old books? Music? Instagram? "You're drooling." I pointed to the toothpaste that was dripping onto her pajama top.

She set down her phone and leaned toward me.

I straight-armed her. "Ew. Gross. Get away."

She laughed, spit into the sink, and rinsed off her mouth and toothbrush.

"Anyway," Lauren said, grabbing the hand towel and dabbing at her shirt. "Guess what I found out?"

"What?"

"That the dinner band is practicing tonight in the lodge theater."

I swallowed hard, my loaded toothbrush still waiting in my hand. "Who told you that?"

She hung the drool towel back up and I made a mental note not to use it. "Tia. That girl who served us rolls last night. She was handing out worksheets at the motivational thing."

"And you asked her about the band?"

"Of course. They are the only cute guys I've seen since we got here. She gave me all sorts of good info. So we're going to go."

"To band practice?" Brooks had invited me to crash band practice when he thought I worked here, but I knew that the invitation was all but revoked when he found out I didn't.

"Yes, to band practice."

Finally, I put my toothbrush in my mouth and started brushing. "Mom and Dad won't let us."

"Seriously?" she said.

"Yes."

"It's a camp-sanctioned event."

"It is?"

She rolled her eyes. "It is now. Keep up, Avery. Besides, a cute

42

band in the middle of the woods is going to make the best series of videos ever."

"Is that how you make your decisions? Based on whether they'll be good videos?"

"Why not? It pushes me outside my comfort zone. You should try it once in a while." She raised her phone, pushed record, and pointed it at me. "What about *your* life would people actually want to watch?"

I blinked twice. *Nothing,* I wanted to say directly into her phone. *I'm of no interest.* Isn't that why Trent left, why Shay was willing to risk everything? I swallowed down those words. "I don't need people watching my life."

Dad appeared in the doorway. "Who wants to go to Grass Games with me right now?"

"I'm going to the Slip 'N Slide," Lauren said. "I sense I can get some good *videos* there." She tucked her phone in her pocket and left.

"What was that about?" Dad asked.

I spit out my mouthful of toothpaste and straightened up. "All the world is her stage."

He smiled. "And some of us are meant to work behind the curtains." He pointed at me with the comment, then back to him.

I pictured my dad, the coach, pacing the sidelines at the junior high basketball games, yelling out encouraging words to the players or snide remarks to the refs. I'd never thought of him as a behind-the-curtains kind of guy. "Right," I said anyway.

"So, Grass Games?" he asked.

"Sure, let me get dressed."

43

Dad and I ended up on the lawn behind the lodge playing cornhole with two total strangers—a husband and wife from Idaho Falls. We had already learned that they had three grown kids and eight grandkids, each more accomplished than the last. At least Dad and I were crushing them in cornhole, because we weren't winning in conversation at all.

"You all live in Los Angeles?" the man, Mr. Masters, was asking. "My oldest lives there. He designs sets for movies."

Of course he did.

"That's amazing," Dad said. "I have a feeling my second daughter will be in the entertainment field. She has this super-creative brain. She's constantly thinking outside the box and can turn anything into a compelling story. She has this incredible passion for what she does. And she's only fifteen." My dad's eyes lit up as he described Lauren to this man. It's not that I didn't want my dad to be proud of Lauren—of course I did—but I had always assumed he and my mom thought the videos were a waste of her time. It was shocking to hear him brag about them.

"So what about you, young lady?" Mr. Masters asked. "Are movies in your future?"

"What? No." I squeezed the beanbag I held, feeling the insides slip through my fingers.

My dad waved his hand through the air. "Avery is more laid-back. She takes the path of least resistance, happy to stay in her comfort zone. She's going to be a professor, just like her mom."

I froze, my brain trying to catch up with the words my dad was saying.

"That's neat," Mrs. Masters said. "What do you want to teach?"

"I . . . I'm not sure," I said. "Literature . . . maybe." Why did I suddenly feel like I was on trial? I'd been asked this question dozens of times. I was going to be a senior, after all; it seemed like it was the only question any adult knew how to ask.

"I bet you're so busy planning and applying and testing," Mrs. Masters said.

I opened my mouth to agree when Dad said, "My wife works at UCLA, so it makes it easy."

Easy? Sure, I'd get to go to school for free because my mom was a professor there, but he knew I still had to have a certain GPA and that I had to fill out applications and creatively answer essay questions and register and actually get accepted, didn't he? I stared at him for a moment, then bent down quickly to pick up the hrinbag that had dropped to my feet. I tried to mask my expression because I didn't want him to see that this whole conversation had hurt.

"Well, that's great," Mr. Masters said. "I hear UCLA is a really good college."

"It is," Dad said.

"Sometimes it's nice to have your future already picked out for you, isn't it?" Mrs. Masters said, patting my arm.

It took everything in me not to yank away from her touch. "Yep. Super nice," I said.

❁ ❁ ❁

I paced the living room alone, seething. It had been several hours since Grass Games with my dad but I couldn't stop thinking about what he'd said. Path of least resistance? Happy to stay in my comfort zone? Did he think that was a compliment?

I did hard, new things all the time. Like that time I . . . My mind went absolutely blank as it scanned the last few years of high school. Suddenly I couldn't remember the last time I did something outside of my routine. Even here at camp I was sticking to things I'd done before: badminton and floating on the lake and campfires. Was I happy in my comfort zone?! Is that how I chose my entire future—by default?

I plopped down on the couch and pulled out my phone. I stared at my boring apps. I gritted my teeth and swiped to my photos, hoping to pull up a pic of me and Shay doing something fun or inspiring, but my finger froze on the first pic on the camera roll.

Brooks.

He'd taken a pic the other night when he'd had my phone? It was a goofy selfie with his cheeks puffed out and his blue eyes shining. I rolled my eyes and slammed my phone down on the couch cushion next to me. "Don't act like you're funny and cute, Brooks," I muttered.

My legs twitched, angry energy coursing through them. I stood again, taking the same path as before between the overstuffed couch and the irregular-shaped coffee table.

The front door swung open and Lauren walked in. Her cheeks were pink from the sun and she had a towel wrapped around her. She watched me complete a back-and-forth path. "What are you doing? Where are Mom and Dad?"

"They went to pick up the laundry room key. I guess the owner gave them permission to use it because we'll be here all summer."

"Ugh!" Lauren groaned. "And here I thought we'd be able to get out of this place every once in a while."

"Guess not," I returned.

"So what are *you* doing?"

"I'm trying to think." And it definitely wasn't working.

"O-kay," she said, obviously not impressed with that answer.

"You know what I need," I decided, sitting back down and picking up my phone. "I need a playlist." That's what would help me think.

"I thought all your songs were stuck in the clouds."

"They are, but that's not the point."

"What's the point?" She walked into the kitchen and opened the fridge, staring inside as she waited for me to answer.

"Inspiration."

"Inspiration?"

"I'm going to prove I don't just go with the flow."

"Um . . . what?" She turned around, holding an apple.

I opened my Notes app. "I need a title first. Something like *I'm Not Your Ice, Ice Baby,* or *Failure to Launch.*"

"Are those supposed to be inspirational?"

"They will be to me." I started typing in songs that I could add when I had internet. But even just having the list would remind me.

"And then what?" Lauren asked, biting into her apple.

"Then I'll . . . I don't know. Try new things or something." I'd prove I knew how to live deliberately.

"While listening to your *I'm Not Your Ice, Ice Baby* playlist?"

I held up a finger. "While *not* listening to it."

She smiled. "Right. While *thinking* about it."

"Yes." I went to the kitchen counter and began riffling through the welcome packet, looking for the schedule of activities. I'd make my own schedule—things to try this summer.

"I have a new thing for you to try," Lauren said.

"Okay, what?"

"Band practice tonight."

"No . . . I can't . . ." We could *not* go to band practice. At least, *I* couldn't. Brooks was going to think I was obsessed with him. I wasn't. Right now I'd be happy if I never had to see him again. But I had to admit, when he dropped his judgmental walls, there was something there that intrigued me.

She raised her eyebrows, challenging me. She was right— I couldn't turn down the first new experience presented to me. The goofy selfie of Brooks on my phone flashed through my mind. "Fine. I'll come."

Chapter 6

"YOU READY?" LAUREN SAID, POKING HER HEAD IN OUR room.

I sat up, putting the book I had been reading facedown on my bed. I'd found it on the TV stand in the living room where a television was supposed to sit but where only books and board games could be found. "Good news. I still like to read," I said to Lauren. That was the initial reason I'd thought of a career as a lit professor. It later became about how literature and words and ideas had shaped history and how they could shape people.

"I thought you were trying new things, not old things," she said.

"Yes, I am. I just . . ." *What, Avery? You just what?* Had still been trying to convince myself that I had chosen my future and it hadn't chosen me? That I wasn't as pathetic as I felt right now? "Nothing, you're right. New things. Let's go."

Mom and Dad were sitting in the living room as we headed to the front door.

"Where are you girls off to?" Dad asked. I'd been avoiding him since cornhole. I'd begged off dinner in the dining hall, opting for a bowl of oatmeal here, and had been in my room ever since. I'd get over what he'd said eventually. He had no clue he'd insulted me; if he knew, he'd feel bad, and I really didn't want to make him feel bad. I just needed some time.

"They're telling ghost stories at the lower fire pit tonight," Lauren lied effortlessly.

"Ooh, fun," Mom said. "Maybe I should come with you."

Lauren leveled Mom with a stare.

"But I won't," she said, laughing.

"See you later." Lauren pulled the door closed behind us and aimed a flashlight on the path ahead. As we walked, trees loomed dark on either side of the path, like large sentinels.

"I have a really good ghost story. Do you think it's audience participation tonight or no?" I asked with a straight face.

"We're not really going there," she said. "I just picked something from the schedule in case they checked it."

"I know."

"Oh, right. You and your dumb jokes." She pulled out a notebook. "So, you trying new things got me thinking."

"Yeah?"

"There's been something I've wanted to try forever now." She took a breath and showed me the notebook. In black Sharpie on the front cover was the word *Documentary*. "I think I've found my subjects."

"Subjects?" I asked.

"The band."

"A documentary?" A loud toad croaked in the distance in a deep baritone. "About the band?"

She nodded. "Yes. I love doing videos. You know that. And I love all those true-crime documentaries. I've watched like a million of them. So this will be perfect."

"Ooh, what crimes has the band committed?" I asked.

She rolled her eyes, proving once again that she didn't appreciate my jokes very much. "None, but the same principles apply, right?" She flipped through the book and I could see she'd taken notes, pages and pages worth. She really *had* been thinking about this for a while. "Find out their backstory, what makes them tick, what brought them here. Address their obstacles, what's holding them back, what conflicts they're facing. Then watch them succeed . . . except . . . not at being convicted for murder. At the whole band thing, obviously."

"Obviously."

"You don't think it's a good idea?"

"What? No, I mean yes." I was a horrible person for being jealous right now. Jealous that at fifteen, my sister seemed to be full of creative, thoughtful ideas and all I'd come up with so far was the title to a motivational playlist full of songs I couldn't even listen to. "It's a great idea, Lauren. Really."

"It will be, I think."

As we came to the main path leading up to the lodge, the walkways became more crowded. People filed in through the large, propped-open doors.

"What's happening here tonight?" I asked.

"Bingo?" Lauren suggested.

As if she knew D might object to our band practice invasion, Lauren hung close to a large group of people as we entered the lodge and then peeled off to the right without looking back. Like the first night we'd arrived, I could hear the music as we approached the hall.

The stage was lit and the seating area was dark, so nobody saw us at first. The four guys were playing through a song, with Brooks on guitar, Kai on drums, the bleached-blond guy on bass, and the guy with floppy brown hair on vocals. The song had a punk rock feel to it with more energy and grit than the tune Brooks had played on his guitar the night before by the campfire.

When the song was finished, Brooks turned and said, "Better, but the chorus should be faster."

Much to my horror, Lauren called out, "Hello!" The single word echoed through the mostly empty theater, and all eyes were now on us. Lauren walked forward and up the stairs to join them onstage, saying, "That was so good! And here we thought you were going to be practicing dinner songs."

I wasn't as fast to follow but eventually was standing next to her.

Brooks looked at me. I wasn't sure what I was expecting him to do. Nod? Wave? Acknowledge that we'd had a conversation before this moment? Maybe he was expecting the same from me, but seeing him now brought back all the feelings of frustration from the night before.

"Avery!" Kai said from behind the drums; then he beat out a *ba-dum-dum* on the tom-toms.

Now Lauren's eyes were on me.

"Hey, guys," I said. "This is my sister, Lauren."

"You know them?" she hissed.

"Not really," I said under my breath. Because I really didn't. I wasn't even sure which guy was Ian and which was Levi.

As if reading my mind, the bleached-blond guy raised the head of his bass in a semi-wave and said, "I'm Levi."

Which by default made floppy brown-haired lead singer . . .

"Ian," he said.

Kai tossed a drumstick in the air and caught it. "Lauren?" he asked with a big smile.

She nodded, her cheeks going pink.

"I'm the heart and soul and life of this band," he said, as though already auditioning to star in her documentary. "But you can just call me Kai."

"Oh please," Levi groaned. "You're the drummer."

"What does that mean? Have you ever heard a song without a drum pattern?"

"Have you ever heard a song without a bass line?"

"Yes. A million," Kai said.

Brooks let out a long sigh. "Do you both need gold stars tattooed on your foreheads?"

"Are you offering?" Kai asked. "Because that could be our band thing."

"You must be Brooks," Lauren said. How did she know that? Tia?

Brooks's eyes went from my sister to me. Great, he thought I'd been talking bad about him. "Yeah," he said.

I pasted on a big fake smile. "You said to come watch practice, right?" Now he'd have to admit that he really didn't want me here and tell everyone it was because he thought I was a snob.

"We're not supposed to hang out with guests," he said.

Oh right. Or there was that.

"Off the clock!" Kai yelled out. "We're not supposed to hang out with guests off the clock."

Brooks shot Kai a look.

"Exactly," Levi said. "They can stay. We need feedback anyway. Are you two any good at feedback?"

"I am excellent at feedback," Lauren said. "Avery is not. She'll just tell you what you want to hear."

"Excuse me?" I said.

"What? It's true. You don't like to hurt people's feelings. I am great at hurting people's feelings."

"Well, that's true," I grumbled.

A smile played on Brooks's lips and I narrowed my eyes at him.

"But if I'm going to give you feedback, I require something in return." Lauren looked around, found a stack of chairs by the curtains, and freed one, moving it closer to the guys. "How do you all feel about being recorded for my channel?"

❀ ❀ ❀

Surprisingly, they'd all agreed, with varying amounts of enthusiasm, that my sister could record their practice sessions. I was pretty sure Brooks only agreed so that he could have videos to analyze. But my sister didn't care what the reason was; she'd been practically

54

skipping around the stage for the last thirty minutes recording while I sat in the chair off to the side.

They'd just finished a song for the third time and now Lauren was over by the drums interviewing Kai. I couldn't hear the questions from where I sat, but there was a lot of laughing.

"So I don't get it," I called out to the guys. "How come there are only a couple lines of lyrics? And if you can't play this song in the dining hall for people, why are you practicing it?"

Levi leaned down to his guitar case, which was open beside him, and produced a neon-green piece of paper. He walked it over to me. I collected it from his outstretched hand and unfolded it.

Do you have what it takes?
A band? A song? A sound?

If you answered yes to those questions, audition for a chance to be part of the showdown. Winning band takes home ten thousand dollars. Additional cash prizes available in several categories. It all happens Saturday, August 1, in Roseville!

To purchase tickets to the Festival of Undiscovered Bands, call the number below.

Or visit us online at **festivalofundiscoveredbands.com**

"You're trying out for this?" I wasn't sure why I looked at Brooks when I said that but I did.

"If we can actually write words to this song," Brooks said, slowly twisting a tuning key on his guitar and then testing out the string.

"You're a band with no finished songs?"

Levi answered, "We all just met a couple weeks ago. Kai and Brooks play back home together, but Ian and I were hired this year for the house band."

I held up the flyer. "And after your first magical night together you decided to try out for this?"

"That was Brooks's idea," Levi said as I handed him back the paper.

"But we're never going to finish a song, so it was a stupid idea," Brooks said in a tired voice, like he'd pointed this out a hundred times.

"We'd finish a song," Levi said, "but Brooks doesn't like anyone else's lyrics."

Ian, who seemed much more comfortable singing than he did talking, nodded at this. I laughed.

"Oh, you're on his side?" Brooks asked me while throwing his guitar pick at Ian.

I held up my hands. "I didn't realize there were sides."

"There are!" Kai called out as though he'd been following along, even though he was being interviewed. "There's Brooks's lame lyrics and then there's—"

"Nobody being able to build on them," Brooks finished. "Because you all get distracted too easily."

Lauren's camera had now panned to the group, recording this exchange. I backed up so I was out of the shot.

Levi stepped closer to Lauren's phone and said, "I will sing you his lyrics." He pulled the microphone from where it sat in a stand and sang, "Hope is the lie that keeps us hanging on to madness."

56

"What's wrong with that lyric?" Brooks asked.

I lowered myself back into the chair, feeling bad I had started a fight with my questions. It obviously wasn't a new fight, though.

"We don't want to suck the life out of the audience," Levi said.

"But that's my number one goal," Brooks deadpanned.

"What was that other lyric?" Kai said. "Something about love being for fools?"

Brooks, who had been tuning his guitar that didn't need tuning for the last several minutes, said, "Love is just child's play for the dreamers and the fools."

"Yes, that one," Kai said.

Lauren laughed along with the other guys. I wondered if any of these lyrics were drawn from life experience. Was that how Brooks really felt, or were they just words for a song?

"Levi," Ian said. "Put the microphone back."

"Uh-oh," Levi said, holding the microphone in the air like a game of keep-away. "I've touched Ian's pretend instrument."

Ian just rolled his eyes, which seemed to work because Levi tossed the mic to him. He barely caught it with a fumbling grasp.

Kai rubbed the back of his neck and looked at Lauren. "Did you have any more questions for me?"

"Oh, yeah." She rejoined him.

Levi patted his stomach. "Think there'll be food at the campfire?"

Maybe I actually *was* on Brooks's side of the lyrics argument because I hadn't heard them come up with any ideas, just criticism. Plus, I actually liked the lyric. *Love is just child's play for the dreamers and the fools.* Out loud, I added, "You want me to play your game but won't teach me all the rules."

Brooks's hands stilled on the strings of his guitar and he looked at me. "What?"

I shook my head. "Nothing. Just thinking out loud."

"No, say it again."

"It was just a passing thought. I don't write lyrics."

"But she loves words," Lauren said. "And poetry. You write poetry sometimes."

"It was a lyric idea?" Levi asked. "Let's hear it."

Kai pounded a beat on the drums and started chanting, "Avery, Avery, Avery."

I felt my cheeks heating up with so much focused attention on me and wanted to crawl inside myself.

Brooks, as if sensing this, said, "Kai! Stop."

He immediately did. "Too much?" He smiled sheepishly at me.

Brooks swung his guitar to his back and dug through his guitar case, coming up with a notebook and pencil. "Something about rules?"

He wasn't going to drop it, so I said, "Your lyric was 'Love is just child's play for the dreamers and the fools.' And then I added, 'You want me to play your game but won't teach me all the rules.'"

"That's good," Levi said.

Ian nodded. "I'd sing that."

Brooks scribbled it down, then gave me a curious look. His eyes scanned the group. "See, *that's* how you build."

With those words, they all broke out into another argument, talking over each other. "Who needs a gold star now?" "You never listen!" "We just need to finish the other song!"

I stood. "Lauren, we should get going."

Brooks's head whipped around. "You're leaving?" And I couldn't tell if his intense expression was saying, *Finally* or *Don't go yet.*

"We have a few ghost stories to think up," I said.

I could see Lauren wanted to argue, but she knew I was right. "We'll come back next time," she promised, and that was either the best news or the worst news for Brooks.

Chapter 7

A SHARP TAPPING NOISE BROUGHT ME OUT OF SLEEP. THE spiral edging of my notebook dug into my cheek, reminding me that I had fallen asleep the night before trying to write out a schedule of new things to try this summer. I pushed the book aside and rubbed at the bumpy indentation it had created on my skin. The tapping noise was back. It took me several sleepy moments to realize it was something hitting the window.

I sat up. My sister groaned and turned toward the wall. I checked my phone on the nightstand—six-thirty. What woodland creature was waking me up at six-thirty in the morning? I started to lie back down when another series of taps made me jump.

I moved the curtain to the side, expecting to see a bird or a squirrel or something, when I met a face. My hands flew to my mouth, barely containing my squeal of fear, the curtain dropping back into place. With my heart racing, I took several deep breaths, then moved the curtains again. My brain hadn't made it up—Brooks was standing outside my window, an impatient expression on his face. This time, he pointed. I assumed that meant he wanted me to go to the front door. I nodded.

Why was he here? Was he going to reiterate the fact that we shouldn't have been at band practice the night before? That we had caused too much tension and distracted everyone? It seemed like an extreme way to get that message across. Maybe this was just the time he started his workday.

I slid out of bed and tiptoed to the bedroom door. I opened it as quietly as possible and shut it slowly, using both hands. I walked toward the front door, then found myself stopping at the bathroom and checking my reflection in the mirror. It wasn't good. My normally straight brown hair stuck out in a spectacular display of bedhead, and sure enough, a long line of notebook-spine bumps decorated my cheek. I rubbed at them without any luck, and even though he'd already seen me, I quickly ran a brush through my hair, grabbed a tie, and pulled it up. I moved to leave, then stopped and squeezed a bead of toothpaste onto my finger. Morning breath was not good for anyone.

The rest of the house was quiet, my parents obviously still asleep, as I finished my walk through the living room and went out the front door. I didn't see Brooks right away and was beginning to think I had imagined him. That he was part of some weird dream my brain had concocted and that maybe I was still in that dream.

Then a movement down the path caught my eye. He was leaning against a tree, waiting. I realized I hadn't put on shoes. I held up my finger to him, opened the front door again, and grabbed the first pair of flip-flops I could find by the wall. I slipped them on and walked down the gravel path. A squirrel scurried across the rocks in front of me and up a tree. A crow squawked what seemed to be a morning wakeup call from a high perch in a pine tree up ahead. But other than that, the morning was quiet, not the normal low murmur of camp.

"Hi," I said when I stood in front of Brooks.

His eyes were on my too-big shoes.

"They're my dad's," I said.

"Are you going to be able to walk in them?"

"Yes. But why do I have to walk in them?" I looked down at my feet. I really didn't want to have to walk too far in them. Why was he even here? "About last night, I know my sister is a lot. And I didn't mean to start a fight . . ."

He narrowed his eyes in confusion. "What? You have a phone call."

"Oh." I had a phone call. "Wait . . . What?"

"A phone call. Someone called you at the pay phone."

"What pay phone? Is there a pay phone at the lodge?"

"No . . ." He seemed to assess my sincerity. "Up at the employee cabins."

"Someone called me? Who?"

"I don't know."

"And they asked for *me*? By name?"

"No, they asked me to find just any cute brunette and I chose you," he said. "Of course they asked for you by name. Why else would I be here at six-thirty in the morning unless some person made the phone ring for ten minutes straight?"

"I . . ." He probably wanted me to just say thank you and take my phone call so he could move on with his day, but my stomach was now in knots and all the blood seemed to drain from my face. "Who was it?"

"I don't know. Probably whoever you gave the phone number to."

I shook my head. "I didn't give it to anyone. I didn't even know it existed."

"Okay," he said like he didn't quite believe me. "Do you want to take the call or not?"

"No . . . Yes . . . I don't know."

"Are you always this indecisive?"

I'd never thought I was before a few days ago, but now it seemed that's all I was. His question motivated me to action, and I started walking in the direction of the employee cabins. He matched my pace.

"What did she say?" I was assuming it was Shay, somehow figuring out how to get ahold of me. But what if it wasn't? What if it was Trent?

"Who?" Brooks asked.

"The person on the phone." A morning jogger ran past and Brooks put some space between us. "Was it a girl?"

"Yes."

"Did she say anything?"

He laughed without humor. "She was very demanding. Told me she had to talk to you or her life would be over. Told me I had to go down and wake you up despite the fact that she'd just woken up the entire employee village. Told me she's been trying to get ahold of you all weekend."

"I'm sorry," I said. Why did something else have to happen that made him think I was super entitled?

"It's fine," he said, seeming to realize how grumpy he sounded. "It's just early."

I gave a breathy laugh. "Too early."

He pointed at his cheek. "What's on your face?"

I rubbed at the marks again. "Oh, a project I'm working on."

"Um . . ."

"No, this isn't the project. I was writing in a notebook. This is the notebook."

"Oh, yeah, I can see it now. Spiral bound. Seventy pages?" He smirked.

"An amazing guitar player and a notebook expert? Stop stealing all the talents."

He gave a half-smile. "I'll try."

As we headed up an incline, my feet slid in the flip-flops. I curled my toes to hold them in place.

He noticed me falling behind. "Why didn't you grab your own shoes?"

"Because you were standing there waiting for me and I didn't think we were going on a hike and I'm an idiot."

"No, an idiot would have also left her cabin in a tank top. . . . Oh wait." His smile widened.

I reached over and shoved him, very satisfied when he stumbled a little from the force. I actually wasn't cold at all. Maybe it was because my heart felt like it was pumping a hundred miles a minute.

"So that's all Shay said?" I asked.

"Shay?"

"The girl on the phone."

"Right. She said she'd keep calling if I didn't get you and she said she was your best friend, so I figured you'd want to talk to her."

I hesitated.

"Would you like me to ask her what she plans to say to you?"

"Will you? Please," I joked.

He saw through me. "You don't want to talk to her."

"I don't." I closed my eyes and blew out a slow breath. All the anxiety I'd felt since the moment I'd found out about Shay and Trent seemed to have grown into an elephant sitting on my chest. I leaned over and braced my hands on my knees.

"Whoa. You okay?" Brooks asked. It sounded like he was speaking underwater.

"Yes, fine. I just need to . . . I just need to sit for a second." I lowered myself to the dirt path just as a woman walked by with a small child. I could feel her eyes on me. My cheeks heated up as my eyes stung with tears. Small rocks dug into my palms.

Brooks squatted down in front of me. "What is it?" he asked quietly, concerned.

"I can't talk to her," I said. "She just called to make herself feel better. This is not going to make me feel better." A tear slipped down my cheek and I swiped at it in frustration.

"There's a bench up there. Let me take you." He helped me to stand, then led me up the hill, past the EMPLOYEES ONLY sign, and to the back side of the bathrooms. I could hear showers running inside as he pointed to the bench.

I lowered myself down and took several calming breaths. "You guys don't have bathrooms in your cabins?"

He let me change the subject. "No. We have good old-fashioned communal bathrooms and showers." He patted the log building behind me.

I nodded and toed a pine cone by my foot. I pushed it one way and then the other several times. "I'm sorry. I'm okay."

His eyebrows lowered. "You don't have to talk to anyone you don't want to."

But didn't I? It may have felt like I was a million miles away at the moment, but summer wouldn't last forever and I'd have to go home and deal with this. It would be easier to just get it over with now, not let it stew all summer. She felt bad. I just needed to talk to her. "Where is this pay phone?"

He waited a beat, seeming to gauge my sincerity, but when I stood, determined, he led me around the corner. Sure enough, on the far side of the bathrooms stood a single pay phone. The black handle was dangling at the end of the stiff metal cord. Had she been waiting for me this whole time?

Even though I hadn't seen it happen, a flash of Trent and Shay kissing invaded my brain. It was just an accident, she had said. They had been talking about how much they would miss *me*. Another memory I had almost forgotten about flooded my brain along with this one. Last summer, at a pool party, I had overheard Shay and another girl talking bad about me. Shay had assured me she was just trying to get all the information so she could set the record straight. For *me*.

My eyes went to the dangling phone again. I took several sips of air, not able to fill my lungs fully. I leaned a hand against the wall, bracing myself, trying to force my other hand to grab the handle. That's when Brooks picked up the phone and held it to his ear.

"Hi, Shay, is it?"

Shay must've responded.

"How did you get this number?" He listened for a moment, a dark expression, the one I realized I hadn't seen since the campfire, on his face. "Google?"

He met my eyes, his brows rising in question, and I just stared, frozen.

"Avery is unavailable at the moment. She'll call you back at her convenience, not yours. Please respect her request." With that, he hung up. I leaned my back against the wall, then slid down to the ground in relief.

"Should I have done that?" he asked.

I nodded over and over, grateful. "I'm not normally this dramatic." I let out a shaky laugh. "That's my sister's role."

He shrugged. "It's not drama if it's real."

I gnawed at the inside of my cheeks. It was so real. I'd just been pushing it down, trying not to think about it. Now it was demanding to be thought about. "Well, thank you. For that." I nodded toward the phone. "And that." I gestured back toward the bench.

"No problem." He looked to his left, where someone was exiting the bathroom, her hair wrapped in a towel, carrying a caddy of toiletries. He waited until she was out of earshot before saying, "Are you okay? I mean, obviously you're not okay, but can I . . . Do you need anything?"

I stood and brushed the dust off my backside. "I've made you feel enough pity for me that you don't hate me anymore?"

"I never hated you." It took him a second to realize I was kidding. The crease between his brows relaxed and he said, "I really was a jerk. I just have a lot going on. I'm four hundred miles from home and I can never quite leave it behind." He stared into the distance as if he could see some scene playing out in front of him.

"You want to?" I asked.

He held his hands out to the sides as if this entire forest was the answer to my question.

"What are you running from?"

"Life, reality . . . responsibility." He looked at the pay phone. "What about you?"

I thought about that for a moment. "Life, reality . . . decisions . . . apparently."

Just as I was about to ask him to expand on his answer, Kai's loud voice rang out from somewhere beyond the nearest cabin. "Brooks! You out here?"

Brooks glanced over his shoulder and then back to me. "You sure you're good?"

"You mean aside from the poor clothing and footwear decisions I made this morning?"

His eyes lit up. "See you around." He started walking, then turned, moving backward for a moment, his magic smile on, reminding me of the very first time we met. "Write some more awesome lyrics for me, will you?"

"Only if you screen all my future phone calls."

He laughed and disappeared around the cabin. I sighed and stared at the phone that I hadn't known existed before today. I wished I still didn't know.

Chapter 8

"HEY, MARICELA!" MY ORIGINAL PLAN TODAY HAD BEEN TO work more on the "Try New Things!" schedule, but after the failed phone call that morning, I felt emotionally drained. I decided the correct alternative was to float on the lake for hours. It was the right choice. The vitamin D and rocking motion of the lake had left me with a serotonin buzz.

"Avery! Hey! Cute suit."

I was wearing a floral one-piece, the straps ruffled. "Thanks."

"Walk with me? I'm heading to my cabin to get out of this." She pointed to her red lifeguard suit.

"Sure." I changed direction. "How was work?"

"You don't want to know. Some kid vomited in the pool today and I had to evacuate everyone."

"I'd think people would willingly evacuate a vomit pool," I said.

"It was like herding chickens. And have you ever tried cleaning up vomit with a pool net?"

"No, and I hope I never have to."

"Yeah, I'll have nightmares about it." Maricela stopped at the fifth cabin and pulled out a set of keys. Before she inserted the key into the lock, she knocked on the door. "I'm coming in. Hope you're not naked!" She swung open the door to an empty cabin. It was just one big room. Three twin-sized beds lined one wall and a dresser and changing screen were on the other, plus two suitcases, overflowing with clothes.

"You have roommates?"

"Just one this year. You want to move in?" She pointed at the far bed that obviously hadn't been slept on but had become another dresser of sorts—piled with clothes.

"Sure, but will I have to clean up vomit?"

"Yes, number one requirement." She collected a pair of shorts and a tee off the foot of one of the beds, then pulled out some under-clothes from the top drawer of the dresser. She ducked behind the screen.

As I stood there in silence for several moments, I suddenly wondered if Brooks had told her about the embarrassing breakdown I'd had that morning. Was he the type to talk? I really didn't want her to ask me about it.

"So?" she said after a few more quiet moments, still behind the screen.

I sat on the end of her bed. "Yes?"

She stepped out, dressed, then retrieved a tube of lip gloss off her dresser and applied it. She took out her ponytail and finger-combed her hair. "How do I look?"

"Amazing." She really did. Her natural curls were full of body and her emerald-green T-shirt looked great against her skin. "Are you trying to impress someone? Aside from me, of course?"

I asked it as a joke, but the way her smile slipped off her face before reappearing again let me know I'd guessed right. "Who?" I asked.

Her eyes shot toward the door, then back to me. "Shhh."

I looked around. "Nobody is here."

"I know, but I swear this place has ears everywhere."

"Someone off-limits, then? A coworker?"

She smiled. "Don't tell anyone."

"You haven't told me anything."

"I know, and I can't. It's still super new. After summer is over, I'll tell you everything."

"That's torture," I said. "But I get it."

She picked up her wet swimsuit from the floor behind the screen and hung it on a hook by the door. Then she stretched her arms above her head. "Do you have dinner plans or do you want to see if the campfire is happening again tonight?"

"Is it already dinnertime?" I'd stayed out at the lake longer than I thought.

"Yes."

I snapped the strap of my swimsuit. "Let me go change. Can I meet you up there in like thirty?"

"For sure."

❀ ❀ ❀

I opened the door of our cabin to yelling.

"I said I'm not hungry!" Lauren called from what I assumed was our bedroom.

"Then just get something small," Mom said, swiping her key from the counter and sticking it into the pocket of her jacket.

"Just bring me back something if you're worried about it!"

Dad, sitting on the couch and tying his shoes, called, "Lauren, don't talk to your mom like that!"

"I wasn't trying to be rude! I was being serious!" she called.

Mom scoffed.

"Hey," I said from the doorway, where nobody had noticed me yet.

"Oh, hi, Avery," Dad said. "You ready for dinner?"

I looked from Mom, who seemed tired, to Dad, who was obviously frustrated. "Yep," I said.

His face relaxed. "We've missed your go-with-the-flow energy today."

I took a deep breath, trying to decide how to respond to that, when Lauren yelled, "Bring me back one of those garlic knot things!"

I sighed. "Let me go change."

When I got to our bedroom, I shut the door. Lauren was sitting on her bed, laptop on her knees.

"What's going on?" I asked.

"Nothing. I don't want to go to dinner. I'm working on editing Kai's interview from the other night." As she said it, her smile widened. She turned the computer toward me, where a close-up of Kai's smiling face filled the whole screen. "Here's my star."

"Yeah, he's pretty charismatic," I said. "But would it hurt to take a break and go to dinner?"

"Yes, it very well might."

"It would make the parents happy."

"That's your game, Avery. *You* do things to make people happy," she said, as if making people happy was a bad thing. "Maybe you should add *start saying how you really feel* to your list of new things to try."

"Thanks." I pulled out some clothes and headed for the bathroom to change.

"I'm sorry," she called after me. "I didn't mean it like that!"

I just lifted my hand in a wave but didn't turn around.

After I'd changed and joined my parents, I hooked my arm in my dad's as we walked to the front door.

"Everything okay with you?" he asked.

Lauren was right—I needed to tell him how the things he said sometimes hurt. I opened my mouth and said, "Yes, I'm fine."

❁ ❁ ❁

The campfire group was smaller tonight, so Maricela was easy to spot, sitting in a chair on the opposite side of the flames, talking to a girl next to her. I scanned the rest of the faces and didn't see D, so I relaxed as I made my way around to them.

"That was the longest thirty minutes ever," Maricela said when she saw me.

"I know. I got roped into dinner with my parents."

"This is my roommate, Tia," Maricela said, pointing to the girl next to her.

She looked familiar. "Hi, I'm Avery."

"Did you know that *tía* means 'aunt' in Spanish?" Maricela said to her.

Tia laughed.

Maricela looked up at me. "I tell her that like five times a day."

"And yet it never gets old," Tia said.

Maricela clucked her tongue. "Sarcasm is the ugly stepsister of humor, Tia."

"Are we not allowed to use sarcasm around here?" I asked.

"No, it's my third language," Maricela said. She leaned her head back. "Sit, already."

There was an empty chair to her left. I pointed at it and she nodded.

"Your sister does the videos, right?" Tia asked.

That's why she looked familiar. She was the roll girl in the cafeteria from day two. And the one who'd given Lauren all the info on the band. "Yes, she does."

The fire crackled and the smoke shifted. I waved it away and moved the chair before I sat.

"I forgot to ask you earlier—how is that home drama going?" Maricela asked.

"Brooks told you," I said, more disappointed about that than I wanted to be.

"Brooks? No, you told me the other night." She turned toward Tia. "Avery is knee-deep in some mysterious drama at home."

"Welcome to the club. Pretty sure that's why most of us come up here in the first place."

Someone across the way threw a stick into the fire, causing sparks to fly.

"Hey, watch it, Clay!" Maricela said.

"Sorry, ladies!" he called out, and the guys on either side of him laughed.

"Is that what people think is flirting these days?" Maricela asked us. "Because if that's it, we have no hope."

"Or maybe we do," Tia said.

Brooks and the band rounded the cabin at the end of the row. Brooks with his long hair and confident stride. My stomach did an unexpected flip that surprised me.

"How come there's no music playing?" Kai asked the group.

I hadn't realized the music had stopped until he pointed it out. And just like that, the guitar was being strummed again. I thought Brooks would take it over, since he was obviously the best guitar player here, but he didn't. He let his gaze wander until it landed on me. He smirked and sauntered over.

"Hey," Maricela said. "How was the dinner music sesh?"

"The audience was mesmerized."

"I thought it was great," I said. At least the forty-five minutes I had heard.

"Oh good, we have one fan," Brooks said with a flash of the smile that made my stomach flip again. I scolded it.

"No food tonight?" he asked, peering at the empty picnic table.

Maricela pointed. "I have some Oreos in the bear box outside my cabin if that sounds like a meal to you."

"What's a bear box?" I asked.

"Kai!" Brooks called. "Avery wants to know what a bear box is!"

Kai came lumbering over as if he were an actual bear and Brooks walked away, presumably to get the Oreos. "Bear boxes are those metal boxes you see outside each of our cabins. We put our food in them and lock it up so the bears can't get it."

"There are bears here?" I asked, and the entire group of people sitting around the fire roared with laughter. My cheeks heated up.

Maricela patted my leg. "Oh, you poor city girl. The name of the camp didn't give it away?"

"We mostly do beach camping. I didn't think about it."

"Don't be too embarrassed—Kai here cried like a baby when he first heard that a bear could break into his cabin. That's why he's the one who likes to tell others."

He tapped Maricela's shoe with his. "Hey, I didn't actually cry, but there was lots of whining."

"*Lots* of whining!" Clay called out.

I was stuck on the previous bit of information. "A bear can break into our cabin?"

Tia smiled. "Not yours. You're in the new and improved, double-pane windows, dead bolts on doors, well-populated area of camp: the guest cabins. The bears don't like people much. We're on the outskirts of camp with the paper-thin windows and flimsy doors."

Maybe I didn't look convinced because Maricela added, "And we haven't had a bear sighting in a long time. They mostly just pass through on their way to the Dumpsters that are clear on the other side of the employee parking lots."

"That's comforting," I said, full of sarcasm.

Brooks came back holding the package of Oreos and sat in an

open chair by Levi and Ian, nowhere near us disappointed.

open chair by Levi and Ian, nowhere near us. I tried not to be too disappointed.

"Any other dangerous animals I should know about? Mountain lions or something?" I asked.

"If you think bears are shy," she said.

"Wait," Kai said. "There are mountain lions up here?"

This had everyone laughing again and I wasn't sure if he did that so I didn't feel as stupid or if he really didn't know, but either way, I appreciated it. He pulled up a chair and we all started talking about the things we were most scared of. Kai—snakes. Tia—ghosts.

Then it got to Maricela. "I think I'm most afraid of disappointing my parents."

"Wow, that went dark fast," Kai said. "Don't go all deep on us."

She nudged his elbow. "I'm serious. My parents have big plans for me and honestly I just want to mess with hair."

"Mess with hair?" I asked. "As in, cosmetology?"

She nodded.

"That's a great career," I said.

"My parents won't see it that way."

Tia chimed in. "I'm sure your parents will be happy if you're happy. That's what most parents want, right?"

"Yes, for sure," I said.

"Okay, you're right," Maricela said. "I went too dark. Your turn, Avery. What are you scared of?"

I could tell she was trying to get the attention off herself, but how was I supposed to go after that? "I don't know . . . bears?"

They laughed, but then Maricela said, "No, really. I went there. What scares you?"

I tried to think of a time in my life I was most scared. "In the sixth grade, I was in this elite choir for school and after a few months I got picked to do my very first solo. The time came to sing it and I just stood there, staring at the audience, in complete terror. I ran off the stage and never went back to choir."

"You have stage fright?" Maricela asked.

"I must." It was probably the same reason I froze up every time Lauren's camera was on me. Or panicked when I was the center of attention. I looked at Kai. "How do you do it? Sit up there and play in front of everyone?"

He shrugged and smiled. "I'm a natural, I guess."

"There's your answer," Maricela said. "An abundance of confidence."

"This is truth," Kai said.

"Ian!" Tia called. "Tips for stage fright?"

"Just don't think about it," he called back.

"Helpful," I said.

Levi got up to join us. "Or imagine nobody is listening," he said. "Oh wait, that just works when playing at dinner . . . because nobody is."

"Because all the attention is on me," Kai said.

"With a head that big . . ." He trailed off.

"What's that, Levi?" Kai asked. "Did you want to finish that sentence?"

A movement behind Levi caught my attention and I watched Ian leave the campfire, heading toward the cabins. Brooks was now sitting alone, the Oreos on the ground. He was slouched so far down in the chair that his head rested on the back, and his legs were out in front of him, crossed at the ankles. He looked deep in thought. While the others moved on from their argument and started talking about tomorrow's workday, I stood up and stretched.

"I'm getting one of your Oreos," I said to Maricela. She waved me the go-ahead.

"Toss me one too," Kai said as I walked away.

I reached Brooks.

"Come to steal my food?" he asked, his head still on the chair's back, his eyes pointing up at the sky.

"Are there any left?"

"Yes."

I picked up the package, peeled open the resealable top, and took out a cookie. "Kai! Hands up,"

He turned and I threw one into his waiting hands. I got one out for myself and then put the cookies back down.

"Hey, um . . . thanks for not telling anyone about . . ."

"About what?" he asked, that teasing glint in his eyes.

"About me having a meltdown. I don't normally have those, and especially not in front of strangers."

"Are we still strangers?"

"No . . . we're not." Did that mean we were friends?

"No problem," he returned. "You okay?"

"I'm . . ." *Okay, Avery, you're fine. You were willing to text it to Shay and say it to your dad. Why can't you say it to Brooks?* "I'm . . . still a mess, but I will eventually be okay, I think." For the first time in days, a little tension eased from my chest at admitting that out loud.

And maybe that gave me the courage to say the next thing I blurted out. "I'm going to discover myself this summer." He was the first person I had admitted that to.

"Are you missing?" he asked.

"I'm beginning to think I am." And it was not a good feeling.

He nodded at the chair next to him and I sat down.

"Long story," I said. "Basically, I've become a zombie, I guess. Just doing what I always do because I've always done it. So now I need to, I don't know . . ."

"Live."

I smiled. "Yes. I'm going to try a bunch of new things. Make sure I'm awake while deciding my future. If I'm going to spend the rest of my life doing something, I want to make sure it's what I want to be doing. Like you." I paused as my brain caught up with my statement. "Oh frick, that came out wrong. I don't want to be doing you. I meant, you know what you want to do with your life." My cheeks were bright red.

"You don't want to be doing me?" he asked, obviously enjoying my embarrassment.

"Stop," I said with a laugh.

He was laughing too, but then his laughter slowly trailed off. "You think I know what I want to do with my life?"

"At least what you're passionate about."

"Music?" he asked.

"Aren't you?" I knew he was. I'd seen him playing, that fire in his eyes.

He slowly nodded. "Do you believe in signs, Avery?"

I thought about that question. "Probably not."

One side of his mouth rose into a half-smile.

"Do you?" I asked.

"I do," he said. "After this summer, I was going to give up music. I need a more secure future. People are counting on me."

"But . . . ," I said when he stopped.

"But on the way up here this year, I saw that flyer for the festival at a hole-in-the-wall coffee shop and I made a deal with myself. If I could win that festival, I wouldn't give it up. That was my sign."

"*Win* it? Go big or go home?"

"That's the kind of megasign I need right now. Not some half-hearted maybe."

"Then win it," I said.

He gave a breathy laugh. "If only my band believed in me that much."

"Make them."

He stared at the tips of his fingers that were probably calloused from years of pressing down on strings. "Help me with the lyrics for our audition song," he said in a rush of air.

"Me?"

He nodded. "And I'll . . . I'll help you find yourself. I know this camp inside and out. I know all sorts of new things you could try."

This felt like the easiest decision I'd made in weeks. "Deal."

Chapter 9

"MY SISTER THINKS SHE MIGHT BE THE NEXT . . ." LAUREN paused, the camera pointing at herself while she thought. Then her camera was on me, then on the painting in front of me. "What's the name of the guy with the big hair who paints?"

Brooks may have agreed to help me find myself the night before but we hadn't really formulated a plan, so that morning at the breakfast table I had announced, "I'm going to try a painting class today."

Dad had looked up from his eggs and bacon and said, "Painting? Really?" Did he have to sound so skeptical?

Mom patted the table in front of my plate. "Avery, remember those hilarious potato people drawings you used to bring home from school?"

"When I was like five?" I asked.

"They were so cute," she said. "I put you in this little art class, but you were more interested in the lady's cat."

"You did?" I asked.

"You don't remember?"

I didn't, which in my opinion meant this class still met my criteria of trying something new. So I'd put on a T-shirt I didn't care about (as instructed per the schedule) and gone to the class. Lauren had tagged along. And now we stood in a meadow behind the tennis courts, ankle deep in grass, where we were taught some basic techniques and were told we could paint anything we saw on a thicker-than-normal, but definitely not canvas, piece of paper, clipped to an easel. I chose a group of wildflowers that at the moment looked nothing like the drippy blobs of paint on my paper.

The *thwack* of tennis balls against rackets rang out behind us. Not exactly the serene environment I'd pictured for a painting session.

Lauren raised her hand. "Teacher!"

"Lauren, his name is Mr. Lucas." He'd told us he didn't work for the camp but traveled around doing classes. "And he looks busy." He was pointing out something on someone else's painting I hoped he didn't make it over to mine.

"Mr. Lucas!" Lauren said, ignoring me. "What's the name of that big-haired painting guy from television?"

"Bob Ross," Mr. Lucas said with a smile.

"Yes! Bob Ross. Thank you!"

Back to her phone, she said, "My sister thinks she's the next Bob Ross."

"I don't think that," I said. "And remember when I said you couldn't record this."

She put her phone down. "I don't mean it literally. It's exaggeration, for story effect."

"Hyperbole," I said.

"Yes, that." She looked over my shoulder. "Ooh, I'll be right back."

"Lauren," I hissed as she walked away. "That's super rude." The class was supposed to last an hour and we'd only been here twenty minutes. Lauren left her paper clipped to her easel and I glanced over at it. She had painted a tree. It wasn't great but then again, she hadn't really tried.

Behind me, I saw what had drawn Lauren's attention—the band. She had caught up with the guys at the corner of the chain-link fence surrounding the tennis courts. I was too far away to hear what they were saying. I added another purple blob to a green stem. All the colors on the cardboard palette I held were mixing together and there was nothing I could do about it. Mr. Lucas was getting closer, going down the row of painters, made up mostly of people in their sixties.

I set my paints on the ground and stepped over to Mr. Lucas. "Excuse me, I'm sorry. I'll be right back. I'm going to get my sister."

"That's fine," he said.

"Thank you." I rushed down the path.

"Avery," Kai said when I reached them. "How is your transformation into Bob Ross going?"

Lauren gave me her impish smile.

"The only thing left is a perm," I responded.

Levi snorted.

As casually as possible, I looked at Brooks and said, "Hey."

"Hi," he said, then returned his attention to the clipboard he held, writing something down.

84

"I've never painted anything in my life," Levi said. "You any good?"

"No, not at all." Back in the meadow, my paint blobs were probably dripping onto the tall grass by now.

"It's one of those things that takes practice," Ian said. "You're not born with the skill."

He was right, of course, and I appreciated the first bit of encouragement I'd heard all day.

"I was born with some skills," Kai said.

"Oh, here we go," Levi sighed.

"Good looks, awesomeness, and these." He flexed his biceps.

"That was probably terrifying for your mother," Brooks said.

I laughed.

"That's not what *your* mother says," Kai shot back with a punch to Brooks's shoulder.

"Gross," I said.

Brooks caught my eye and then looked down at his clipboard. I followed his gaze and saw a paper with the words *pay phone, tomorrow, noon.*

I gave him a short nod, hoping that was just where he wanted to meet for the deal we'd made the night before, not that I'd gotten another phone call from Shay.

"How'd my footage from the other night turn out?" Kai asked Lauren. "Need some better angles?" He spun a slow circle and of course Lauren laughed.

My big sister mode came out. It was one thing to talk about how cute the guys were, like Lauren had done the first night she saw them, but my dad was right—Lauren was only fifteen and Kai was eighteen, and I needed to make sure nothing came out of Lauren's documentary other than some killer footage.

"Yes, actually," she said, dragging him closer to the chain link. "Outside shots would be good."

Ian and Levi followed and I stayed close behind.

"What's with the clipboard?" I asked Brooks, noticing him move with me. "Do you do something aside from band stuff here?"

"We're gofers. We go wherever we're needed."

"But you have to do it together . . . as a group?" I asked. "You're inseparable?"

He smiled. "Yes, we're very codependent."

"As every good band should be," I said.

He lifted the clipboard. "No, we don't have to stay together but we usually do in the mornings so that we can talk over songs and stuff for that night."

"Oh, is that the reason?" Levi asked. "Then I have a discussion point."

Ian had wandered over to the fence and was watching a tennis match.

"What's that?" Brooks asked.

"Kai has gotten heavy-handed with the drums in the bridge. I think you should talk to him about it."

"I'll listen for that tonight."

"Will you?" Levi asked. "Because Kai seems to do what he wants."

"Seriously, Levi?" Kai said, leaning around the phone my sister had been holding up. "Just because you make zero contributions to the band doesn't mean you have to crap all over mine."

"Bass is a key element."

"Is it, though?" Kai said with a cheerful smile.

Levi turned to Brooks. "This is what I mean—you let him get away with everything."

"Last I checked, I wasn't band mom," Brooks said.

"Spoken like a true leader," Levi said in exasperation, and stormed off.

I watched him go and then assessed the remaining band members. Kai was focused back on my sister. Ian had never stopped watching tennis, and Brooks was crossing out items on the list he held.

"Is he going to be okay?" I asked when it was obvious nobody was going to say anything.

Brooks looked confused for a split second before he said, "Oh, Levi? Yeah, he'll get over it. Always does."

"You all seem to fight a lot."

"I wouldn't call it fighting but yes, there are many strong opinions here."

It had seemed like fighting to me. And conflict wasn't my favorite; I tried to avoid it when I could. Lauren's laugh rang out and my brows drew together as I watched her and Kai, heads close, watch a video on her phone.

"Lauren, we should probably get back to our class." I gave Brooks the *Help me out here, she's only fifteen* look.

It was a lot to expect him to understand without words but he seemed to at least understand the first part because he said, "And we have a mouse in cabin four to corner, boys."

They left, and as Lauren and I walked back to the meadow and our paintings, I said, "You know he's eighteen, right?"

"Who?" she asked.

"You know exactly who I'm talking about," I said, because she did; she was just trying to play innocent.

"Okay, Dad," Lauren returned.

"Seriously, Lauren, any boy in college interested in a sophomore in high school is only interested in one thing."

"Now you can read minds?" She sighed as she picked up her paint palette off the grass. "It's not my fault that I'm mature for my age."

"I'm not kidding."

"Whatever. Nothing is happening. Pretty sure you're the only one crushing on someone," she said.

"No, I'm not. We're just friends!" My racing heart and overly defensive reaction seemed to completely contradict my words. So I calmly added, "Plus, Brooks is only a year older than me. There's a difference. But, either way, it doesn't matter. I'm not here to get anyone fired." And that was true.

She reached over and swiped a streak of green paint across my arm.

I gasped. "Brat!" I added purple to her neck and she squealed, then laughed.

I held up my paint palette like a shield, waiting for her retaliation. But before she did, she pulled out her phone so she could get it on video. My smile slipped off my face.

Chapter 10

"WHERE DID YOU GET THESE? YOU JUST HAVE BOWS AND arrows lying around your cabin?" I asked.

Brooks and I stood in a clearing in the woods above the lake. After meeting at the pay phone (which turned out to be just a convenient place, not a waiting phone call), we'd trudged through overgrown brush, away from the crowded trails of camp, away from the docks dotted with colorful kayaks and paddle boats, away from the roped-off swimming area with its lounge chairs and splashing kids, to this spot that seemed far away from everything.

Even though it seemed far away, it had only been a fifteen-minute walk. I picked a few foxtails out of my socks and then stood. Beyond the trees surrounding us, I could see the large lake stretched out below, its jagged borders making it seem like it wanted to escape the confines of its home, the trees its only barriers to freedom.

Brooks picked up a bow leaning against a tree. "I swiped them from the archery range. They won't miss them for a couple hours."

I wondered when he had brought them up here. When he'd had time.

"Have you done this before?" he asked.

"Snuck into the woods with a boy and shot arrows? No, no, I haven't."

He smiled. "And if you take away the boy and the woods?"

Why would I want to do that? "Still no," I said.

He nocked an arrow onto the bowstring and sent it flying into a fallen tree across the way.

"Is that what you were aiming for?"

"Yes," he said.

"I wasn't sure how impressed I should be."

"And you've decided you're very impressed?"

"For sure."

His eyes twinkled as he handed me a bow. "Let's see what you got."

I gripped the bow and stared at the tree across the way. "Tips, tricks, secrets?"

"Are you right-handed?"

"Yes."

"Okay, left arm forward, right elbow straight back, until your hand rests against your cheek, and then aim and release."

"That easy, huh?"

"I guess we'll see." He held up an arrow and pointed to the orange, feathered end. "See this little notch here? That fits over the string."

I lifted the bow, fitting the arrow in place, and managed to stretch the string and arrow back until my hand touched my cheek.

I'd seen enough movies to know at least the basics. There was more tension in the string than I'd imagined there'd be.

Brooks reached out and adjusted my elbow. "Look at your target over the top of the arrowhead."

"Okay, I got it."

"And release."

I released, the arrow flew, and the string snapped hard against my inner arm. "Holy . . . Ouch!" I dropped the bow and covered my stinging arm.

"Oh yeah," he said with a cringe. "I should've warned you about the snapback. People wear forearm guards for that."

"But *we* don't? We're not people?"

He laughed. "I didn't think to grab any."

"Did you not get your arm snapped when you shot?" Without thinking, I grabbed his arm and flipped it to study the underside. There were no red marks.

"If you bend your extended arm just a bit, it helps."

I dropped my hand. "Remember when I said tips, tricks, secrets? That would fall under really any of those categories."

"I'm sorry." He took my arm this time. "Let me see." He ran a light finger over the welt that had appeared on my skin. "Does it still hurt?"

A chill ran up my arm and all the way down my spine. Our eyes met. He was waiting for an answer, I realized. "No, it doesn't." Lauren's accusation about me having a crush on him flashed through my mind and I took a step back, breaking our connection. Then, much too loudly, I asked, "Did I hit the target?" I searched the tree in the distance, which only held his arrow.

"Close," he said.

"Are you lying?"

"Yes."

I walked the path to the tree and found my arrow on the ground halfway there. I scooped it up and finished the walk, pulling his out of the dark wood. Instead of walking back to him, I sat on our target. A large black ant crawled along the bark by my leg, carrying a tiny rock in its pinchers. I shifted out of its path.

"Where did you learn how to shoot an arrow?" I asked as Brooks walked my way.

"Here, actually. My first summer."

"I thought you were going to tell me that you belong to a family of hunters or something."

"No. I've only ever shot paper targets. And honestly, not very well."

"But I was very impressed. Do I need to take it back?"

He nudged at the tree with his foot. "This was a very big target."

"Obviously not big enough for some of us." I held out the arrows to him.

"It was your first time. Don't tell me you're done."

"I'm done for a minute." I rubbed my arm. "I thought you were going to bring your notebook so we could work on lyrics too." But he hadn't. The only thing in the clearing were the bows and arrows.

"That would've been smart."

"When is this festival audition anyway?"

He used the arrows as drumsticks and tapped out a beat on a branch. "July eighteenth."

"That's in less than four weeks!"

"We have the instruments, the players, and the music. All we need are the lyrics. Easy."

I laughed. "Except obviously not, because you guys have had, what, three weeks together and have written two lines?"

"But now we have you."

"You do remember I've never done this before, right?"

"We have almost four weeks."

"No pressure or anything."

He sank both arrows into a rotting section of wood on the fallen tree and left them there. "If it works, it works. If it doesn't . . ."

"It's a sign?"

"Right."

Great, Brooks's entire future was dependent on whether I could help him write the perfect song? "Remind me of the lines Ian kept singing the other night."

"'What's tomorrow look like from over there? Because from here it looks a lot like yesterday, and I'm tired of trying to rewrite history.'"

My eyes were on the ant traveling the log again while I listened to Brooks. "Did you write that?"

"Yeah."

"What's it about?"

He seemed surprised by the question, as if nobody had asked him that before. Wasn't that the kind of thing a band discussed when writing lyrics? "It's about feeling stuck, I guess, like when your future looks exactly like your past and there's nothing you can do about it."

I moved one foot onto the log with me and hugged my knee to my chest. "Is it fiction? Or is that inspired by your life?"

His gaze went out to the lake or at least in that direction. "*Inspired* is such a funny word. Like my life could be inspiration for anything."

"Many stories are inspired by tragedy."

"I guess that's true."

"So what's yours?" I asked.

"What's mine?"

"Your tragedy. Why all the musical angst? Broken heart? Bitter divorce?"

"I haven't been married yet," he said.

I gave a breathy laugh. "You're running out of time."

"I know, I'm practically an old maid, a spinster, a cat lady. . . . Wow, all the *late to marriage* sayings only apply to women, don't they?"

"Yes, should we write a song about all the misogyny in the world?"

"Because an all-male band performing a song about misogyny is a *good* look?"

"You're right, let's focus on your tragic, tragic backstory and then go from there. So spill."

"Yes, where do I start? My pathetic life is full of lyrical inspiration."

I could tell he had started that as a joke, but by the end of the second sentence, his voice had gone so low I almost couldn't hear it. So I put my chin on my knee and waited to see if he wanted to share.

He was back to staring at the lake. "My dad is sick. He had a stroke several years ago and can hardly function on his own. My mom decided to put him in a home that we really can't afford. So now she works all the time and all my money goes to the family fund as well and basically I feel like I'm forty when I want to be eighteen for a minute but she needs me and so does my little brother. But most of all, my dad." He said that all in a breathy rush, like he'd said it a million times and yet hadn't shared it with anyone.

When I didn't respond right away, searching for words that didn't exist, he slowly let his head turn my way. "How's that for tragedy? Is there some good inspiration in there?"

"I'm so sorry," I said. "About your dad."

"It's . . ." He shrugged. "It's whatever."

"I understand why you feel like you need a practical career instead of . . ."

"Selfishness?"

"What? No. Most teenagers I know wouldn't contribute *any* of their paychecks to the family expenses. Brooks, you're not selfish for also wanting to dream."

"I guess the universe will let me know."

Just in case there wasn't some greater power ready to dole out signs, I wanted to help as much as possible. "Lyrics," I said.

"You have an idea?"

"'What's tomorrow look like from over there? Because from here it looks a lot like yesterday, and I can't rewrite history,'" I said, tweaking the last line of the lyric slightly.

Brooks nodded as if he agreed with the change and added, "'Even though I've tried before.'"

I hated that he thought he was selfish for wanting to pursue music. He could be there for his family and still dream. I repeated his lyric aloud a couple times, trying to think what could come next in the song. Finally I spit out, "'It's time for change, for letting go, for wanting more.'"

His magic smile was back. "Look at you trying to add hope to my songs."

"If you don't like that line, it could be something like—"

"No, I like it. It fits. And the guys are always telling me that every song needs at least a little hope in it. I guess we just needed someone in the writing sessions who has some."

I was about to respond when his watch started beeping.

"Time's up," he said, collecting the arrows from the bark, then looking over his shoulder as he headed to the others across the way. "Did you want to try one last shot?"

I stared at the arrows. That was the whole point of this, right? To shake myself awake. I smiled as I realized this experiment of mine was way more fun to do with someone else. And it didn't hurt at all that the someone else was the attractive, confident, guitar-playing Brooks, who I absolutely did not have a crush on at all. "Yes."

Chapter 11

I WALKED DOWN THE TRAIL, TOWARD MY CABIN, MY EYES
on my dusty ankles. We'd been here over a week and I was never
going to get used to how dirty my feet always were.

"Averyl"

The beach area and docks had just closed for the day and several people were tugging canvas totes and tired kids along the path,
blocking my view. I weaved through a group until I saw Maricela
on the beach by the swimming area, dragging a lounge chair back
into its spot. She waved at me when I finally saw her.

"Hi!" I said, stepping over a knee-high rope border and around
the snack hut, where an employee was retracting the awning, to join
Mari on the sand.

"Where are you coming from?" she asked.

"The lodge. Lauren and I made some really lopsided vases."
Again, Brooks and I hadn't made a plan, so instead of some cool
outing, I was left with whatever the camp schedule offered.

"Ah, pottery? Fun."

I patted my bicep. "It was a workout."

"See you later, Maricela," the girl from the snack hut called.

"Bye, Lucy! Thanks for letting me raid the candy stash today."

Lucy held a peace sign in the air.

Back to me, Maricela said, "Speaking of workouts, in a couple days, I have to lead a hike up to the natural slides. The list fills up fast, so I added you and your sister."

"That sounds fun."

"Try to tell your face that." She threw a striped beach towel into a pile she'd started by a standing umbrella.

I followed suit and collected more used towels that had been left on chairs. "No, it does."

"Good because D signed up to co-lead with me and I need to make sure some people I like are going to be there."

"I thought she was front desk duty."

"She is, just like I'm lifeguard, but Janelle is all about employee satisfaction and she lets us pick a few extra things each summer to mix it up. So we don't get bored."

"And you picked a hike?"

"Not just any hike! It's the natural slides. You'll see why I picked it soon."

"Can't wait."

A loud buzzing noise sounded by the docks, making me jump. Clay stood on the end, holding up a megaphone. "Lake activities are closed for the day. Please return."

A lone red kayak was at least fifty yards out, turning in circles.

"You must paddle on both sides," Clay said. "No, both!"

Maricela laughed as she lowered the back of a lounger.

Past the kayak, on the opposite shore, something caught my eye. Some bright, multicolored . . . balloons? They were bobbing and bouncing, attached to or tangled around a tree trunk. "What is that?" I asked.

"It's a person who doesn't know how to work a kayak," Maricela said.

"No, past him."

She was squinting now, too, and sighed. "I swear. People are so rude. Always leaving their trash everywhere. Come on."

She beelined it to the docks, where Clay was now helping the kayaker onto solid ground. The man seemed wobbly as he dropped his life jacket in a pile of others and moved past us.

"You're welcome," Clay mumbled, now tying up the kayak.

"Clay," Maricela said.

"What? You heard nothing," he said, then stood and began gathering the life jackets and tossing them into an open shed by the lifeguard stand.

"How about untying one of the canoes for us?" Maricela asked sweetly.

"What? Why? I need to clean up."

She pointed and when Clay saw what we had, he walked down the wooden planks and freed a canoe at the far end. It was a two-seater but he climbed in after us, sitting on the hump in the middle. They each grabbed a paddle, but since there were only two, I was left empty-handed. As we glided across the lake, it seemed twice as far as it had from the docks.

When we reached the shore, Maricela, who was in the front, hopped out and held on to a handle while Clay and I climbed out. Then Clay dragged the canoe farther onto the sand.

"Is this still part of the camp over here?" I asked.

"No," Maricela said. "This is the state park."

The balloons were tied around the trunk of the tree just past the shoreline and were banging into each other, creating an unnatural rhythm in the forest.

"Anyone bring a knife?" Clay asked as we approached.

"You don't carry one?" Maricela asked.

I smiled. "Is that a man requirement?"

"Yes," she said.

"I guess I've failed as a man," Clay said.

I took hold of a section of the ribbon and tried to rip it in two by sheer force. It didn't work. While Clay and Maricela took turns trying as well, I searched the ground for some sort of tool that might help us. I came back with a rock.

"I got this," I said, shooing them aside. I wedged the sharp edge of the rock beneath the ribbon and tugged, breaking it with a snap.

"Nice." Clay grabbed the balloons and tugged them the rest of the way free. "Now you can add forest ranger to your resume."

We all turned back toward the lake and canoe. "Better yet, I'll use this as an answer to a college essay question," I said. "Describe a time where you saved a tree from the perils of humankind."

Clay shook the three balloons in his hand at me. "You would be so prepared for that question."

"I know!"

"Hold up a minute, you two, I want to see something," Maricela said, and she split off to the left, toward a big boulder fifty feet away.

"You think?" Clay asked.

I was obviously not privileged to whatever information came from their shared history. So when we came upon a group of rocks forming a messy circle, I had no idea why they both laughed.

"What is it?"

"I don't believe this is still here," Maricela said. She toed a rock back into place. "Last summer, a bunch of us did a moon circle."

"What's a moon circle?"

"I'm not sure what it is officially, but for us, we came out on a new moon, sat in this circle, and made promises. The new moon is supposed to represent a do-over. A chance to set new goals or whatever."

"You believe in moon powers?" I asked.

"I believe in putting positive thoughts into the universe, and whether it's the moon that helps me achieve those goals or the energy of the thought itself circling my brain, it makes no difference."

"It worked, then? The goals you made last year were achieved?"

"You know what? They were. I'm coming back here on the new moon because I have a few wishes that need granting."

I wondered what she was referring to. Cosmetology? Her mystery boy?

"What promises did you make last year?" I asked.

"That's between me and the moon, girl," Maricela said with a smirk.

"Everyone's was different," Clay said, catching Maricela's eye. And for a second I wondered if Clay was Mari's mystery guy. But that was the first real shared look I'd seen this whole time, so I doubted my own suspicions.

She squatted down and moved a few more rocks back into the circle. "When's the next new moon?"

"I don't know," Clay said. "We'll have to look it up."

"Look it up?" I asked. "How? Google does not exist here."

She smiled. "We actually go into town on our day off."

"Lucky!" I said.

"Your parents won't let you leave camp?" Clay asked as we headed back toward the canoe.

"You know, I'm not sure. I haven't asked them. My guess is no. I think they picked this camp on purpose. To get us away from social media for a summer." I was almost positive it was because of Lauren. They may have been proud of her creativity, but I was sure my parents wished she was on her phone less.

"So that's what you miss most about life outside of camp?" Maricela asked. "Wi-Fi?"

"Considering this camp is pretty posh, what else could I miss?"

"In-N-Out," Clay said.

"Dairy Queen," Maricela said.

"Chipotle."

"Five Guys."

"You both sound hungry," I said.

Clay pushed the canoe into the water and held the handle as Maricela and I climbed in. "That's because it's almost dinnertime," Clay said.

He was right. The sky was turning gray and I had a small moment of panic as I wondered if we'd actually missed dinner altogether.

And because I wasn't hungry, I knew it had nothing to do with the food and everything to do with the dinner entertainment.

That suspicion was solidified when we reached the docks on the opposite shore and Brooks was standing there watching us. My heart doubled its speed.

Brooks held up a walkie-talkie. "I got a report about life jackets left out."

Clay hopped out of the canoe. "Really? Someone tattled on me? I'm here. We had a civic duty to perform."

Maricela reached up for Brooks, who offered her a hand out. "Aren't you supposed to be playing right now, rock star?" she asked.

He held his hand out for me now. I took it and stepped first onto the seat and then onto the dock, the canoe shifting a bit with my movement, causing me to pitch forward. Brooks caught me by the elbow as I stumbled to standing. "You okay?" His breath tickled the hair by my ear.

"Yes, thank you."

To Mari, Brooks said, "Yes, I'm heading to play right now. Just had to check this out first."

"I'm going to be able to answer the tree saver question on the college essay now," I blurted out, still flustered from the tingling by my ear.

"What?" he asked.

"Nothing," Maricela said, hooking her arm in mine. "I'm going to walk this girl to dinner." She patted my hand as though she understood the effect Brooks could have on people. I needed to get myself in check.

"Hey, Avery!" Clay called before we got too far.

I turned.

"Happy birthday." He handed me the half-deflated balloons.

I laughed. "You're so thoughtful."

My eyes flitted to Brooks and he mouthed, *"Tomorrow? Six a.m.?"*

I gave a quick nod and as my chest expanded with happiness, I decided that getting myself in check was overrated.

Chapter 12

"WHERE ARE YOU GOING?"

My hand was on the knob of the front door and I whirled around with the question. Dad sat at the table in the breakfast nook. I hadn't seen him. It was early—six in the morning. I'd assumed nobody would be awake.

"You scared me," I said as my nonanswer. I was not good at lying and I'd been having to do it more often than not lately when every night at dinner my parents would ask for a summary of our day. But just leaving out a few events was a lot easier than having to think of a fully formed lie. I tried to stick as close to the truth as possible and said, "I wanted to go look at the ropes course. I guess it's less crowded in the morning."

"I don't think it's open this early," Dad said. "I don't think anything is."

"I'm sure you're right. When someone told me to go early, they probably didn't mean this early." Except that's exactly what Brooks meant when, after telling me the time the day before, he'd told me the place. That was the whole reason we were going this early, because it wouldn't open for two hours and we'd have it to ourselves. "Maybe I'll just check it out and see if it's something I even want to do."

"Do you want some company?"

"No," I said too fast, then added, "I'm okay."

The flash of hurt that crossed my dad's face made me feel guilty, so I added, "Maybe later we can reserve a kayak."

"Sounds good," he said.

I left, pulling the door closed behind me. *Why should I feel guilty?* I thought. *You don't care when you hurt my feelings.* I sighed. He doesn't care because he doesn't know.

I was so caught up in my thoughts that I hadn't felt the electricity in the warm air as I set off down the path. But I felt it now. A band of gray, early morning sky shone in the distance, but overhead, piles of dark clouds hung in still silence. I ignored them and trudged ahead. The wind started slowly at first and then kicked up dry leaves and pine needles as I walked.

I looked up at the sky and a drop of rain landed on my cheek. It was just a small drop. I kept walking, wind whipping through my hair. The longer I walked, the more drops of water fell from the sky. The ropes course was on the far edge of camp, past all the guest cottages and the lodge, past the tennis courts and meadow. It was tucked in a section of tightly grouped trees.

Suspended between the trees were wide ropes and hanging tires and wooden slats and rope ladders and cargo nets and my knees felt like they wanted to buckle while staring at it all from solid ground. The obstacles swayed in the wind.

A crack of lightning lit up the sky, followed several seconds later by the rumble of thunder. I ducked, as if the thunder was the part to be worried about. Thirty feet away was a wooden pavilion. I rushed over to it as the rain turned from a sprinkle to a steady drizzle. I stepped under the shelter and shook the water off my hair. That's when I realized I wasn't alone.

Brooks was already there, sitting on a backless bench next to a pegboard of harnesses and helmets.

"Hey," I said, wiping at my shirt and shorts as if that would dry them. "It's raining."

He smirked. "I hadn't noticed."

I walked between two rows of benches and sat down next to him. "I'm guessing ropes courses and rain don't mix."

"Good guess."

"We could've slept in," I said.

"I know."

"I don't wake up this early for anyone."

"Well, you're awake, so that must mean you wake up this early for . . ." He pointed at himself.

I felt my cheeks go warm, but I managed to say, "I mean, technically, it's for me, right?"

"True. Did you have fun with Clay and Maricela yesterday? Are they helping you discover yourself too?" Was that a hint of jealousy in his voice?

"No. I haven't told anyone else about this."

"Was it really your birthday yesterday?"

"What?" I asked, confused for a moment; then I remembered Clay and the balloons. "Oh, no. He was just being funny."

The rain around us intensified, pounding on the roof and echoing through the pavilion.

I turned toward him. "Sooo, what happens when it rains here? Does everyone have to stay in their cabins?"

"No, they open more activities in the lodge."

"And you?" I asked, my eyes catching his before looking back at the bench between us. "Does this mean you get the day off?"

He let out a single laugh. "No, this will keep us twice as busy—leaky roofs and falling tree branches and stranded guests." He pointed at me with his last words.

"Oh, I'm stranded now?"

He looked out at the pounding rain. "It's a long way back to the guest cabins."

"And how are you going to help me, brave Bear Meadow employee?"

"Well, considering I'm not on the clock yet, we're going to hunker down here, hope the rain stops in the next hour or two, and write the rest of a killer song."

I put the back of my hand to my forehead and in a breathy, dramatic voice said, "Is that what you do for *all* the stranded guests or just the lucky ones?"

"It's the least I can do."

I shoved his arm. "It sounds like I'm the one doing the saving in this scenario." Of course, I didn't mind helping him with lyrics, but Lauren had been right—I did write poems and liked words, so this felt familiar to me. Not something new like I was supposed to do today.

Whatever metal parts existed on the course above were clanking together like oversized wind chimes. I stared up at the ropes course. It seemed massive, looming, terrifying. It felt like it was taunting me. Like it was saying, *You wish your life could be bigger and more exciting but it can't be because you're the one living it.* I swallowed hard.

"It will be here all summer," he said, seeming to read my mind.

"True. So, a killer song."

He dragged a backpack in front of him that I hadn't noticed he'd brought. "I have my notebook this time." He pulled out a tattered hundred-page green notebook.

"Ah, is this where all the soul-sucking lyrics are kept?"

"Yes. You might not want to look too close." He flipped a few pages.

"Wow, soul-sucking is super-messy."

He studied a page as if this observation surprised him. "Are you one of those people who writes in perfectly straight lines in your notebook?"

"I don't have a notebook. . . . I mean, I have a notebook, but it's only for class notes, so yes, my lines are pretty straight."

"My class notes look very much like this." He patted the page filled with different colors of ink and scribbled out words and sideways words.

"Do you ever expect to actually find the things you write down after you write them?"

"It's organized chaos. Trust me." He flipped to a page where the lyrics we'd worked on at the beginning of the week were written. "Any inspiration strike since last time?"

I read through the lyrics twice. "Yes, actually. I was thinking about how the lines so far are about history and starting over, and then it says 'It's time for change.' What if we continued with that theme of time?"

"Yeah . . ."

"I know this song was inspired by your life and your dad, but could we also make it apply to relationships? Then it will become instantly relatable to nearly everyone who hears it."

"If people can relate to it, they like it more."

"Exactly."

"Okay, so whose past relationships are we going to draw inspiration from? Mine or yours?"

I froze with the question, then finally stuttered, "It . . . it's *your* song."

"A reaction like that has a story. Let's hear it."

An image of Trent played in my mind. He was smiling and laughing. And then he was looking past me, his eyes softening. I followed his gaze to Shay. Was this a memory playing in my head or just something I'd conjured up since the betrayal? I didn't even know anymore. "I trust too easily in relationships," I said. "I like to think the best of people. And maybe I need to stop that."

"Why would you need to stop that?" he asked.

"Because it hurts more when they're not as invested as I am. When I learn things that I was too blind to see." I shook my head. I did not want to talk about this. I nodded toward his backpack. "Got a pen in there somewhere?"

❀ ❀ ❀

"And we have a verse and a chorus," I said with a big smile. We had moved to the ground and were using the bench like a table.

Brooks looked happy, too, a smile on his face, his eyes lit up. "I haven't had that productive of a writing session in forever."

"We make a good team." I leaned back on my palms, even though the ground was dirty. For the first time since we'd started, I became aware of our surroundings. The rain was mostly gone and water dripped off the edge of the roof. I moved my head one way and then the other, stretching my neck. I opened my mouth to ask how much time we had left when his watch alarm went off.

He pushed a button on the side, silencing it. "I need to go."

"Are you going to turn into a pumpkin?" I whispered.

"Does that make you the princess?"

"I'm sorry. Did you want to be the princess? You do have great hair."

He laughed, then stood, brushed off the back of his shorts and his hands, and reached out for my hand. He pulled me to standing, but just as I was about to turn back the way I'd come, he cursed and yanked me against him, whirling us the opposite way. He practically carried me to the other side of the pegboard, where he pressed my back against the large sheet of plywood and his body against mine.

I looked up at him, wide-eyed, but he was staring over my shoulder, listening, I realized. Had he seen someone? Had someone seen us? I concentrated on the sounds around us, but there was just his heart, pounding against me, and his breath, close to my ear. He smelled like coconut shampoo and something sharp, like soap or deodorant.

"My backpack is out there," he mouthed. *"Stay here."*

I nodded, a little dizzy.

He took a step away from me and I stumbled, not realizing I must've been using him for support. I straightened up and listened hard as he rounded the corner.

"Brooks? You scared me. What are you doing?" I didn't recognize the voice.

"Hi, Desiree."

Who was Desiree? I hadn't met a Desiree. A drop of water from the edge of the roof dripped onto my forehead. I didn't dare move out of the way or wipe at it.

"Just making sure the storm didn't knock down any branches on the course," Brooks said. "You brought towels?"

"Yeah, Janelle wants towels at each station to wipe things down."

"She's not closing them for the day?"

"The storm passed. It's supposed to be clear now."

"Right."

Another drop of water hit my cheek this time.

There was a scuffing of feet like she was walking away; then she said, "Kai was looking for you earlier. Did he ever find you?"

"Uh, yeah, band stuff."

"Cool, see you later."

"Bye."

A few minutes passed and I stayed in my hiding spot, more water collecting on my hair and face. I could hear someone moving around out there and I was pretty sure it was Brooks, but I didn't want to risk it.

"That was close," he finally said as he appeared at my side.

"Is everything okay? Did she see me? Who's Desiree?" I asked.

He smirked. "Take a breath." He wiped at some water on my

cheek with the back of his hand. My breath caught. "Want a towel?" he asked.

"No." I used my sleeve to mop up more water. "Who was that?"

"You know D, right?" he asked. "Works at the front desk."

I took several deep breaths. "That was D? Tell me she didn't see me."

"She didn't see you. It's fine. But we should go." He held out his hand and nodded toward the forest. "Time to rescue my stranded guest."

Chapter 13

THE NEXT DAY BROUGHT PERFECT WEATHER. BROOKS HAD led me all the way to the edge of the guest cabins the day before. We'd stayed on the back side of buildings, cut through trees, well off the trail, and away from people. He kept hold of my hand the entire time as we tripped over roots and stepped in hidden puddles, laughing and shushing each other as we went.

The rain, which had continued sporadically throughout the day, canceling all outdoor activities, had finally cleared. And now the camp smelled like damp dirt and tangy pine. When Lauren and I entered the lodge to meet up with the hiking group, D was standing on the bench that surrounded the tree, holding a clipboard.

"Fredrick Sampson," she called out.

A man in his midthirties raised his hand. "Here."

"She's taking roll?" Lauren whispered.

"Guess so."

Maricela stood by a folding table full of snacks.

"Laney Swan," D continued.

A woman with a big sun hat waved. "Yeah."

D put a mark on the clipboard; then her eyes were on me. "This excursion is already full, sorry."

"We're on the list," I said. "Avery and Lauren Young."

D shook her head as she ran her pen along the page. "I don't—"

"They're on there," Maricela said.

"Oh yes, here you are, at the very bottom."

Maricela rolled her eyes and nodded me over.

"I don't think she likes me very much," I whispered.

Maricela waved her hand through the air like it was nothing. "Nah. That's just her."

"If you say so," I said. "By the way, this is my sister, Lauren. Lauren, this is Maricela."

"Hi," Lauren said. "Are these snacks for the hikers?"

"Yes, help yourself."

Lauren eyed the snacks warily. "Free snacks must mean it's a long hike. Is it long?"

"It's not hard," Maricela assured her.

"That's not what I asked. Is it over a mile?"

"A mile?" Maricela said. "A mile would hardly get us out of camp!"

"So two miles, then," Lauren said with a smile. "I can do two miles."

"Are you negotiating?" Maricela asked.

"I am," Lauren said. "What would it take to get a ride to the halfway point in one of those air-conditioned shuttles I saw in the parking lot?"

"It would take a road. There is no road to the rock slides."

Lauren looked at me like this would change my mind. Like no road meant no civilization. "The camp has its own water slide and we only have to go about a hundred yards for it," Lauren said, as if she needed to remind me.

"I promise it will be worth it," Maricela said. "They are amazing."

"I'm holding you to that." Lauren grabbed several granola bars and a couple packs of trail mix off the table and put them in the backpack I was carrying.

"Okay!" D said. "Everyone gather 'round. I just need to go over a few rules."

❁ ❁ ❁

Maricela was right. Regardless of the fact that my feet hurt and sweat was beading along my upper lip and gathering at my temples, it was worth it. Between spindly pine trees and tall grass and wildflowers was a wide stream of flowing water. And in that stream was a natural phenomenon that I had never seen before—large sheets of rock smooth enough to slide on. And that's exactly what people were doing—sliding over the slick surface of the flat rocks to a pool ten feet below. Beyond the pool was another slide and another drop.

"This is amazing," Lauren whispered, her camera scanning the scene in front of us.

"Remember what we talked about!" D called out to the group that was already moving toward the slides. "Look for people below before you slide, and no diving!"

I squinted my eyes upstream toward the first slide. "Wait, is that . . . ?"

"Kai!" Lauren called.

He turned at his name and a big smile took over his face. "Hey!"

D shaded her eyes with one hand, her other hand flying to her hip. "What is he doing here?"

"It's my day off!" he called, as if he'd really heard D's question. Maybe he could read lips from fifty feet away.

"Wait for me!" Lauren called, throwing off her tank and sliding out of her cutoffs. She wore an adorable high-waisted two-piece.

D sputtered a bit, as if she was going to object, but Lauren was gone before she uttered a word.

I picked up her phone, which she had tossed onto her pile of clothes, and tucked it in the front pocket of my backpack.

Maricela, who had been walking at the back of the group with some slower hikers, stopped at my side, out of breath.

D whirled on Maricela. "Did you know they were going to be here?"

They? My eyes followed the flowing stream down the smooth rocks, and I saw a couple other employees I knew and several I didn't.

"Who?" Maricela asked.

"Kai, Clay, Ian, Lucy, Mario." She pointed at each as she said their names.

"No, but if it's their day off, they can go wherever they want."

D shook her head. "Janelle said—"

"D, there are a ton of people here. You know Janelle just means that we can't hang out with guests alone."

D's eyes slid to mine and my heart seemed to stop in my chest. She had seen me the day before behind that pegboard. Brooks thought she hadn't but it was obvious now she had. Was she going to call me out?

"You're right," she said. "That is the *official* rule."

"So see, we're all good," Maricela said. "Go have fun."

"I'll go make sure the guests are enjoying themselves," D said, and left us standing by the pile of backpacks and clothes that the hikers had abandoned near us.

"That's not what I suggested," Maricela said under her breath, "but almost the same thing."

I tried not to laugh too loud.

"I thought it was Brooks's day off too," Maricela said, proving that even though she'd played innocent with D, she may have known some of the other employees would be up here. She moved to her tiptoes and scanned the heads in the water. "I wonder why he didn't come."

"Pretty sure he hates most of the guests," I said.

"Who hates the guests?"

I tried to contain the smile that wanted to take over my face as I looked to the right and saw Brooks walking up from where he must've just completed the series of slides. His hair was wet and he wore a swimsuit and water shoes. And he looked really good. Really, really good.

"We were just talking about you," Maricela said unhelpfully. Then she had the audacity to be distracted by a group of campers standing on an outcropping of rocks by the water. "That's super slippery, guys, be careful!" She walked away.

Brooks stopped in front of me, water dripping off the bottom of his shorts. "You think I hate everyone?"

"I mean everyone but me, obviously."

He gave a sharp laugh. "Obviously."

"You didn't tell me you were coming to this today," I said.

"You didn't tell me *you* were coming."

"I guess that's true." Because I hadn't known today was his day off.

He jerked his head toward the slides. "You going to try it?"

I realized I was just standing there, sweat on my face, gripping the straps of my backpack, my shoes and shorts and T-shirt still very much on. "Yes, of course." I let my backpack slide down my arms and onto the ground by the pile of other backpacks. I was very aware that Brooks was still there as I took off my shoes and shorts.

"Do you do this a lot?" I asked.

"The slides?" he responded.

"Yes."

"I've done it a few times."

"It's fun?" I didn't know why I was so nervous.

"For a girl with the Granny app on her phone, you can't be scared of this."

I laughed. Granny was a game where a scary cartoon grandma hunted down the player and killed them if they didn't hide well enough. I hadn't played it in forever. "I was wondering when you were going to start calling me out for my apps."

"Not nearly soon enough," he said.

"You owe me reciprocation." I narrowed my eyes. "You do actually have a phone, right?"

He chuckled. "Yes. I do."

"Don't laugh. This place messes with my head."

"It *is* super weird not seeing people on their phones all the time."
He held up a finger. "Except your sister."

"True, she keeps us all in this decade."

"Is she serious about making a band documentary?"

"As serious as Granny is when she discovers your hiding place."

His lips twitched a little and he said, "So your sister is going to *kill* us?"

I shoved his shoulder. "And I thought my joke was bad."

"Your joke *was* bad. It was terrible. It deserved that comeback."

As we headed up an incline toward the first slide, D turned away from the group she'd been talking to and jolted to a stop when she saw us. I inched to the left, putting more space between me and Brooks.

"Hey, Desiree," Brooks said.

The hard look she'd given me slipped off her face and she showed all her teeth to Brooks. "Hi, be safe."

He nodded and we continued up.

When I was sure we were well past her, I said, "She saw me yesterday."

"What?" he asked.

"At the ropes course. With you."

The muscle in his jaw jumped, then relaxed. "Are you sure?"

"I mean, no, but I think." I watched as his brain seemed to work through things. I cringed. "That's bad, right?"

"She didn't see us. She would've reported me."

"Yeah?"

"For sure."

"And if she had reported you?"

"I wouldn't be here," he said.

"Then we need to be more careful." I almost suggested that we shouldn't spend any more alone time together. That we always needed to be with other people if we were going to hang out. But I couldn't force myself to say it out loud and I knew that made me selfish.

He nodded. "Agreed."

Chapter 14

I SLID DOWN THE ROCK AFTER BROOKS. IT WASN'T QUITE as smooth as it looked but it was fun. Especially the drop at the end. I landed in the large pool below with a splash, my breath sucked out by the cold.

When I surfaced, Brooks was talking to Kai and Lauren, who were treading water off to the side. I swam over to join them, out of the way of the steady stream of people sliding after me. Most of the sliders didn't linger in this drop zone but continued through it and on to the next.

"How deep do you think this is?" Kai asked. "As deep as the school pool?"

Brooks looked down as if he could see the bottom but the water was dark. "At least."

All I could see were our legs, pumping to keep us afloat. "Did you two go to high school together?"

"Yep, Bulldogs for life." Kai barked and held out a fist, but instead of bumping it with his own, Brooks pushed down on Kai's shoulder, sending him underwater. Kai must've pulled on Brooks's leg from beneath the surface because Brooks went down fast with a laugh.

My brain was just thinking about the fact that one of our rival schools back home were the Bulldogs when Lauren said, "They live in Pasadena."

"You do?" I asked Brooks, who had resurfaced.

He wiped off his dripping face with one hand. "I do what?"

"Live in Pasadena?"

"Yes, why?"

"We live in Arcadia," I said. How had we never talked about this before? When he said he'd traveled four hundred miles to get away from home, for some reason I thought he lived north of here. Oregon or something.

"You do?" he asked. Our cities were basically neighbors.

I nodded. Brooks was hard to read but there was a brief flicker of something in his eyes—surprise?

"Come on, Brooks," Kai said. "Let's show them the echo chamber."

Lauren, who was floating on her back now, said, "What's the echo chamber?"

"Follow me." He swam toward the curtain of water falling from the edge of the slide above, and then he swam through it, disappearing from sight.

Lauren followed him.

I put my hand on Brooks's arm. "Hold up."

"Yeah?"

"Should I be worried about that?"

"About what?" he asked.

"Lauren is fifteen. Kai knows that, right?" Now that I knew Kai lived in the next town over from us, I was worried even more that Lauren had gotten some ideas in her head that this could actually be something real.

"She's fifteen?" he asked, as though this was news to him.

"Yes. Too young for Kai."

"Too young for . . ." His eyes got wide. "No, Kai would never. You guys are guests here. He's just really friendly."

I paused, wanting to correct him for lumping me and my sister into the same category. Wanting to remind him that I was two years older. But he was right, of course. He wasn't hanging out with me because he was interested. We hung out because we were helping each other. We might have been breaking the basic rule, but he was telling me now, in not so many words, that anything more than that was too big of a risk. And, of course, I agreed. We'd just gotten through saying we needed to be more careful. "Okay, good."

I moved toward the curtain of water.

"Wait," Brooks said, stopping me this time. "She's not into him, is she?"

"I don't know. She's very intense about a lot of things. I'm hoping this time her enthusiasm is about the documentary."

Brooks held my gaze, trying to read into what I wasn't saying, but I was telling the truth. "I'll talk to him," he said.

"Thank you." I forced myself to look away from his stare to where Lauren had disappeared. "Let's go."

Behind the falling water was a shallow cave. Before I had time to move onto the rock with Kai and Lauren, Brooks broke through the curtain behind me. His momentum pushed me forward, my knees scraping rock.

He swore. "Sorry. Are you okay?"

"Yes, no big deal." I climbed the rest of the way into the cave and he followed.

"Cool, right?" Kai said.

"A bit coffin-like," I said. Not because it was small or anything. It easily fit all four of us and would easily fit several more. But the ceiling was low, and being surrounded by stone and water felt constricting. Plus it was at least twenty degrees cooler in here.

"I think it's awesome!" Lauren said, and her voice echoed off the walls along with the water.

"Check it out," Kai said, and he sang. "La la la la la!" His voice bounced around the space.

He held a fake microphone to Lauren.

"Twinkle, twinkle little star," she belted out.

Then his fake microphone was in front of me. I stared at his fisted hand for a moment, the familiar tension I always felt when being put on the spot tightening my chest.

Maricela's head appeared through the curtain of water, saving me. She let out a loud growl. Lauren screamed and I covered my ears.

Mari climbed in, pulling Ian along with her. "Are you giving voice lessons in here?"

Ian settled in next to Mari and pushed his sopping wet hair off his forehead. "Kai is giving *voice* lessons?" he asked.

"What are you trying to say?" Kai asked. "You know, if you weren't the lead singer, I would be next in line for sure."

Both Brooks and Ian scoffed.

"Pretty sure you're tone-deaf," Maricela said.

"All the years of pounding on drums has made me lose a bit of hearing." Kai stuck his pinky in his ear and wiggled it.

"Is that the excuse you're going with?" Brooks asked.

Kai took Ian into a headlock and rubbed his head with his fist a few times. "Are you saying I don't have the voice of this songbird right here? Sing for us, our pretty little songbird."

Ian pinched Kai's side and he yelped and released him.

"Yes, sing for us!" Lauren said.

"Any requests?" he asked.

"Something from *Dirty Dancing*," I said, rubbing at the goose bumps on my arms. "I've been getting *Dirty Dancing* vibes since we got to camp."

"Is that the name of a band?" Ian asked. "I don't know them."

Everyone in the cave made some sort of shocked noise.

"It's a movie!" Lauren said.

"Never seen it," Ian said.

"Come on," I said. "You had to have at least *heard* of it." I held up the fake microphone this time and sang, " 'I . . . had the time of my life.' "

I was staring at Ian, who was still very lost, and it took a second to realize everyone had gone quiet. I looked from Kai to Maricela and finally to Brooks, whose expression was once again unreadable.

"What?" I said.

"You can sing," he responded in a low voice.

I rolled my eyes, feeling my cheeks heat up. "This cave is like a shower. Everyone sounds better in the shower."

126

"Not everyone." He shoved Kai's arm, and Kai responded with something about Brooks's mother in the shower.

Brooks punched his arm this time and Kai let out a hooting laugh, then yelled, "Last one down all three slides is on bathroom duty tomorrow!" He burst out of the curtain of water, followed closely by Maricela, Ian, and Lauren. That left me and Brooks, who didn't move, alone behind the waterfall.

My heart seemed to jump to my throat. "We should probably . . . D might . . ."

He was quiet for a moment before his eyes went to mine. "You keep surprising me."

"Considering your initial impression of me, it hasn't been that hard."

"My initial impression of you? Standing in that theater in a staff T-shirt?"

"No, I guess I meant starting the next day in the dining hall." Wait, why had I said that? Why hadn't I asked what his initial impression of me in that theater was?

It was too late; the moment was past and he was moving toward the curtain of water and saying, "Ready to finish this circuit?"

I nodded and followed him out of the cave. It was eerily quiet as we waded through the pool. We were about to go down the second slide when Brooks pointed to our group on a lower bank, out of the water and gathered off to the side.

"Avery!" My sister's high-pitched scream filled the air, making my face go numb. I crawled to the shore and took off down the hill faster than I had time to process. My heart raced in panic. I felt Brooks at my heels. Rocks and twigs dug into the bottom of my feet as I went, but I didn't slow down until I reached the group, which I could now see was surrounding someone on the ground.

The first thing I noticed was that Lauren was one of the people in the circle, perfectly fine. Relief washed through me. But then I saw that the person on the ground was Ian, his hand on his head, blood dripping out from under it, down his eye and chin and onto his chest.

"Everyone take a step back," D was saying, her face pale.

Brooks jostled past me and kneeled at Ian's side.

Maricela pointed up the hill. "I'm going to get the emergency kit."

Brooks nodded. "Ian, hey, look at me."

Ian groaned. "It's fine." He pulled his hand away from his forehead and looked at all the blood. "Did I win?" Blood continued to gush from the open wound.

"You totally lost, dude," Kai said in his cheerful way, trying to calm the group.

Brooks, water dripping off his hair, directed Ian's hand back to his forehead. "Just keep that there for one more minute." His voice was perfectly steady, which I was sure helped Ian.

"This is why there is a no-diving rule," D said, her panic immediately counteracting Brooks's presence. "We always say no diving."

"D. Maybe you can go grab a towel for Ian," I said, hoping that would remove her from the scene.

"Yes, I will. I'll be right back. Everyone just stay calm," she said as she sidestepped away.

"What happened?" Brooks asked.

"He dove off the last slide and hit a rock," Lauren said, burrowing into Kai's side. "Is he going to be okay?"

Ian pulled his hand away again. "I'll be fine."

"Keep it there," Brooks said, now using his own hand to hold Ian's in place. Then he smiled at Lauren with his magic smile. "He'll be fine." How was Brooks this calm under so much pressure? His dad, I realized. He took care of his dad.

Maricela appeared with a black backpack. She opened it and several things fell out. I dropped down and collected the fallen items. One was a big square gauze pad.

I ripped it open and went to Brooks's side. "Here, use this. Is there a roll of gauze in there, Maricela?"

"Yes," she said.

Brooks took the gauze pad from me and pushed it against Ian's forehead. "We just need to keep the pressure for a minute."

Ian lowered his bloody hand to his thigh.

"Janelle is going to kill us," someone said.

Brooks shot the guy a dirty look.

"Ian," I said. "Do you know what day it is?"

He rolled his eyes. "What?"

"Aren't you supposed to answer questions like that when you hit your head?"

"Do *you* know what day it is?" he asked.

"Friday . . . right?" I actually wasn't positive about that. It felt like we'd been at camp forever but I was pretty sure it had only been two weeks. "Fine, bad question. How old are you? Where do you live?"

"Now you're just trying to get personal info out of him," Kai said.

The group laughed. Even though Brooks had been playing calm this whole time, I could see the tension in his jaw. I found myself wanting to put my hand on his shoulder, tell him it was going to be okay. I folded my arms across my chest to resist.

Maricela had found the roll of gauze and helped Brooks wrap Ian's head.

Ian's eyes began to droop.

"Ian," I said. "Stay awake, okay?"

"Of course I'm going to stay awake," he said. "I don't sleep on rock beds."

That produced another worried look from Brooks. "Let's get you back to camp." He stood and slowly helped Ian to his feet, draping his arm around his shoulder. Kai went to Ian's other side, doing the same. Maricela repacked the first aid bag.

"You know what would be helpful in a situation like this?" Lauren asked.

Kai looked at her and smiled. "Cell phones?"

"Exactly!"

Chapter 15

MY SKIN FELT HOT. I KNEW WITHOUT EVEN HAVING TO LOOK, as I lay there in bed, eyes closed, that I'd gotten sunburned the day before. It was a long hike, after all, made longer by how slow we'd walked back with Ian. But we'd made it and Ian went straight to the nurse. And that's the last I'd heard. The band hadn't played at dinner and my sister and I had exchanged worried glances all night.

My hand went to my collarbone. I wondered if we had any aloe.

The door opened and so did my eyes. Lauren swept into the room, shut the door behind her, and sat on her bed, cross-legged, facing me. "So, Ian's still in sick bay being observed," she said without preamble.

"I figured," I croaked in my morning voice. "But he's okay?"

"I haven't seen him."

"Then how do you know he's still there?"

"I saw Kai."

"Where?" I sat up, flinging the blanket off my legs.

"You're sunburned," she said.

"I know."

"I'm going to visit him," she said.

"Who?"

"Ian. Who else? Are you awake?"

"Don't let Janelle catch you," I said.

"Or D, I know," she said.

I narrowed my eyes at her. That sounded like someone who'd had experience avoiding those two.

Seeming to read my mind, she said, "I'm doing the documentary. I've been around the band more than you."

Maybe I was overreacting about Kai. Maybe, like I had told Brooks, her enthusiasm about getting to know the guys really was about her documentary.

"And D caught you?" I asked.

"They were on the clock and practicing, so there wasn't much she could say."

I nodded. So D had caught both me and my sister hanging out with band members. I had a feeling that was going to come back and bite us.

"Do you want to visit Ian too?" she asked.

I hesitated, not wanting to make things worse. But I knew Lauren was going to go with or without me, and maybe it would be better if she wasn't caught there by herself. "Yes."

"Then get ready and let's go."

○ ○ ○

We knocked on the door with the red cross on it. An older woman answered. "Can I help you?"

"Is Ian still in here?" I asked, hoping this woman didn't know who all the staff members were and would assume we were two of them.

"That boy gets more visitors than the Pope." She opened the door wide, resigned. We stepped inside, walked down a short hall and to the only room in the small building. A half-closed curtain left only a foot visible at the end of the bed.

"Hello," Lauren called out.

"Hello? Come in," Ian responded.

We stepped inside and around the curtain.

"Hey. How are you feeling?" I asked.

Ian now had a more professionally bandaged head, but his eyes looked sleepy and his face was a bit gray. "I'm okay. You guys didn't need to come."

Lauren shook her head. "We were worried. And we brought you some get-well chocolate." She pulled a candy bar out of her back pocket. She must've gone to the camp's general store or the snack hut sometime that morning.

"Thank you." He seemed genuinely touched by the gesture. He took the candy and put it on the table next to his bed. Then he cringed like it hurt to move.

"You okay?" I asked.

"Headache."

"That's what happens when you go hitting rocks with your head," I said.

"I know. Not smart." He settled back into his pillow, then pointed to a folding chair that was leaning against the wall. "I guess only one of you can have a seat."

"We don't want to bother you," I said. "You probably want to sleep."

"No, I don't want to sleep. I've been sleeping so much."

The door creaked open and the nurse grunted. "Grand Central station."

"She can't wait for me to leave," Ian whispered.

Brooks came into view. He took in the room: the curtain that hung from the ceiling, the glass jars of Q-tips and cotton balls, the blood pressure machine quiet in the corner. Then his gaze shifted to me and Lauren, like he was surprised to see us.

"Are you here to break me out?" Ian asked.

"How are you feeling?"

"Good enough to leave sick bay."

"Nora won't let you out until Dr. Casablanca clears you."

"That sucks."

For the first time since I'd met him, Brooks looked uncomfortable. Like he didn't know how to stand or where to put his hands. He ended up leaning carefully against a counter, knocking over several boxes of gloves and then quickly righting them. "She's coming from town, so it will be a while. Plus, Nora's trying to get ahold of your parents."

He sighed. "Great. My mom will demand I spend the rest of the summer in a layer of Bubble Wrap." Apparently that wasn't a joke because when I laughed, he turned his attention to me. "Your parents aren't overprotective?"

"Not too bad."

"Are you sure about that?" Brooks spoke up. "They brought you here of all places. Far away from home, no way to communicate with anyone." His eyes were smiling, so it caught me off guard when he added, "Who were they trying to get you away from? Crappy friends? Bad boyfriend?"

I flinched a little without meaning to.

"Are you kidding?" Lauren said. "This is supposed to be a reward for her. Avery's last big trip before she abandons us for life, apparently. They're already mourning her inevitable departure. She's always been their favorite."

"Not true," I said, a clear replay of how Dad had bragged about Lauren repeating in my mind. But was Brooks right? Was the "epic adventure" narrative my parents had been feeding me just a cover for the real reason we were here? This trip had been planned months ago. Had they not liked Trent? Shay?

"Totally true," Lauren said. "I mean, look at her puppy dog eyes. She gets everything she wants."

"Yes," I said, straight-faced, knowing the longer I resisted, the longer Lauren would insist. And I was ready to be done talking about this. "That's why I have a barn full of ponies and a convertible Porsche back home."

"What *would* you ask for?" Ian said thoughtfully. "If you could have anything in the world?" I knew he wasn't posing the question to me specifically, but to the room.

"Fame," Lauren said without hesitation.

"Money. Lots of money," Brooks said. That would definitely solve a lot of his worries.

Ian hummed as if thinking, then said, "I guess I'd want to hear myself on the radio once. Or be recognized in some way for my voice."

"Like winning a music festival?" Lauren asked.

"That would be nice," Ian said.

Now it was my turn. Everyone was waiting for me to say something. But wasn't that the whole issue I was having this summer? That I had no clue what I really wanted? That I had zero passion for life? "I already said mine: ponies and Porsches."

Before anyone called me out, the big voice of Kai was at the door. "Hey, nobody told me there was a party happening."

Lauren laughed louder than the statement justified. Then the nurse was in the room, saying, "This is too many people. All of you out. He needs to rest."

Brooks freed the walkie-talkie from his waistband and set it on the table next to the chocolate Lauren had brought. "Let me know if you need anything, Ian."

"Okay."

"I hope you get out soon," I said.

"Me too."

"Bye!" Lauren called. "See you at band practice once you get cleared."

He nodded.

Kai smacked his leg and smiled. "Stop faking it. We have a song to finish."

As we left the building, Kai and Lauren fell into step side by side, Brooks and I walking behind them.

"You're sunkissed," Brooks said, his eyes traveling my face.

"What?" Hearing Brooks say the word *kiss* in any form made my stomach flutter.

"My mom always tells me that's the nice way to say *sunburned*." He held his suntanned arm next to my pink one.

"Oh yes, me and the sun totally made out." I poked at his arm, making a white fingerprint appear. "You get that tan from here?"

"Hours outside every day."

"You should wear more sunblock."

"Another thing my mom tells me."

"I think I'd like your mom," I said.

"Yeah . . ." His expression went dark with some unexpressed thought. "Yeah . . ."

When he didn't go on, I nodded over my shoulder. "Have you spent a lot of time in hospitals with your dad's illness?"

"Why do you ask?"

"You seemed . . . jumpy in there."

"Huh," he said. "Didn't think I was that transparent."

"You're not. Normally you're a little harder to read," I said back without thinking.

He smirked over at me. "Are you trying to read me?"

A group of kids ran by with water guns, laughing and squirting each other. I wiped at my arm after an errant splash of water hit me. "Yes. Yes, I am," I said in my sarcastic voice, but I really did feel like I was constantly trying to read him and coming up short.

Brooks's gaze was ahead of us now, aimed at Kai and Lauren.

"Did you get a chance to talk to him?" I asked.

"I did. You have nothing to worry about."

I watched Lauren for a bit. She and Kai weren't walking super close or anything, and from the snippets of conversation I could hear, it sounded like she was asking Kai about his history with music. I ran my thumb over my opposite palm a few times. "So did the band like the lyrics we came up with?"

"Yes, it was a miracle."

That made me happy. "Just one more verse, then?"

"Yes."

"So we should . . ." *Jeez, Avery, you aren't asking him on a date. You're helping him. Just spit it out.* "Get together again soon."

"For sure," he said without a second's thought. His eyes were on Kai and Lauren again. "Kai! Break's over! Let's go!"

"Yes, Mom!" Kai called over his shoulder.

To me Brooks said, "Soon," and then he was gone.

Chapter 16

"DO YOU THINK HE'LL FEEL WELL ENOUGH TO PRACTICE?"
Lauren asked as we headed for the theater the next night. Maricela
had told me Ian was out of sick bay, so we were hopeful band practice was back on.

D was busy checking in a family at the desk, so we easily passed
through the lobby unnoticed. When we walked through the theater
doors, the first thing I saw was Ian standing by the microphone. Kai
was sitting at the drums, and both Levi and Brooks were strapped
into their guitars. But nobody was playing.

"You're here!" Lauren called out, and ran ahead.

Ian turned his smile to her.

By the time I joined my sister, Ian was squatting down and digging through his backpack. He pulled out some papers, then moved
to stand and wobbled on his feet. Lauren reached out to steady him,
but he waved it off with a laugh and handed Brooks the papers.
"Those are the lyrics you gave me." He cringed and pinched the
bridge of his nose, in obvious pain.

"You should sit," I said.

"He's leaving," Brooks said, rolling the pages and tucking them into his back pocket.

At first I thought he just meant that he was leaving practice, but when Ian's eyes shot to the floor, worry edged its way into my mind.

"What did the doctor say?" Lauren asked.

"Long story," Ian said, "but my parents are here and the doctor said I have a concussion and Janelle won't let me stay. Something about liability."

"Wait . . . you're *leaving*, leaving?" Lauren asked, her eyes becoming big and even more concerned.

"I know, it's stupid."

"Concussions are pretty serious," I said. "You should listen to the doctor. Take it easy."

Suddenly all eyes onstage were on me. Lauren's held a look of betrayal.

"But what about the music festival?" she said. "My documentary?"

"I know," he said. "That would've been really cool."

Lauren looked pleadingly at Ian. "What if you just stayed around Roseville? Then you wouldn't have to work but you could try out with the band. You'll probably feel better in a few days anyway."

I knew that it could take weeks to fully heal from a concussion.

Ian seemed to consider this but then said, "I don't think my parents would go for that. And I have no place to stay."

Kai, who had been uncharacteristically silent, started tapping ever so lightly on the drums, over and over, like the buildup to some big announcement.

"But, Brooks," Ian said, "you should still audition. You just need to find a replacement singer." He looked around and ended up lowering himself onto a chair, obviously still dizzy.

"Oh yes," Levi said sarcastically. "Because that's easy."

"Yes!" Lauren said, ignoring Levi's sarcasm or maybe not hearing it at all. "This still needs to happen. There has to be someone else who can sing around here. We've already established Kai can't."

"Hey," Kai said with a final clashing strike on his cymbals.

Lauren flashed him a smile. "Brooks? Levi? You don't sing?"

"No," Brooks said. Levi shook his head as well.

"What about you?" Levi said, staring at Lauren. "You could sing for us. You're loud and fun and have lots of charisma."

I sucked in my lips, waiting to hear what Lauren thought about that. Knowing her, she would probably jump at the chance even though we both knew she couldn't sing to save her life.

She surprised me by saying, "If only I was given a singing voice to match my star power."

Kai groaned. "This is so pointless."

Even though Brooks was playing this all off like it was no big deal, out of the corner of my eye, I watched his jaw tighten.

"I'm sorry, guys, I know I said I could sing one last rehearsal with you, but I have to go." Ian was cringing again as he reached for his backpack.

Lauren gave him a gentle hug. "Get better, okay?"

"Thanks."

"Bye," I said from afar, not really a hugger.

The band must've already said their goodbyes before we got there because they all just nodded. Brooks walked him all the way to the theater doors, probably worried about his balance, before Ian waved him off.

"Well," Kai said, stretching his drumsticks into the air. "My nights just opened *wide* up."

"Brooks didn't say we're done," Levi said. "Maybe we really can find a replacement."

"Brooks didn't say we're done?" Kai asked. "We have half a song and now half a band."

Brooks climbed the stairs back onto the stage.

Kai twirled a drumstick. "Brooks, Levi says you have to call it or he won't believe it."

"Call what?" Brooks asked.

"The end of this band."

"You've been ready to blow up this band from night one," Levi said. "Maybe we should find *two* replacements."

"You think a drummer is just going to walk in here off the streets? It'd be way easier to replace *you*. Who was that guy playing at the campfire the other night? He'd work."

Lauren and I exchanged a wide-eyed look. I was surprised she hadn't pulled out her phone yet to record. I just wanted to back down the stairs and leave.

"Kai, stop," Brooks said, sounding tired.

"Really?" Kai said. "It's *me* who needs to stop? Brooks, love you, brother, but I can't work with him."

"*You* can't work with *me*?" Levi asked, voice raised. "I don't know how anyone has ever worked with *you*."

"Brooks and I have been in a band back home for two years

now without any problems. Who's the new factor in this equation? Oh, that's right: you."

"You're impossible!" Levi shoved his guitar back into its case so hard that one of the strings snapped, producing a twanging sound. This just made Levi angrier. He slammed down the lid of the case and picked it up. "I'm over this," he said as he stormed out.

Kai sputtered a laugh. "He's so dramatic."

"You do like to pick fights with him," Brooks said.

Kai shrugged his big shoulder. "It's not my fault he runs hot."

"Yeah, well, you didn't help."

"And neither did you, Brooks. You always just sit back and watch. You never step up."

"I'm tired of stepping up. I'm not in charge here. Take care of your own self for once." The words were sharp and heated and they hit their mark.

Kai blinked. His eyes found Lauren, then me, and he offered a smile. "That's my cue, ladies." He tucked his drumsticks into his pocket and bounded down the stairs.

Lauren ran after him.

Brooks went to his guitar case and dropped the pages from his pocket into it, followed by his guitar.

"You okay?" I asked.

"Sure, treating my best friend like garbage always puts me in a great mood."

"I'm sorry."

He sighed. "No, don't be."

"I get it, your whole band just imploded in one night."

"Teaches me to ask for signs," he said with a breathy laugh.

"You don't have to fake it for me."

He collapsed into a chair, put his elbows on his knees and his head down. "He's right. I should've stepped up."

I inched forward, the desire to comfort him, like up at the rock slides, taking over. This time I didn't stop myself and put a hand on his shoulder. "This is your escape, right? You don't want to have to be responsible for everyone here like you are back home."

He seemed to still with my touch, his breaths becoming shallow intakes. One of his hands brushed the side of my leg and I wasn't sure if it was by accident or on purpose, but every nerve ending in my body sprang to life.

A voice called out by the door, "Ugh. Kai is being so stupid!"

I jumped back, nearly tripping over my own feet to put some space between me and Brooks. Lauren was either too preoccupied to notice or she chose to ignore it because she continued, "How big does your band have to be to try out for the festival?"

"What?" Brooks asked. Was he as disoriented as I felt?

"How big does your band have to be to try out?" she repeated. "You have a song and you. All you really need is a singer at this point, right?"

"I don't have time to find one," Brooks said, standing. "We hardly had time as it was."

"Avery can do it," Lauren said with confidence.

"Excuse me?" I asked, my head whipping around toward her.

"You can. You sing all the time. In the shower and in the car and with your AirPods in. You love music. You should do it. And then maybe Kai and Levi will rejoin too."

"No," I said.

"Come on, Avery," Lauren pleaded. "Try it."

"No . . . just, no," I said firmly.

"Why not?"

"Because I can't, Lauren. I can hardly say hi to your phone without freezing."

Lauren crossed her arms with a huff. She didn't care that the second I got on that stage I would crash and burn. That would probably make a better documentary, actually. She'd be rooting for some drama. Because that's why she was pushing this—for her video. No other reason. Not for the guys, not for the music, and definitely not for me.

I met Brooks's eyes. "I'm sorry."

He shrugged an *It's okay*.

Every bone in my body wanted to yell, *Fine, I'll do it*. I knew that was only because I didn't like seeing people unhappy. Especially people I cared about. But I would never be able to sing on a stage in front of a crowd and that was the only thought that kept my mouth firmly closed.

Chapter 17

"IT'S NOT TOO LATE TO CHANGE YOUR MIND," LAUREN SAID as we walked back to the cabin after leaving Brooks with another apology. "Everyone, and I mean *everyone,* is counting on you." By *everyone* she meant her.

"I'm not changing my mind."

She clicked on her flashlight as we left the glow from the lodge. The nighttime sounds of camp echoed around us—crickets and distant squeals and laughter. "I thought you were trying new things," she said. "Stepping out of your comfort zone."

"I am. Just not this." Her voice was rising, so I tried to keep mine calm.

"Oh, so you just meant you'd try fake new things that really didn't push you at all—making vases and sliding down rocks and painting blobs."

"Singing isn't a new thing. I've tried it before."

She whirled on me, stopping us both in our tracks. "Just step up and do something unpredictable for once in your life."

"You only want me to do this for *you,* not for me."

"Fine, I won't make a documentary out of it. Will that change your mind?"

"No."

"That's what I thought." With that, she marched ahead of me in a dust-kicking cloud of indignation, taking our flashlight with her.

I stopped in the middle of the path, the anger I'd been holding back coursing through my veins now. I pulled up the flashlight on my phone and turned in the opposite direction. I didn't want to see her for a while. I wasn't sure what stupid thing I'd say if I did.

Five minutes later, I found myself standing in front of the pay phone. Before I could talk myself out of it, I picked up the handle and dialed Shay's number.

A monotone voice came through the earpiece. "The call you have made requires a coin deposit. Please hang up momentarily, listen for a dial tone, deposit coin, and dial your call again."

"Deposit coin?" I hung up the phone and shone my light around. On the top was a small slot next to some weird lever. Beneath that a blue strip said *.50.* Another sticker with red letters said: *Collect calls dial *11.* What did that mean?

"Fifty cents." I patted my shorts as if some money had magically teleported into my pockets. They were, of course, empty.

I glanced back down the trail. Lights shone from the employee cabins all along the path. I found myself walking to a porch and knocking on the door. It swung open and Tia stood there in a pair of plaid pajama pants and a tank.

"Avery," she said. "Hi."

"Hi, is Maricela here?"

"Hey, babe," Maricela said from the background. "Come in."

Tia opened the door wider and I stepped inside. Maricela cleared a space on the extra bed and I sat down. "What's going on? You look like your dog just died."

"No, I was trying to use the pay phone."

"You need some quarters?"

I nodded.

"It also takes cards," she said, walking to the dresser and opening the top drawer. She dug through it.

"I don't have a card either," I said.

Maricela walked over to me, change in her open palm. She picked up my hand and dropped four quarters into it.

"I only need two."

"Most out-of-area calls take four."

"Oh, okay. Thank you so much."

"No problem. Is everything okay?"

"Yeah . . ." I took a deep breath. "Did you hear about Ian?"

"The concussion?" Maricela said. "Yes, that sucks."

"He's leaving."

"He's leaving?" Tia asked, surprised. "For how long?"

"For the rest of summer."

"So no festival," Maricela said, catching the implication right away. "Brooks must be torn up. He's been going on about signs and how the stars all aligned for him this summer."

"Yeah." My stomach twisted with guilt again. I clenched my fists, the quarters pressing into my palms. This was not my problem to own. Why was I feeling guilty? "Anyway, thanks for the quarters." I stood. "I better go make that call before it gets too late."

"Okay, good luck with that."

"Good night."

Back at the pay phone, now that my anger had subsided to the less motivating emotion of frustration, I wasn't sure I wanted to make this call. Why did I think talking to Shay would help anyway? Because she knew my sister and would talk me through this? Did being angry at my sister make me less angry at Shay? I pressed my back against the brick building and looked up at the sky.

The stars were exceptionally bright tonight, and it took me a while to realize it was because there was no moon. I stepped out from under the eve of the building and searched every inch of sky I could see through the dark trees.

My heart thudded twice in my chest and I ran back to Maricela's cabin. The light was still on so I tried the handle. It gave and I flung open the door. Maricela was by the mirror on the wall, tucking her hair into a sleeping cap. Tia was sitting on her bed reading a book. They both looked at me in surprise.

"It's a new moon!" was my only excuse.

A slow smile spread across Maricela's face, and she dropped the sleeping cap on top of her open suitcase.

"What's that mean?" Tia asked.

"It means we need to take a trip across the lake."

❁ ❁ ❁

The group was eerily quiet as we sat, knees touching in the circle. The water lapped against the shore behind us, where we'd left a couple canoes. Maricela had collected several people as we had

149

made our way to the docks—Clay, Brooks, Kai, and Lucy, a girl I'd seen around but had never officially met.

There was still a marked tension between Kai and Brooks. They had come across the lake in separate canoes and now weren't sitting by each other. Much to my disappointment, Brooks wasn't sitting next to me either. I hoped that didn't mean he was mad at me. I tried to catch his eye but his focus was on Maricela.

"Welcome," she said from where she sat on my right.

Tia, on my left, giggled, then put her hand over her mouth to stop. I wondered if she was nervous. I found myself a little nervous, sitting in the dark, only a single flashlight pointing at Maricela's face. She looked like a ghost.

She shot Tia a look, then continued. "For those of you who weren't here last year, this is our moon circle. As you can see, there is no moon in the sky, which makes it a perfect time for renewal. Tonight is like a fresh start. Or just a time to think about what you really want and to remotivate yourself. Everyone hold hands."

Kai was on Maricela's right, and I watched him take her hand. I wondered if her speech had softened him. If he and Brooks would make up. Brooks was next to Tia and as I linked hands with her, so did he. I reminded myself that jealousy was not a good emotion to bring to a night of renewal.

"Now, everyone close your eyes," Mari said, switching off the flashlight and then taking my hand.

It was so dark I almost didn't need to close my eyes. I could barely make out my own crossed legs. But I closed them anyway.

"Let go of the things that are holding you back," Maricela said.

"And fill your mind only with the things that will take you forward."
She fell silent.

I tried to clear my mind, think about my future, college, teaching, like my mom. But all I could see was Lauren's disappointed face when I'd said I couldn't sing. And Brooks's shrug when I'd said I was sorry. I tried to picture myself onstage, a microphone in hand, a crowd of people waiting, watching, and panic immediately gripped my chest.

Maricela squeezed my hand and I realized I was breathing fast. I relaxed my shoulders and shook away those thoughts. I needed to try something new tomorrow, I decided. Get back to my goal of discovering myself. *Picture something new you can try*, I told my brain. But I was left with only blackness. Brooks would help me think of something.

I froze.

Wait, Brooks wasn't doing the festival anymore. I no longer needed to help him write a song. Did this mean our deal was off? He wouldn't help me anymore either?

My eyes flew open to look at him, but I couldn't see a thing.

Maricela let go of my hand and picked up her flashlight. "I hope the moon grants you everything you desire," she said.

"I don't trust the moon," Kai said. "She's shady."

"Was that a pun?" I asked.

Tia giggled again next to me. Maricela playfully hit Kai's arm and he laughed.

Clay, across the circle, said, "My wish right now is to get back across the lake without getting caught."

Maricela, light pointed at her face, rolled her eyes. "None of you took this seriously. No wishes for any of you." I could see the hint of a smile on her lips as she said it. "Let's go."

I climbed to my feet. And as the group dispersed, I took several quick steps, trying to see which shadowed form was Brooks, when Clay stepped up beside me.

He draped his arm across my shoulder in a friendly manner. "Need any more random experiences to answer obscure college essay questions?"

"You have no idea," I said.

Maricela, who was now on the other side of Clay, said, much louder than necessary, "How about a late-night swim in the light of a new moon?"

"How about a late-night skinny-dip in a new moon?" Clay said with a laugh.

"Did someone say skinny-dip?" Kai asked.

My light was pointing ahead, so when Brooks glanced back, I could see his face clearly—a flash of hurt or disappointment or maybe something else entirely.

I shrugged Clay's arm off my shoulder and quickened my pace, wanting to clarify that what just happened had nothing to do with Clay or Mari helping me to discover myself and was just a stupid joke. But Brooks stepped up to the canoe that already had Lucy and Tia inside and pushed it farther into the water. Then he climbed inside and they were off.

"Who's ready for crazy Fourth of July week?" Mari said, stepping into the other canoe.

"Is it worse than normal?" Kai asked.

"Our highest occupancy rate of the year. And everyone seems to think celebrating their independence means demanding free things."

Fourth of July. Was it already almost the Fourth?

"What did you ask the moon for?" Maricela said, taking the seat in front of mine.

"That's between me and the moon," I said with a smile.

"Well, I hope you didn't ask it for a certain boy we both know, because he's a mess."

"I didn't." And that was the truth.

As we rode back across the dark lake, I stared up at the sky full of stars. *Just help me to know what I want. A few signs wouldn't hurt.*

Chapter 18

I SHOULDN'T HAVE ASKED FOR SIGNS, EVEN IF I DIDN'T BE-lieve in them, because it made me read into everything that happened that week. It started the next morning at breakfast.

I was stirring my oatmeal when my mom asked, out of the blue, "Remember when you used to sing in that elite choir at school?"

My eyes shot to my sister. She held up her hands. "I did not say anything."

"What?" Mom said.

"Why did you bring that up?" I asked, adding another scoop of brown sugar to my bowl.

"I don't know. I just remembered how much you loved it."

"I remember that. What made you quit choir?" Dad asked.

"You honestly don't remember?" I asked, my agitation growing. Lauren had to have said something to them. She obviously didn't spell it out because if she actually told them she wanted me to sing in a festival with an employee, they would say no. Maybe I should tell them and shut this down right here and now.

"No, I don't remember," Dad said.

"I ran off the stage in the middle of a concert because I froze up. Forgot my part," I said. "The whole audience laughed."

"Oh yeah," Mom said. "I had forgotten that too."

How could they have forgotten one of the most humiliating days of my life? "Well, I haven't," I said.

"Maybe it's time," Lauren said, "to replace that awful failure with a triumphant success."

"Maybe it's time," I said, standing up, "for you to think of a new documentary you can create this summer." I placed my half-empty oatmeal bowl in the sink and filled it with water. "Maybe it can star the lifeguards or the cooks."

"Stellar ideas, Avery," Lauren said. "Those sound like block-busters."

"What is going on with you two?" Dad asked, but he was really staring at me. He wasn't used to seeing me lose my cool. "What documentary?"

"Nothing," I said, and Lauren chimed in with, "Beyond nothing."

❁ ❁ ❁

Maricela was right—Fourth of July week had the camp bursting at the seams with the influx of new guests. Every table in the dining hall was full that week. The walkways were teeming with people, the lodge activities had sign-ins and waiting lists, the swimming pool reached its max capacity. But that didn't stop me from putting on my swimsuit and heading for the Slip 'N Slide midweek. We'd been here awhile and I still hadn't tried it.

There was a line at the slide. It snaked halfway down the hill and then took a sharp turn at the bathrooms and twisted back onto itself. The majority of line occupants were kids under ten. As I took in the attraction, I realized this was not just a piece of plastic with a cheap pool at the end. This was a hundred feet of plastic, heading down a slope before it leveled off again into a huge splash zone. No wonder the camp bragged about it.

I stepped up to the end of the line and the little girl in front of me turned around and peered up at me.

"Hi," she said. She couldn't have been more than six or seven.

"Hi."

"Have you done this before?"

"No, it's my first time. What about you?"

"Mine too." She rose to her tiptoes and then back down again several times.

She seemed nervous, so I said, "Look at all the people getting off and coming back in line again. It must be really fun."

She nodded as we inched forward in line. "My brother says it's fun."

"That's good. I was a little nervous but that makes me feel better."

"Me too!"

"You can show me how to do it when we get to the top."

She smiled, revealing two missing top teeth. "You're pretty."

Suddenly waiting in line with a bunch of kids didn't seem so bad. "Thank you. So are you."

"You look like Belle," she said.

"You have a friend named Belle?"

"No, Belle from *Beauty and the Beast*."

"Oh." I'd never gotten that one before. Lauren always got all the Disney princess comparisons. "Thank you."

"Do you know any of her songs?"

"Um . . ." It had been forever since I'd watched *Beauty and the Beast*. "There's that one she sings in the village. And the one where all the dishes sing."

The girl giggled. "Sing one!"

"What?" I changed my mind. Kids were the worst. "No, that's okay."

"Please!"

Had Lauren somehow put her up to this? I searched for my sister in the crowd. "Look, we're almost to the front," I told the girl, even though we'd only just reached the curve of the line.

That's when she started singing, loudly, drawing lots of stares. A few of the other kids around us joined in. I felt like I was in the middle of a bad musical. By the time I got to the front of the line, I was so ready to be done that I hardly enjoyed the slide.

※ ※ ※

The Fourth of July arrived and as I was heading to change for fireworks, I saw Maricela walking ahead of me, on her way to break or done with her shift, I wasn't sure. I'd just finished dinner with my family where the band's stage in the corner of the dining hall sat quietly empty again tonight until a boy, maybe twelve or thirteen, had stepped onto it and called out, "Where has all the music gone? Someone bring back the music!"

His friends had laughed and eventually his parents had pulled him down. Surprisingly, my sister said nothing about it, didn't even look at me. Lauren hadn't said more than a handful of words to me since our fight.

I picked up my pace until I was walking next to Maricela.

"Hey, stranger!" she said, her face brightening. "Where have you been all week?"

"In hiding. There are too many people here." And the universe or the moon or someone by the name of Lauren was out to convince me to do something I didn't want to do.

"Tell me about it."

"You done for the day?" I asked.

"Yes! You should come with me! We watch the fireworks from a clearing up the hill."

"Pretty sure my parents wouldn't be super excited if I didn't watch the fireworks show with them. They reserved a spot by the lake last week."

"Oh, right. Sometimes I forget your whole family is here."

"Very much here," I said with a smile. "Don't you have to help with the fireworks?"

"No. Janelle hires a company for that. She doesn't want us burning the forest down. Go figure."

"She expects so much." I scanned a group of people in front of us as we walked but there was nobody I recognized—only guests. "How is everyone?"

"Everyone?" she asked.

I bit the inside of my cheek. She was really going to make me spell it out. "Brooks. How is Brooks? Have he and Kai made up? Has he talked about the festival at all?" I hadn't seen him all week, despite doing everything to search him out except knock on his cabin door, and it was killing me.

She smirked. "It's been so busy this week, I haven't talked to anyone much. But he seems like his normal self, from a distance. I saw him talking to Kai just yesterday, so I think they're good."

The amount of relief I felt at that was more than the news deserved.

We passed a bench tucked between two pines where a guy was singing to a girl. She was giggling, her hands over her mouth. "Seriously?" I said.

"Music is a love language, isn't it?" Maricela said with a sincere smile.

"Not you too," I responded with a groan. "Has my sister been talking to you?"

"About what?" she asked, oblivious.

"About me singing with Brooks for the festival?"

"What? No! Is that a possibility?"

"No, it's not. I'm a chicken."

"You're not a chicken," she said.

"I really am," I said.

She nodded slowly as if thinking this through. "So now you're worried Brooks is mad at you."

"Do you think he is?"

"No, I don't. Brooks is probably mad at himself for entertaining the idea of performing at the festival in the first place. For getting his hopes up about it. He probably even has some stupid idea that his dreams are what caused Ian to get hurt. Like I told you before, Brooks is a mess. And I thought I told you that meant you

159

should steer clear." Just how well did Maricela know Brooks? With a speech like that, more than I realized. I panicked when I realized he could easily be her mystery guy.

"You don't think I should sing?"

"It doesn't matter what I think. It matters what you think."

If only I knew what I thought. "I better go. My parents will be waiting."

"Okay, if you can sneak away tonight, follow the signs to Shadow Ridge." She rushed ahead.

"I don't need to follow any signs," I mumbled.

Chapter 19

I'D CHANGED INTO JEANS AND PULLED ON A HOODIE, AND now, as the light was quickly fading from the sky, I searched the crowded shore around the lake for my parents and Lauren. They said they would be near the snack hut but I didn't see them anywhere. All I saw were families sitting on colorful blankets awaiting the main event.

The lake was dotted with sailboats and paddle boats and motor boats, filled with people, all anchored and waiting as well. On the dock, an older woman tapped a microphone, then said, "Will everyone please stand for the national anthem." I wondered if this was the infamous Janelle. She was in a flannel and jeans and her gray hair was pulled back into a ponytail.

She passed the microphone to a young girl while everyone around me climbed to their feet. And then this girl, who was probably only eleven or twelve, began to sing, with an entire camp and lake full of people staring at her. And she didn't miss a single note.

"Jealous?" Lauren's voice asked in my ear when she was done.

I turned to see Lauren's smirk. "Yes, actually. I think you think I choose to have stage fright."

"I think you choose not to do anything about it."

"Where are Mom and Dad?" I really didn't want to have this conversation. I just wanted to watch fireworks. I loved fireworks.

She spun on her heel and led the way to a blanket halfway down the beach area.

"Avery," Dad said with a smile. "We thought you got eaten by a bear."

"I almost did, but luckily I threw someone else in the path and kept running."

"Good call," Dad said.

Lauren blew air between her lips. "You two and your dad jokes."

I met Dad's eyes. It had been a while since we'd shared some friendly banter. Things had been awkward between us. I dropped my gaze and lowered myself to the blanket.

Mom was using a wadded-up sweatshirt as a pillow and she looked up and raised one of her hands. "I thought it was funny."

"Thanks, Mom," I said.

"Where are these fireworks going to be blasted from anyway?" Lauren asked.

Dad pointed. "Way out in the middle of the lake. You going to record tonight?"

She shrugged. "Things like this don't translate very well to video without super-expensive equipment. It's like when you try to take a picture of the moon. It's just not the same as seeing it."

I narrowed my eyes at her. Had someone told her about our

moon circle or was it just a coincidence that she was bringing up the moon? Had she seen Kai or Levi . . . or Brooks this week?

"You feeling any better?" Dad asked, putting his hand on my mom's head.

She had her forearm draped across her eyes as she lay on the blanket.

"What's wrong?" I asked. "Are you sick?"

"I think that salad at dinner and my stomach aren't getting along," she said.

"I'm sorry," I said.

"Me too," she said. "But I'm going to stick it out for at least one firework."

"You're leaving?" Lauren asked.

"One firework," Mom insisted.

"Well, we all know they start with the best fireworks and end with the crappy ones anyway," I said.

Mom laughed and then held her stomach. "Don't make me laugh."

The lady in the flannel shirt was weaving between blankets, talking to people now.

"Who's that?" I asked.

"That's the owner of this camp," Dad said.

Lauren's eyes shot to Janelle, probably wanting to put a face to a name as well. A huge red firework lit up the sky to oohs and aahs from the crowd around us.

Mom groaned.

"Girls," Dad said, "would you feel the need to talk to your future therapist about being abandoned on a holiday if your mom and I went back to the cabin?"

"Definitely," I said.

"Right after I tell them about the summer my parents took away my access to the internet," Lauren said.

"Oh good, you'll have plenty of fodder," Dad said, standing as another firework lit the sky behind his head. "Come home right after the show is over. It's too crowded to stay out here late tonight."

"I'm sorry," Mom said to us, letting my dad help her to her feet.

The two of them slowly picked their way through the crowd. Lauren and I sat there in silence for several minutes staring at the sky. Then, as if we both knew the other had found out about the staff party happening right now, I said, "Should we go?"

And she said, "Absolutely."

❀ ❀ ❀

"Who told you about this?" I asked as we walked, pointing our flashlights at the trail ahead.

"I don't remember. Levi? Kai, maybe?" Lauren said.

"You're still talking to them even though the documentary isn't happening?"

"Yes. We're friends now. I wasn't just faking it for the documentary. I'm not a user, Avery."

"I know." A sadness washed over me with her words and I knew why. I had thought Brooks and I were friends, but now I wondered if he was only helping me because I was helping him. I mean, that's exactly why he was helping me; that's how it started at least. But I

164

had hoped we had moved on from that. This week, not seeing him once, proved to me that we hadn't.

"Did you hear that?" Lauren asked, stopping in the middle of the path. Fireworks were still going strong in the sky, the smell of explosives stronger up here on the ridge.

"I didn't hear anything."

Her flashlight swept over the trees on our right. "What if there's a bear out here?" she whispered.

I almost told her that she was being dumb, but maybe there *was* a bear up here, scared by the loud blasts. I pointed my light to the trees as well. I didn't see anything, but now I heard what she had: a rustling of leaves or underbrush. My heart slammed into my rib cage.

"Are we supposed to run?" she asked. "Or play dead?"

"I have no idea." Every instinct in my body told me to run. Why hadn't I asked Maricela what to do if I ever saw a bear? That seemed like some good information to have.

Lauren, who hadn't touched me all week, gripped my arm and smashed herself against my side.

"It's fine," I said. "It's probably just a squirrel or something." It did not sound like a squirrel. It sounded like something much bigger. "Let's keep walking."

"They sell bear spray in the general store. Why haven't Mom and Dad bought us any of that?"

"They probably didn't think we'd wander away from camp after dark." We weren't that far from camp, just on one of the trails that cut through the woods above the lake. I took the first step forward and Lauren followed me.

We walked for several more minutes that way—slowly, with Lauren clinging to my arm and the sound of rustling to our right. When I finally heard voices up ahead, I almost cried out in relief. Lauren relaxed beside me as well.

But then the rustling noise got louder and more intense. Lauren yelped and we started running. In my periphery I saw a huge shape leap out from the woods, followed by a very human sounding "Roar!"

I swung the flashlight around in time to see Kai land on the trail in front of us, laughing.

"You are the literal worst," I said evenly.

Lauren melted into tears and Kai's happy face crumpled to remorse.

"You deserve that," I said to him.

"No," he said. "I'm sorry. Come here." He pulled Lauren into his arms. "Shhh, I'm sorry."

"You. Are. Such. A. Jerk." She hit his chest with each word.

He tried to stifle his laugh. My suspicions about the two of them came roaring back to life. I wanted to pull Lauren out of his arms, but just as I stepped forward to take her hand, he released her and said, "Come on, you're missing the show. There's food too." Then he led the way to the clearing.

It was brighter than I expected. Lanterns had been strung up in trees. Someone had even hiked a folding table up here and it was covered with snacks and drinks. And to the left, like the trees had grown to create a perfect window, was a large circle of blackness that kept bursting to life with fireworks.

Lauren walked to the food and I walked to the colorful display in the sky. I wasn't the only one who had wanted a closer look. Several others were standing at the edge of the clearing, watching the sky.

"You made it!" Maricela said, giving me a big hug. "Your parents were cool with this?"

"Not at all." My eyes were scanning the others in the group, but none of them were Brooks.

"He's over there," Maricela said. I obviously wasn't as subtle as I'd thought.

Brooks sat on a large rock just outside the glow of the lanterns.

"Do you mind if . . . ?" Was I asking her permission because I thought she and Brooks had something more going on?

"No, go ahead," Maricela said. "He wasn't very chatty, but maybe you can crack him. He seems like he could use a friend."

I wasn't sure that was me, but I walked over anyway.

He glanced my way, looked back at the fireworks, then did a double take. "Avery?"

"Hey." I sat down on the rock next to him. "This place is pretty cool."

"Yeah. And the killer show doesn't hurt." A green flower lit up the sky, layered with a red star.

"I've seen better," I said with a smirk.

"Snob," he teased back, and then, seeming to think I'd take offense, said, "I didn't mean that."

"I know." I stared at the sky when really I wanted to be staring at Brooks.

Last year for the Fourth, Shay and I had gone to the local water park and watched fireworks while sitting in tubes in the wave pool.

For the first time since I got here, I realized how bad I missed her. My anger had been masking it before, but it was there. I missed my best friend. And what scared me more than anything was that maybe I'd never get her back; maybe things would never be the same between us again.

"I usually watch the fireworks with my friend Shay," I said. "Pay phone girl."

"Is that going to be her new name? Pay phone girl?"

"Only for you."

He smiled but his eyes stayed glued to the sky. "Before I worked here, I'd watch with my brother."

"How old is your brother?"

"Fourteen now."

"You miss him," I said. It wasn't a question.

"My mom had to work tonight, which got me wondering if she worked last year or the year before. Has my brother had to sit in our apartment alone and watch fireworks out the window for the last three years? I've never asked him."

"He probably goes to a friend's house or something."

"Maybe."

"You should ask him so you can stop putting more guilt on yourself."

His eyes left the show in the sky and met mine. "Maybe I won't like the answer."

"I understand that fear." I really did. I mean, wasn't that part of the reason I was avoiding Shay? Because I didn't want to know if what had happened had ruined everything? Wasn't that part of the reason I hadn't asked Maricela earlier if Brooks was her mystery guy? "But you're already thinking the worst, so it can only go up from here."

He gave a breathy laugh.

"Don't listen to me. I really don't know what I'm talking about considering I'm in the middle of some pretty major avoidance myself right now."

"Pay phone girl?"

Among other things. "Yes."

He nodded, then surprised me by saying, "We should do the ropes course early Monday. Things will be slower next week."

"Oh, I thought . . ."

"What?" he asked when I didn't finish.

"I just thought since we didn't need to write the song anymore that our deal was off."

He paused and then said, "That's right. I had kind of forgotten it was a deal."

A smile took over my face. "You had? You were just helping me discover myself to be nice?"

"Well, I mean, it seems like all the employees in camp are helping you now. They've taken over my gig, but whatever." His magic smile that I had missed so much made an appearance.

I laughed. "Nobody else is helping me, dork."

"Uh-huh, sure."

The fireworks finale halted our conversation as it rumbled through the sky and vibrated in my chest. I watched them light up the dark night and then I watched them color Brooks's eyes purple and green and orange. He wanted to help me just because. Even without our deal. My heart seemed to triple its speed and my lungs filled to capacity.

"I'll sing," I said.

Brooks turned a questioning gaze on me, his eyes still reflecting the colors. He hadn't heard me. I waited until the night went quiet, until his eyes were back to just one color—their intense blue—and I said again, "I'll sing."

Chapter 20

"WHAT?" BROOKS HAD GONE STILL, LIKE HE THOUGHT THAT if he moved too fast, I would change my mind.

The rock we sat on was digging into my tailbone and I adjusted my position. "There's still two weeks until tryouts, right?"

He stared at me for a long moment. "You don't have to do this."

"Did you find someone else?"

"Yes, I mean, no . . ."

"You just don't want *me* to do it?"

"I just thought you didn't . . . *Can* you sing?"

"You heard me sing."

He leaned back onto his palms. "Yes, but only one line in a cave with killer acoustics."

"Fair enough. Well, I *can* sing. I just hope I *will*."

"What do you mean?"

"I have major stage fright, so if you can help me figure that out, I'll probably be decent."

"*Decent?* That's the adjective you're going with?"

"I'm not you. I'm not a prodigy or anything, but I'll do my best."

He rolled his eyes. "I'm not a prodigy. I just practice a lot."

"Then I should start practicing . . . a lot."

His expression became serious, sincere. "Avery, I don't know what to say."

"Say *Thank you, you're the best, and if we win, I owe you all my future children.*"

He raised one eyebrow and one corner of his mouth. "You want to have all my future children?"

I laughed and blushed. "That's what it sounded like, didn't it? I say dumb things sometimes." My attention was drawn back to the dark sky. "I need to find my sister. My parents are expecting us right after fireworks."

"Tomorrow night practice? Nine p.m. on the stage?"

Nine was going to be hard to justify to my parents but half the time they were in their room for the night at nine anyway. Having no television had aged us all thirty years in our sleeping habits. "Okay, I'll see you then." I stood and started to walk away.

"I owe you all my future children!" Brooks called after me.

I spun, walking backward for two steps, and said, "Yeah, you do," before I turned and left in search of my sister. As I went from group to group with no luck, I realized I couldn't stop smiling. It was Brooks's fault.

I saw Kai disappear behind a tree on the far side of the clearing and I wondered if Lauren was with him. They were probably about to do his bear prank again on someone, with Lauren recording it this time.

I smiled and as quietly as possible made my way over to the tree

I'd seen him duck behind. When I made it, I rounded it with a big "Roar!"

Kai jumped back but not before I saw his lips smashed against someone else's. That person let out a sharp scream with my imitation bear sound. At first, I thought it was Lauren because that's who I had expected to see. But as my brain caught up with the scene in front of me, I saw it was Maricela.

A panicked look took over her face. "Avery," she hissed in a low whisper. "You scared me."

Kai was her mystery boy? A huge amount of relief and happiness poured through me. "I didn't mean to scare you. I'm sorry."

Kai looked over my shoulder, obviously checking to make sure nobody else had followed me. "You won't talk, right?" he asked.

"Please," Maricela said. "You can't tell anyone about this. If people start spreading this and Janelle finds out, we'll both be fired."

I looked over my shoulder too, but nobody else had seen or followed me. People were hanging out in different groups, each group having been drawn to a lantern and now lit by a hazy glow. And that's when I finally saw Lauren. She was talking and laughing with Levi. Was she really just friends with the band? Kai's feelings were apparent now, but would Lauren be sad to learn about this? "No," I said back to Kai and Maricela. "Of course not. I won't tell anyone."

Maricela gave me a hug. "Thank you. You're awesome."

"I'll see you soon," I said, backing away. "And be more careful."

Lauren was in the middle of explaining some editing software to Levi when I joined them. "Hey, you know Dad will search the whole camp if we're not back soon."

She gave a drawn-out sigh. "Fine."

"Hi, Avery," Levi said. Last time I'd seen him, he was storming out of band practice.

"Hi," I said. "How are you?"

For a second I thought about telling him and Lauren right there that I was going to fill in for Ian. That the audition was still happening. But something stopped me. I wasn't even sure if I could pull this off yet. I hadn't had a single practice. I didn't need the added pressure of my sister recording and the guys fighting.

"So much better," Levi answered. "It feels more like a vacation here now that I'm not dealing with band practice."

Oh, right. Levi had quit the band. He wasn't coming back just because I was a part of it now. Brooks and I would have to make this work on our own. And I was perfectly fine with that.

"What?" Lauren asked. "Why do you have that goofy smile on your face?"

"Do I?" I let it drop off. Tomorrow couldn't come soon enough.

As we made our way back toward the cabin, I looked over at Lauren. "Hey, you and Kai—"

"Gah. Avery, seriously, you're going to go on about this again?"

"No, I'm not." Because I'd just promised Maricela I wouldn't tell anyone. "I just worry about you."

"Well, stop. It's annoying."

I wished it were that easy.

Chapter 21

"NOBODY IS IN THERE," D SAID THE NEXT NIGHT AS I WALKED toward the theater a little after nine. The day had dragged on, but it had been just as easy as I'd hoped to leave the cabin—my parents had been in their room, and Lauren had crashed after a day in the sun.

I could've sworn D's shift ended at nine. I thought that was half the reason for the time Brooks had chosen.

I turned. "Oh. I know. I think I left something in there the other night."

"What?"

"I think I left something," I repeated.

"No, I mean, what did you leave?"

I was a crappy liar. "My hair clip."

She lowered her eyebrows.

"It's my favorite."

"Okay, good luck."

"Thanks." I opened the door to the theater and the room was dark. No stage lights, like there usually were. I held the door open with my foot and turned on my phone flashlight. Behind me, D stacked a few piles of papers together and said a few words to the night-shift person. As she rounded the desk for the exit, she caught my eye. I moved my foot, letting the door close between us.

"Hello?" I whispered, shining my light ahead. It only lit a ten-foot area around me. "Brooks?" Where was he?

With my hands stretched in front of me, I made it to the edge of the stage and felt my way along it to the stairs. Off to the side, I saw a tiny sliver of light from a small gap between two curtains.

Once backstage, the light led me to a room down a short hall. The door was cracked open and I poked my head around it to see Brooks sitting on an old couch, his guitar in his lap. I let out a sigh of relief.

He looked up with the noise.

"Was this my first test?" I asked.

"Sorry, I didn't mean to hide. I just saw D hadn't left, so I made sure she saw me walk out the front. Then I came in through the back."

I stepped all the way inside and pulled the door shut behind me.

"Is your sister coming? I wasn't sure."

I cringed. "I didn't tell her yet. I don't need my failures posted online."

He flashed me a smile. "Such positive thinking."

I walked the perimeter of the room, letting my hand run over the stacks of boxes that lined the walls. One of the boxes was open, revealing piles of colorful T-shirts.

I wanted to think positive, to know that I could do this, but I was struggling. "Where do you find your confidence?"

He held up his hand and circled it over his chest. "Somewhere under all this BS."

I let my eyes travel the length of him. "That's a lot to wade through."

He gave a single laugh. "It really is."

"So, seriously? You're not going to tell me your ways?"

He tilted his head. "You just have to stop caring."

"About what?"

"About what anyone thinks about your performance."

I finished my lap around the room, then lowered myself next to him on the couch. It was threadbare and smelled of dust. "So you don't care what *anyone* thinks about your music?"

"No."

"What about your mom? Do you care what she thinks?"

"She doesn't really listen to my music, so no."

"Your brother?"

"No."

"Your teachers? Or the girl you like, what about her?"

"What about her?" he asked.

I looked down, then back at him. "You don't care what she thinks?"

He gave me a slow smile. "If she likes me back, she probably doesn't do a lot of thinking."

"It *really* is a miracle you can get through all that BS," I said, circling my hand close to his chest like he'd done earlier.

He grabbed hold of my wrist and directed my hand back to me until it covered my heart. "Try this. Repeat after me." He raised his eyebrows and I nodded. "You're fun, brave, and hot."

"You're fun, brave, and hot."

He dropped my wrist and rolled his head. "No, you were supposed to say *I*."

"You said repeat after you."

"You're right, I did. Well, in that case, thank you."

I whacked his arm. "You're such a punk."

He picked up his guitar again. "Now that we don't have a full band, I'm going to play acoustic instead of electric."

"Okay," I said.

He strummed a chord. "You ready to try?"

I smiled. "No."

"But you're going to do it anyway?"

"Yes," I said. "Because you're fun, brave, and hot."

He barked out a laugh. "And don't forget it."

"You have the lyrics? I want to make sure I remember them right."

He reached over and pulled the loose pages out of his guitar case and handed them to me.

"Okay, count me in because I don't know my cue yet."

He strummed several chords, then said, "One, two, go."

I opened my mouth and then shut it. "Sorry."

"It's okay. Again."

I grabbed hold of the edge of the cushion on either side of my legs with both hands. And when he counted me in this time, I sang. I sang while staring hard at the lyrics, so hard that my eyes started to water. But I was doing it and it didn't feel foreign at all. It felt like something I did. Because my sister was right. I sang in the shower and with my AirPods in and while I did homework. It wasn't perfect—I stuttered and went off-key a couple times—but I made it through the whole song. I didn't look up from the pages of lyrics for three long beats, and finally, I raised my eyes to his.

He was staring at me, his unreadable expression back. "You can sing," he said with a hint of relief and a hint of excitement in his voice.

"I told you I could sing. That's not what I'm worried about."

"Oh, right." He looked up as if replaying our conversation in his head. "Stage fright. We need to work on that."

My legs were jittery and I realized that even though the singing felt better than I expected, I was still beyond nervous about this. "Can we go through it again?"

"Of course. As many times as you want."

"It feels . . . I don't know, fast?"

He hummed. "Yeah, I can see that. We don't have a band to fill it out. You want to try it slower?"

"It would feel less punk rock," I said.

"I'm okay with that. Are you?"

"This is your thing."

"This is our thing now, Avery. We'll make song decisions to-gether." He held his fist out.

"Are you asking for a fist bump?" I said with a laugh.

He bumped his fist against my hand that rested on my leg. "Was that so hard?" His smile made me happy inside.

He pulled on a piece of string hanging off the bottom of my flannel shirt, but it was attached and stayed very much in place.

"You know what else we need to work on?" he asked.

"My wardrobe?"

"No . . . Well, I mean, obviously we're not wearing camp clothes to the audition."

"You're right. Just let me go to the section in my suitcase I packed knowing I'd need something other than camp clothes."

"Huh. Maybe Maricela will have something you can borrow."

I wondered if Brooks knew about Kai and Maricela. Kai was his best friend; he'd probably told him. "I'll ask her. So if it's not my wardrobe, what else do we need to work on?"

"Figuring out how you're going to disappear all day for the audition."

The blood seemed to drain from my face. I hadn't even thought about what the audition would entail. "*All* day?"

"Roseville is about an hour away, and no matter when we audition, we have to stay until the end for results."

"That really is all day."

"Can you make it work?" he asked.

I wasn't sure I could. "I'll figure something out."

Chapter 22

THE LOBBY OF THE SPA SMELLED LIKE CHLORINE AND IN-cense. The large windows behind the front desk framed the lake. I imagined that same view was visible from the massage room and the pedicure room and the mud-bath room. Well, maybe not the mud-bath room. That probably had no windows.

I stared at the prices in the leather folder the lady at the counter had handed me. They were way beyond my price range; even a simple forty-five minute massage was something I couldn't afford to gift my parents. And that definitely wouldn't fill up their entire day. I'd have to think of another way to keep them busy on the Saturday I auditioned.

"Thank you," I said, handing the folder back to the woman.

"You don't want to book anything?"

"No, I'm okay." As I left, a group of older women walked in wearing swimsuits and talking about cold therapy.

I exited through the glass doors and down a wide set of wooden steps and back along the dusty path around the lake. I tried to think of other activities the camp offered. Maybe it was time to enlist the help of my sister. It was possible I'd need her to cover for me. But when I went back to the cabin, all I found was her phone on the nightstand. That worried me. She rarely left her phone. Was she bored without her documentary project? It really was time for me to tell her what I was doing. To suck it up and let her record me.

❄ ❄ ❄

"Everyone stand perfectly still!"

When I finally found Lauren, she was on a paddle board, twenty feet from the shore with two other girls around her age. My sister was in the middle and trying to slowly stand along with the other girls. Two boards floated beside the one they now occupied, abandoned.

Lauren let out a squeal and they all fell in the water. She came up sputtering and laughing. "We are going to get this!" she said, climbing back up. "Again!"

"Huh," I said. She didn't need her phone or this project. If I believed in signs now, maybe I could believe the festival had always been meant for me. Maybe it was the thing that was helping me wake up, find myself, find my passion. I sure felt more alive lately. I smiled and walked away.

❄ ❄ ❄

"I brought Oreos tonight to celebrate finishing the lyrics yesterday," I said, walking into the back room of the theater and sitting on the side of the couch that I had been sitting on all week. I now considered it my side of the couch.

"Nice," Brooks said. He was studying his messy guitar tab paper. He strummed a progression of chords. "Does that sound better?" He played a different one. "Or that?"

"I liked the second."

He looked over at me and his eyes that were normally light and playful were dark and intense.

"What's wrong?" I asked, my smile immediately disappearing. I set the cookies on the ground next to the couch and moved to the middle cushion.

"Nothing." He closed his eyes and shook his head. "Nothing new, I should say. I checked in with my dad's caretaker today and he has a fever. It doesn't sound bad, but for him, any sickness has a way of turning into some sort of secondary infection. I'm sure he'll be fine, but it's just one of those things that reminds me that my life is bigger than me, you know?"

"Yeah . . . Well, honestly, I don't know. I've never had anything close to that in my life, but I can imagine." I reached out and patted his arm, not sure what else to do. His guitar was a barrier between us. "Does he get sick a lot?"

"He doesn't, but when he does, it makes everything harder." He paused as if debating whether to share something with me or not. "I'm trying to convince my mom to go see him."

"Why do you have to convince her to do that? Doesn't she want to?"

He let out a heavy sigh. "I think half the reason she put him in a care facility is so she doesn't have to deal with everything. The other half is so she can pretend he's already gone." There was anger in his words but also so much sadness.

My breath caught in my throat. "I'm sorry, Brooks."

"It's why my mom and I have been at odds for the last several years."

"I can understand why."

"You probably think I'm selfish for coming up here when I'm really all he has."

I shook my head. "No, I don't think that at all. I understand why you might need to get away from the pressure of all that for a little while. Maybe you hoped that if you left, she'd step up." I suddenly understood why Brooks had snapped at Kai the other day, telling him he needed to take care of himself.

He strummed his guitar, even with my hand on his arm. "I need to stop thinking about it. Let's just practice."

"Are you sure? We don't have to do this tonight."

He kept strumming as his answer.

"Brooks, talk to me. This can wait."

"I don't want to talk. I want to work."

"Then let's work . . . I guess." I pulled out the lyrics, which I had folded into a square, and unfolded them. He immediately snatched them from me and crumpled them into a ball. I gasped. "Why did you do that?"

"You don't need them. You wrote this song."

"Technically, I only wrote parts of this song . . . and we only finished it yesterday."

He threw the crumpled ball over his shoulder. "You know you

don't need the lyrics. You're using them so you don't have to look at your audience."

He was right; they'd been my crutch all week. I turned toward the boxes across the room, my head up. "Okay, fine. I'm ready."

He sighed impatiently. "*I'm* your audience."

"I won't be looking at you the day of our audition. I'll be looking ahead." I gestured toward the boxes like they would be there at the end of the week, judging me.

"A person with a face will be your audience. You need to get used to it. Today, that person is me."

Even though I didn't think a beautiful boy with bright blue eyes and gorgeous hair would be my audience, he was right. I needed to get used to looking at eyes that would be looking at me. So I stared at him as he started to play.

"You missed your cue," he said.

"I know." Tears stung my eyes. "I'm sorry."

"Why?"

"Because I can't do this right now. You're snapping at me, and normally you have happy eyes and right now your eyes are super intense. And even though logically I get that it's because you're in a bad mood about really important things, it's stressing me out."

"Seriously?"

"Yes, Brooks, *seriously*." I stood. "Let's just come back tomorrow."

"Whoa, hold up."

I had started to walk away and he jumped up and caught my arm before I could leave. He put his hands gently on my shoulders. "Look at me for a second."

"I can't," I said.

"I'm sorry I'm taking my bad mood out on you."

I shrugged.

"But that's not why you're leaving."

I finally looked up, my brows drawn low. His eyes were no less intense.

"You're leaving," he said, "because you don't want to look at me and sing. Doing that would make this feel real. You're scared."

"What if I can't do this? What if I freeze up?"

"I get it. You don't want to look stupid."

Shay and Trent popped into my head with his words—an image of them kissing. "Yes . . . ," I said, knowing more than anything that's how Shay had made me feel—like a fool. Like a naïve fool. My stinging eyes threatened to become actual tears, so I pulled away and sat on the floor in front of the couch.

"Avery, you can do this. You've been doing this all week. You sound amazing." He joined me on the floor, shoulder touching mine.

"You'd tell me if you didn't think I could do this, right? You wouldn't just let me walk up there and do something I shouldn't be doing."

"Yes, I'd tell you. I promise."

I leaned my head back on the cushion. The light overhead was a chandelier—tiered, with white teardrop jewels hanging from each level. I'd never noticed it before because the ceiling was pretty high. It looked fancy in this small room, out of place. "My best friend kissed my ex-boyfriend two days before I came here."

"Um . . . Wow."

"Telling you that makes me feel stupid. Maybe that will warm me up for singing."

"Wait." He turned, putting his elbow on the couch cushion and propping up his head. "Why would that make *you* feel stupid?"

"Because I should've seen it coming."

"You should've? Does your best friend have a habit of betraying you?"

"No."

"Your boyfriend? Does he?"

"No."

"Then you most definitely shouldn't have seen it coming. The only people who should feel stupid in that scenario is them." It was quiet for two beats and then he said, "What did you do when you found out?"

"What *could* I do? It happened and I came here."

"Pay phone girl?" he said.

"Yes, Shay."

"Is that why she was so desperate to talk to you?"

"Yes, and I should've just talked to her, got it over with, let her apologize, because now it's just lingering."

He gave my knee two bumps with the side of his closed fist. "You're allowed to be mad."

"I'm not."

"Why not?"

"Because I don't like to be mad. And honestly, I don't like it when people are mad at me."

He nodded toward the door I had nearly walked out of minutes ago. "I was never mad at you. I'm mad at myself."

"I know. I don't like that either."

He laughed. "Nobody is allowed to be mad ever?"

"In my perfect world."

"Your perfect world sounds exhausting."

I shook my head even though I was still lying back on the couch. "No, it would be amazing."

"So you're ready to forgive your friend because anger is better if nonexistent?"

I smiled. "Yes."

He raised his eyebrows.

I smacked his arm lightly. "I mean, anger *is* better if nonexistent, but it's not about that. She's my best friend."

"So then *she* should be the one to fix this."

"There's only so much we can do five hours away from each other without—"

"Internet," he finished for me.

"Exactly. And now you officially know more about my summer drama than anyone."

"More than your sister?"

"Yes."

"I feel so special."

"You are." That was supposed to come out like a joke, to match his tone. It didn't. It came out like a lovesick sigh. I cleared my throat. "Anyway." My eyes went back to the chandelier. "Make me feel better about spilling my guts. What scares you, Brooks Marshall?"

He lay back, too, and stared up at the chandelier. Then he said, in barely above a whisper, "Hope."

"Hope? Isn't hope supposed to bring peace?"

"It was a joke."

I turned to look at him. "No, it wasn't."

"I guess I don't like to be disappointed, and it feels like the more I hope for something, the greater the disappointment will be when it doesn't happen."

"So you just, what, stop hoping?"

"I don't know, I guess I sort of have, yeah." His shoulder brushed mine lightly and he didn't pull away.

"Hope doesn't exist in your perfect world? That sounds exhausting."

"It really is."

I smiled over at him. "We're super depressing."

He chuckled. "Did you know there was a chandelier in here?"

"Saw it for the first time tonight. They probably just installed it yesterday," I deadpanned.

"Yes, that's the only thing that makes sense."

"I should sing now while staring into your eyes."

This time he laughed outright. "Please do."

Chapter 23

MARICELA AND I WALKED TOWARD THE LODGE TO PICK UP her paycheck, holding Popsicles we'd just purchased at the snack hut. It was such a hot day that mine was already dripping down the stick and onto my hand. I tried to keep on top of it, my head sideways, but was failing.

"I've been thinking about your parent problem," Maricela said. She was the only one I'd told I was auditioning and she'd seemed genuinely excited about it.

"Oh yeah, did you miraculously solve it for me? Can you kidnap them for the day? Hold them in camp jail?" The audition was happening the next day regardless of the fact that I still hadn't thought of how to pull it off. My plan at the moment was to sneak away and make an excuse once I got home—I was in a kayak all day or at the pool or on some obscure excursion.

"No, I liked your spa idea."

I slurped at the bottom of my Popsicle. "I told you that's impossible."

"My child, nothing is impossible," Maricela said, and pulled an envelope out of her back pocket.

"What is it?" I asked, not wanting to grab it with sticky hands. But written on the outside, in scrolling letters, were the words *Bear Meadow Spa*.

"I got you two day passes."

"How . . . You didn't pay for them, did you?"

"I didn't pay for them. We have employee reward points we can spend on ourselves or gifts and stuff for family. A couple of us pooled ours together."

"A couple of you? Who?"

"Tia. Clay. Don't worry, they won't tattle."

"Maricela, you guys didn't have to do that. Save your points. I should just tell my parents."

"Really? You're just going to march in there and tell them the day before the audition? Risk them saying no? Risk them being mad you've been hanging out with a strange guy alone?"

"No. You're right. I'm not."

"What does your sister say about all this?"

I became preoccupied with a group of kids walking ahead of us yelling out different words: "Bird!" "Cloud!" "Dirt!"

"Eyelash," I said.

"What?" Maricela asked.

"They're playing the alphabet game. *E* is a hard one."

"Are you avoiding my question?"

"Yes." I smiled over at her. "Lauren doesn't know."

That news shocked her. "She doesn't?"

"I know. I'm a horrible person. She made a couple new friends and for once she hasn't been preoccupied with her phone. I'll tell her if we get into the festival. That will make for a better documentary anyway."

She nodded slowly.

"You don't think that's a good idea?"

"No, it was probably important for you to have zero distractions the last two weeks."

"It was."

"And it will be even more important for you not to be distracted on Saturday." She tucked the envelope into my back pocket. "Give this to your parents. I already booked them from noon to eight. You can make up some excuse for the morning and then they'll be busy all afternoon and evening."

"Thank you so much. This . . ." I patted my pocket. "This means a lot."

She rolled her eyes. "Don't get all sappy on me. It was free."

"I know it wasn't." She could've used those points for herself or for her own family. "So just say *You're welcome, I'm the best.*"

"You're welcome. I *am* the best."

As we neared the lodge, the half of my Popsicle that was left clinging to the side of the stick fell onto the dirt at my feet. "Frick," I said.

"Have you ever eaten a Popsicle before?" she asked.

I laughed. "Shut up."

"It's just you're really struggling."

I kicked some dirt over the remains and looked around for a garbage can for the stick. Clay was leaving the lodge, envelope in hand, obviously having just picked up his paycheck. "Thanks, Clay!" I called out.

He changed direction and joined us. "For what?"

"For the spa thing. I really appreciate it."

"You're welcome. Kill it at the audition, okay?"

Mari squeezed my arm. "Do you know this girl heading our way with a very serious look on her face?"

"What?" I first looked at Maricela and then followed her gaze to the lodge parking lot where someone was very obviously walking straight at us. "I don't think so . . . ," I started to say, and then my cheeks went numb. "Shay."

"Who?" Mari asked.

My initial instinct was to turn and run, but wasn't that what I'd been doing all summer? So I stood my ground.

"Avery!" Shay said. Her serious expression turned into a smile when she saw me. "How lucky is this? I thought I was going to have to beg for your cabin number in the lodge, but here you are. You're so tan!" I could tell she was nervous. She was my best friend, after all. And right now she was talking fast, her voice an octave higher than normal.

"What are you doing here?" It probably wasn't the friendliest greeting but I was shocked. She had to drive nearly five hours to get to Bear Meadow from her house. And she didn't have a reliable car. My eyes scanned the parking lot but I didn't see her old blue Corolla anywhere.

"I needed to see you," she said. "Your sister said there was no internet and that's why you haven't been able to text me back."

"Lauren? When did you talk to Lauren?" Did she call the pay

phone back and ask for Lauren? This thought made me angry. I was allowed to be angry.

Shay turned to Mari. "Can I talk to Avery alone for a minute?"

And because Shay said things with such confidence and command, Mari responded, "Um . . . sure."

I wanted to grab her hand and tell her to stay, back me up, but she had no idea what was going on because I hadn't told her. I cursed my private nature as she and Clay walked away.

Shay waited until they were gone, then said, "You weren't talking to me. What was I supposed to do?"

"Wait until I was ready."

She flinched, surprised. She was used to me trying to smooth things over, immediately accepting her apology. That's why she was here, after all, because I hadn't and she was probably positive that she could make it happen in person. "You're my best friend, Avery, and this has been really hard for me."

"Hard for *you*? You kissed my boyfriend."

"He wasn't your boyfriend at the time."

My mouth fell open, but no words came out. I realized I was still gripping my Popsicle stick, my hands splattered with orange. This felt like it was adding to my humiliation.

"I'm sorry," she said. "I know it was still wrong."

I let the anger live, bubble inside me, and said what I'd been wanting to say all summer. "It feels like you don't know that it was wrong. I thought I was going to get back together with him. I told you that. But even if I hadn't told you that, you shouldn't have kissed him. You hurt me, Shay."

"I know."

"Was it the first time?"

"What?" she said, even though I was sure she knew exactly what I was asking.

"Had you kissed him before? When he and I were together?"

"No!" Shay said. "No, we didn't. We talked a few times but we never—"

"What does that mean? You talked about what? When?" I felt a presence to my left and looked over to see Brooks, paycheck in hand. I thought I'd feel even more humiliated thinking about him overhearing this conversation but instead I felt a huge amount of relief.

He gave me a single look that said *You okay?* When had I started being able to read him?

I honestly wasn't sure what I was, but it wasn't okay. My eyes must have said as much because he took a step closer to me.

"Avery and I were having a private conversation," Shay said with a smile at Brooks. She was pretty. I'd forgotten just how pretty, and how she could get guys to cave with her smile.

He shrugged. "I'll leave if Avery wants me to."

"Stay," I said.

Shay's eyes were sad as she turned them to me. "Avery, can't we work this out? Alone."

Could we? *She's your best friend. And you miss her.* I sighed at my own thoughts. Now that I'd said my piece, maybe I should take her to our cabin, where we could sit and have lunch and talk. Maybe . . . My eyes narrowed as I looked over her shoulder and saw someone in the distance standing by a car. "Shay? Did Trent bring you here?" My voice was even, cold. I almost didn't recognize it.

"I had no other way to get here! He wanted to help. He feels bad. We did this for you."

I felt the Popsicle stick crack in my grip. This is what she always did. She pretended her selfish actions were for my benefit. "You need to leave."

"I drove five hours for you."

"For *you*. You drove five hours for you. I'm not okay with what you and Trent did, what you'd obviously been doing for a while, and I'm not okay with you showing up here trying to force me to forgive you for it."

"I'm not trying to force you, Av. I thought you wouldn't want to throw our entire history away."

"Yeah, I thought the same about you."

She paused and then asked, "So that's it? We're done?"

"Yes . . . No." I took a deep breath. With Trent standing in the background, my initial instinct had been to say yes, but she was right, we did have a history, and I wasn't going to make a rash decision, especially one that involved a boy. "I don't know right now. I need time."

"You've been here like five weeks."

"I need more time. Are you going to give me that?"

She clenched her fists, but then her eyes shot to the ground. "I'm sorry. I'll give you more time."

I nodded.

She took a step forward as though she wanted to give me a hug but my entire energy must've repelled her because she swallowed hard, did a one-eighty, and ran back to the parking lot. I immediately felt guilty. She was obviously trying. Why couldn't

I get over it? It's not like I was still hung up on Trent. I was so over him.

"Don't do it," Brooks said, and I realized I had taken a step toward the parking lot.

"Why did she have to do this today of all days?" It's like she knew the audition was the next day. Knew this would mess with my emotions and my confidence.

"Avery, look at me."

I turned toward him and met his eyes.

"Repeat after me. You're fun, brave, and hot."

I tried to smile but it fell flat. I leaned my forehead against his chest and it wasn't until his shoulders tensed that I realized we were out in the open. I took a step back. "I'm sorry," I said, looking around to see if anyone had seen us. A few guests walked the path and a car was backing out in the parking lot, but that was it.

"No, it's fine," Brooks said.

"I just need . . ." I pointed over my shoulder. "I'll see you tomorrow." I left without looking back.

Chapter 24

THE MORNING OF THE AUDITION ARRIVED AND AS MARI-cela braided small braids along the side of my head and clipped them with fat bobby pins behind my right ear, my stomach did a million somersaults. I'd spent the night playing and replaying my conversation with Shay in my head. Wondering if I should've said more or less. Wondering if those were the last words we'd ever exchange. Then I reminded myself about the audition and proceeded to forget all the words to the song I was supposed to sing and had to say them over and over again until I convinced myself that I hadn't forgotten them. I had hardly gotten any sleep.

"What about these?" Tia held up a pair of combat boots. They'd already picked out my whole outfit and were now accessorizing it.

Maricela looked over, a bobby pin in her mouth. "Yes, I love those. What size are you?"

"Seven and a half," I said.

"They'll be a little big, but you'll be sitting on a stool, right?"

"Right."

Tia shoved them in a backpack along with some other supplies they'd equipped me with—bright red lipstick, some silver bangle bracelets, glittery eyeshadow. Basically the things I couldn't waltz through camp in or it would be obvious.

"How did things go with your parents this morning?" Maricela asked. "And what did they say about the spa tickets?"

"I told them I was going to a hair tutorial."

"You did not," Tia said.

I smiled. "No, I didn't. I actually didn't have to tell them much. Just said I was checking out the archery range. And they were so excited about the spa but wondered how I got the passes."

"Oh, right," Maricela said. "Didn't think about that."

"Yeah, neither had I. So I ended up telling them I won them at some lake competition."

"Wow, nice save."

"Yeah, thanks. I actually can't wait until this is over because I hate lying to my parents and my sister."

"So you're planning to lose today?"

I gave a breathy laugh. I hadn't analyzed it, but she was totally right. I had been viewing today as the end.

"That looks so good, Mari," Tia said, studying the braids.

"It does, doesn't it?" She patted my shoulders when she was finished. "Well, even if you lose, at least you'll look good doing it."

Tia laughed. "Great pep talk."

"Come on, you need to go."

After Brooks and I checked in at the venue in Roseville—an art deco–style theater—I went to the bathroom to apply the finishing touches to my look. I was surprised I had the whole counter and mirror to myself. I looked under the doors to the stalls; those were empty too. "Huh."

I unloaded the contents of the backpack onto the counter and suddenly wished Lauren was with me. She could've helped me get ready and her constant chatter would've eased my nerves.

I held up the black tank Maricela had decided on, making sure the holes wouldn't hit me in the wrong places. It looked pretty safe, but I was still going to wear the red and blue flannel over the top of it.

It took me maybe ten minutes to finish everything and when I stepped back and looked in the mirror I felt . . . like I was going to puke. I looked good, but my stomach was rolling and my head felt light. I rushed to the first stall and stood above the toilet for a moment. Nothing happened.

"You can do this, Avery. You've been doing this. You've been having fun, even." I drew in a deep breath, collected my backpack, and went to find Brooks.

Brooks sat on one of the folding chairs that had been set up in a holding area. The room was full of bands and their friends, waiting for their turn to try out.

"Hey," I said, sitting next to him and dropping the boots on the floor, the last thing I needed to put on.

Brooks looked up from his phone (it was weird seeing him distracted by one of those), gave me a once-over, and said, "That works."

"Really? That's the best you got?"

"You look hot," he said with a smirk.

"Better."

"Oh, I have our numbers." He retrieved a white square with the number thirty-seven on it from a stack of papers. He peeled off the back and was about to stick it on my shorts when he must've realized what he was doing. "Sorry, here."

"It's fine," I said, pulling on the bottom of my shorts to create a flat surface.

He stuck it on and smoothed it out. His eyes went to mine and then shot down again and he resettled himself in his chair. "I'm really excited," he said. "Because it seems there are very few girl lead singers. I think we might have a chance at this."

"Yeah, the bathroom was a ghost town." I leaned over and pulled on my boots, then started lacing them up. "Wait, you think we might have a chance because I'm one of the only girls?"

"Yes . . . Well, I mean, no, that's not the only reason. We have good material and you sing great. I'm just saying, I think it gives us an even better shot."

"Remind me never to ask you to give a motivational speech," I said.

"I'm sorry. You're right, I'm really bad at this. It's because I feel super confident in you."

"Okay, okay, you're warming up," I said, but my stomach was

still rolling around, somehow having freed itself from the rest of my organs.

Brooks was staring at his phone again. I held my hand out in front of him and it took a moment for him to look at it, confused.

"Let me see it," I said.

One side of his mouth lifted into a smile and he placed his phone in my upturned hand. I looked at the apps on his first screen. There were several social media icons, a maps program, and a few games.

"Super boring, right?" He held out his hand as if he thought I was going to give it back without checking out the next screens. I swiped.

I could tell right away that this was the screen that held his life. He had a music editing app and a songwriting one. There was one for hiking and one that mapped the stars. He even had a poetry app. The last two at the bottom were a medical dictionary and something about signs and symptoms. They probably helped him navigate talking to doctors for his dad.

A text message popped up as I held his phone and my eyes scanned it without thinking:

$530 by the 1st. Are you sure you're going to have all of that? You forgot to forward the hospital correspondence. Also, while you have service, call Gwen. She's been trying to get ahold of you.

The smiled slipped off my face and I felt like a jerk.

"I'm sorry," I said, handing it back.

"Why?" he asked. "Karma, right?"

"You got a text. I didn't . . . I accidentally read it."

He laughed a little. "It's fine." He read the text, tucked his phone in his pocket, and smiled at me. "It's nothing you didn't already know."

Wasn't it something I didn't already know? Because I was certain he'd never said the name *Gwen* before.

A side door opened and music, which had been muffled before, became clear. A man stuck his head out the door. He was wearing a headset and carrying a clipboard. He referred to that clipboard now. "Brooks Marshall, you're on deck."

"Is that our band name?" I teased.

"No," Brooks said.

"So vain," I continued.

"You're such a brat," Brooks said, poking my side.

I laughed and grabbed his wrist. "The Brooks Marshall Band."

He twisted his hand, releasing his wrist and entrapping mine. Our eyes locked. "Come on. We're on deck."

"Yes, on deck," I said. "What does that mean?"

He flashed his teeth. "That we're next."

"Oh, right."

We stood and walked toward the stage door. "Your brilliant word brain needs to think of a good band name," he said.

My chest warmed with his compliment. "I'll work on it."

We walked up the stairs to the stage and waited in the dark wings as the band performing finished up their song. Then it was our turn. A row of lights nearly blinded me as I stepped onto the stage. I resisted the urge to hold my hand up and block them. I didn't want to look like I was new to this. Brooks dragged a stool from the side of the stage to the middle, in front of a microphone that was set up. I sat down and he adjusted the microphone to my height.

"Whenever you're ready," a voice said over a speaker. I could just make out a table and five dark shapes behind that table in the middle of the theater chairs. It was actually kind of nice that I couldn't see their faces. I hadn't been expecting that.

Brooks leaned into the microphone in front of me, his hair brushing my cheek as he did. "Hey, I'm Brooks Marshall and this is Avery Young, and we'll be performing an original song for you today called 'Rewriting History.'"

"Sounds good," a female voice said. "Go ahead."

Brooks stepped away from the microphone, gave my shoulder a quick squeeze, and then swung his guitar around to the front of his body. I moved both hands to the microphone, stilling my breath. My legs were shaking even though I was sitting down. Brooks played the opening chords and I closed my eyes.

I sang the first lines with my eyes closed. "What's tomorrow look like from over there because from here it looks a lot like yesterday. . . ." My mind went completely blank and my heart jumped to my throat. My eyes flew open but still the words escaped me. "I'm sorry," I said into the microphone. "Can we start again?"

That was it, I'd just lost this for us.

"Yes, please do," a disembodied voice said curtly.

Brooks stepped in front of me. "Hey, look at me. You got this."

Tears welled at the bottom of my eyes. "I just ruined everything."

"You ruined nothing. Just keep your eyes on me the whole time, okay?"

"Okay." I shifted on the stool so I was angled toward him. I could pretend we were in the back room at camp. Just me and Brooks. He offered me his magic smile and every nerve in my body relaxed. He nodded, then strummed the first chord. And as I sang to him, his expression softened and something like pride shone in his eyes. I didn't look away.

Chapter 25

THE HUM OF THE LAST CHORD HUNG IN THE AIR AT THE END of the song and I felt . . . exhilarated. I'd done it. Brooks gave me a quick wink and I turned toward the shadowy figures in the seats.

Finally, a voice said, "Okay, thank you. We'll let you know once all the auditions are complete."

"Thank you," I said into the mic. Then I did a weird bow-curtsey thing and we rushed off the stage and back into the holding room.

My stomach decided it had held on long enough and I ran to the bathroom and straight to the first stall, where I threw up what little I'd eaten that morning into the toilet. Then I stood there, breathing heavy.

The door creaked open. "Avery?"

"I'm fine," I said. But I wasn't and another wave hit me, burning my throat and stinging my eyes as it came out.

"I'm coming in," Brooks said. "Hope you're alone."

"You don't need to come in." I pushed the back of my wrist to my mouth and braced myself on the stall wall with my other hand.

"What can I do for you?" he asked, pumping the paper towel dispenser. "Can I get you a Sprite or something?"

"No, I think I'm better."

He turned the water on and then off and then he squeezed into the stall with me, pressing a cold paper towel against the back of my neck.

"You don't have to take care of me, Brooks. I can do this." I took over holding the paper towel. "I'm sorry I sucked in there."

"You didn't suck. You did really well. I'm proud of you."

I rolled my eyes and left the stall. At the sink, I rewet the paper towel and used it to wipe at some mascara below my eyes. Then I rinsed my mouth with water and spit it out.

"Avery," Brooks said. "Going from having never sung a solo for an audience before in your life to what you did out there just now is amazing."

I sighed. "I might be happier if it was just about getting through it, but it's about more than that." I realized in that moment that even though I'd told Maricela and Tia I wanted to lose so it would all be over, I really didn't. I wanted to get past today, and that thought scared me because I wasn't sure we would.

The door opened and a girl walked in, looked between me and Brooks, and then shut herself in the farthest stall.

Brooks exited the bathroom fast. I washed my hands and followed him out.

"Let's find a vending machine," he said when I joined him. I was too tired to think of a better idea. We found one in a back hall and sat in that same hall with our purchases, our backs leaned against the wall, shoulders touching.

"It's weird not to have to worry about getting caught together," I said.

"Good weird?" he asked.

"Yes." I felt my eyes getting heavy. My lack of sleep was catching up with me. "So good."

"You should lie down," he said. "We have time."

"I'll just rest my eyes for a bit." I pulled my backpack close and used it as a pillow.

When I was nearly asleep, I felt a soft touch on my hair. "I don't resent my dad."

I was way too tired to try to read into what prompted him to say that, so I said, "That's good."

"Sometimes taking care of him can feel overwhelming but only because it's completely one-sided. But even then, he's my dad."

What I said in the bathroom came back to me. I rolled onto my back and looked up at him. "I know, Brooks. I was just feeling stupid. It wasn't about you, I promise."

He smirked. "So next time you barf, you'll let me hold your hair?"

"Let's hope there isn't a next time."

＊ ＊ ＊

"Avery, you're cheating," Brooks said, even-toned.

I'd slept for at least an hour and now we were sitting in a mostly empty hall off the holding room. His guitar case served as our table as we sat cross-legged on either side of it. Our vending machine wrappers littered the floor around us.

"I'm not."

"You're discarding your cards toward yourself so that you know what you're going to put down. You have to do it facing away."

"But then *you'll* see what I'm putting down."

"If we do it at the same time, the same way, it won't matter. Haven't you ever played slapjack before?"

"Yes, I'm the slapjack champion."

"Now you know why. Because you cheat."

I gave an overly dramatic gasp. "You're just a sore loser."

"I am the most un-sore loser I know. I am happy to lose."

"*Happy* to lose?"

"Ask my brother. I let him win all the time."

"If he knows you let him win, then you're not really letting him win, are you?"

"Well, he doesn't know. He'll just tell you he wins, and you'll realize it's because I let him."

"Is that what's happening here?" I held up my fat stack of cards.

"No, you're cheating."

I laughed. "Fine, I will ask your brother when we are both back home."

"Good, then you'll know. I am the most gracious of game players."

"So humble, Your Graciousness."

He laughed, then slid the card in his hand forward. "Should we finish?"

I readied my card and as I put it down, I saw it was a queen going on top of his queen. Huh, he was right. I was seeing the match a second before him. I slapped my hand on top of the pair. His hand went on top of mine almost immediately.

"Do you really think this stack belongs to you?" he asked, not taking his hand off mine. There was a smile in his eyes.

"Yes, it belongs to me." I let my eyes drop to our hands before they went back to his eyes. "Even though I may have cheated."

He lifted his hand. "It's probably good you gave yourself a head start because you are about to go down."

A group at the end of the hall closer to the holding room got up in a rush. "It's time!" one of them called back to us.

"I guess we'll never know if you would've beat me or not," I said.

"I think we both know." He stood, gathered our trash, and discarded it in a nearby bin. Then he looked at me. There was a guarded anticipation in his eyes.

"You better keep that hope bottled up," I whispered. "I can see it in there, wanting to come out."

"I'm just nervous."

I shook his shoulder. "Stop. That's my job."

As we walked, his guitar case between us, he said, "I've decided you're not much better at pep talks than I am."

"It's too late for a pep talk. We no longer have any control." I said that last part in a scary ghost voice.

"You're a huge dork, Avery Young," he said.

"I know."

When we got to the holding room, there was a long line at the door where Clipboard Man had been before.

"What's going on?" Brooks asked the guy at the back of the line.

"They're taking groups of ten in and telling them their fate."

"Good luck," Brooks said.

"You too," the guy said before he turned back around and started talking to his bandmates.

It seemed like it took forever before it was our turn. The spotlights had been turned off and the house lights turned on, so now I could clearly make out the five judges in the audience. Two women, probably in their late twenties or early thirties, and three men, at least that age but most likely older. They didn't look like they'd just discovered the next big music sensation. They looked like they were ready to go home, have a drink, and go to bed.

It surprised me when Brooks reached over and grabbed my hand. He held on to it tight as we stood there with the other nine bands. I squeezed his hand without looking over at him.

"If we call your name, please step forward," the dark-haired judge in the middle said. Then he started listing off names. Each name called added a new wave of tension across my shoulders.

Brooks's grip on my hand became so tight it almost hurt. When the sixth name was announced and we weren't one of them, he dropped my hand. I almost reached back out and grabbed it again when I realized what this must mean. I'd failed us. I was too awkward and inexperienced and not even close to a rock star.

"Front row," the man said. "I'm sorry. You haven't been chosen this year. Back row, report to the fairgrounds on August first at noon. Congratulations."

There was a mixture of shouts of joy and moans of disappointment. I just stood there in shock, not quite understanding what just happened, until Brooks wrapped me up in a hug. "Avery! We did it!" he said against my neck. "We did it!"

I let out a happy squeal and wrapped my arms around him. He

spun me around once, then set me down. His smile was bigger than I'd ever seen it.

"I'm so proud of you," he said.

"Me too!" I said, because I really was. This made him laugh. If joy could be bottled, he would be producing an unlimited supply. I looked around and realized we were the last people on the stage. Everyone else had taken their celebrations or disappointments back out into the side room, leaving a quiet hush.

Brooks gathered up his guitar case from where he'd left it by the back wall and I walked over to the microphone that was still set up. Now that I could actually see the seats instead of just the spotlights, I pretended they were full. I looked over the crowd. I may have sung to five very important people today, but could I sing to hundreds . . . maybe thousands? A calming energy flowed through me and I smiled.

"The chemistry between you and your boyfriend was off the charts," a voice below me said.

I jumped, then looked down to see one of the judges collecting papers off the end of the stage.

"Thank you . . . I mean . . . he's not my boyfriend." I looked over my shoulder to have a laugh with Brooks about the comment but he was gone.

"Well, whatever it was," the judge said, "keep that up for the performance. It was electrifying to watch."

"Thank you." I gave a nod and backed away slowly, not wanting to trip over my too-big boots. She picked up the rest of the papers and walked up one of the aisles.

I turned and left as fast as I could manage out the door, where I found Brooks scanning the crowd of people.

"There you are," he said.

I squatted down and unlaced the boots, sliding my feet free of them. "You know what I forgot?"

"What?"

"Makeup wipes. My parents can't see me like this. You think we can stop at a grocery store on the way home?"

"No problem."

"With your money?" I added, realizing I hadn't brought any cash. "I can pay you back."

"Considering the favor you just did for me, I'm pretty sure I owe you at least one makeup wipe."

I nudged his shoulder with mine. "So generous."

We exited the theater to the parking lot, where everyone was piling into cars. He stepped off the curb in front of me and then cut me off, offering his back. "Want a ride, shoeless?"

I didn't need a ride. I could've just put on my other shoes, the ones now in my backpack, but remembering how good he'd smelled earlier when we hugged, I wasn't about to turn him down. "Sure."

"Okay, here, hold my guitar case in one hand and your boots in the other. Will that work?"

"I think so." I transferred the boots I had been holding in two hands to one and then took his guitar case in the other.

He held his arms to the sides and squatted a little as if bracing himself for some strongman competition.

"You're not about to drag an airplane," I said.

"Jump already."

And so I did. It was a bit awkward trying to position the things in my hands just right over his shoulders, but when he gripped my thighs and hiked me up, my cheek settling against his, I decided that this was the right choice.

Because I knew he couldn't see me, I closed my eyes and breathed him in.

Chapter 26

WE PULLED INTO THE PARKING LOT OF A CVS AND HE turned off the ignition. "I'll just run in," he said, nodding toward my still-bare feet.

I'd deposited all my stuff in the trunk, so I said, "Thank you."

"Is there a certain brand you like?"

"Neutrogena. It will be a blue package in the face care section."

"A blue package? I think my mom might have those ones. Give me your phone number and I'll text you a pic when I find them."

I gave him my phone number and he entered it into his phone. "I'll be fast."

It was seven o'clock. It would take an hour to get back to the camp. My parents' spa day ended at eight. I'd barely make it.

Now that my brain wasn't completely consumed with nerves, I saw that the notifications on my phone were nonexistent. In other words, nobody had texted or Snapped or DMed me in weeks. Nobody had even tagged me in a post. I didn't want to be disappointed by this, but I was.

My phone buzzed in my hand and I nearly dropped it. A pic of Brooks's face next to a pack of makeup wipes appeared on my screen. I smiled, then texted back a pic of me holding up my thumb.

I added his name and number to the contact info in my phone. Then I swiped over to each of my social media accounts, double-checking my notifications. Nothing. I pulled up Shay's latest story, wondering if she'd said anything about our fight. But it was just pics out a car window—trees, a lake, a billboard. Her road trip with Trent, I realized.

Brooks opened the car door and I jumped in surprise.

"Everything okay?" he asked.

"What? Yes. Fine." I turned off the screen and put my phone down.

He tossed the makeup wipes onto my lap.

"Thanks."

"Checking in with your friends?" he said, nodding toward my phone.

"Sort of. No, not really."

He turned on the car and backed out of the spot. "Your boyfriend?"

"No."

"Now that you've made it, you should tell your family and friends about the festival. They can buy tickets and come."

I was super proud that I had helped us make it into the festival, but I didn't think my parents would understand that it was an accomplishment. They'd only see it as a betrayal. I'd been lying to them. The thought of that made my stomach turn. "I don't think that's a good idea."

He pulled out of the parking lot and onto the road. "Why?"

"My parents hate music. They are actively working to have it banned from our town."

"Really?"

"Did that even sound a little bit possible to you?"

He gave my shoulder a push and laughed. "Yes, obviously it did. So then what's the real reason?"

"Because I've been lying, and not just a little bit."

"True. But what about other friends? They wouldn't drive up and watch you perform?"

I flipped the visor down to find the mirror. "Do you mind? Is this blocking your view?"

"It's fine," he said.

I clicked on the light. "I guess I'm not that close to a lot of people," I said, freeing a makeup wipe and getting to work on my face.

"And your boyfriend?" That was the second time he'd asked about a boyfriend. "You and Clay aren't—"

"Clay? No!" I turned to face him. "You thought Clay and I were together?"

"I know he likes you. I just wondered if you liked him back."

"How do you know that?"

"It's obvious."

"Well, I disagree. But we're friends, sort of," I said. "I barely know him. What about you? Are you inviting people up?"

"No."

"You aren't?"

"No, my mom works two jobs. And it would be impossible for my dad."

"You should tell your mom, Brooks. Give her the opportunity to support you."

"I told you, I'm not her favorite person right now."

"I'm sorry."

He shrugged.

I took the bobby pins out of my hair and deposited them one by one into the cup holder in the console. "What about your girlfriend? Gwen? Will she come?"

"Gwen? Who's— Oh! No, she's my dad's nurse."

My shoulders fell with relief.

"I don't have a girlfriend."

"Oh . . ." I undid the braid while trying to hide a smile that wanted to light up my face. "My sister will probably come. I need to tell her now that . . . this part is done."

"And Mari, she wanted to come too."

"That's right. So see, we'll have people there."

I looked down at what I was wearing, knowing my dad would immediately find my outfit suspicious. It wasn't my standard wardrobe. I buttoned up the flannel I wore, leaving the top two buttons undone, then pulled my arms inside of it and snaked my way out of the tank before pulling it out and over my head. I put my arms back in the flannel sleeves, buttoned another button, and threw the tank behind me onto the seat.

"That was impressive," he said, pointing to my flannel.

"All girls have this skill—don't be too impressed."

He was quiet for a little while and I clicked off the light I'd been using to take off my makeup and settled back against the seat. I watched the yellow lines on the road in front of us.

"I *am* impressed."

I let out a sharp breath. "I guess you're easily impressed, then."

"No," he said. "Not the tank top thing. Your performance. You did really good."

"You already said that," I said quietly.

"I can't say it again?"

"It helped to look at you, made me forget what I was doing." The second that came out of my mouth, my cheeks heated up. "I mean, it made me think we were back in the room at camp and I didn't have to worry."

"Good. I'm glad." He stared straight ahead.

"Now we have to write a second song, right?" I asked.

"Yeah, you up for it?"

"For sure." I watched mile markers and street signs rush by as we drove.

I turned a heating vent toward me. Brooks's thumbs tapped a silent beat on the steering wheel. Why had our conversation suddenly dried up? We'd been spending so much time together and never had a problem talking.

Did it have something to do with the fact that I was hyperaware of every breath he was taking? Or every shift he made in his seat. He tucked his hair behind his ear, exposing his jaw, and I wanted to reach over and run a finger along it. I swallowed that desire and turned my attention out the side window.

"Are you still tired?" he asked after a while.

"Yes," I answered, even though I wasn't at all. I was wide awake, my senses on high alert.

"We're almost there," he said.

I checked my phone. Sure enough, the No SERVICE message was back in the corner. We'd made good time. It was ten minutes before eight. I would beat my parents.

The headlights shone on the Bear Meadow sign, and the sound of the turn signal cut through the silence. He turned into the camp and followed the road until he came to a sign that said EMPLOYEE LOT and turned left. We'd driven this part of camp earlier, on our way out. It took us along the back side of the property. Away from the pools and tennis courts and to a dirt lot filled with a dozen or so dusty cars. He pulled next to a pickup truck and turned off his engine.

We both sat there for several moments in absolute silence.

"Thank you for driving," I said at the same time he said, "Thanks again for everything."

We both looked at each other and laughed.

He put his hand out, palm up, and said, "We did it."

I slapped his hand as if he wanted me to give him five. "Yes, we did."

He laughed a little and shook his head, then opened his door, climbing out. I collected the bobby pins and the tank top and got out as well.

He retrieved his guitar from the trunk. I pulled out the backpack and took out my shoes, then replaced all of Maricela's things back inside. "Do you mind if I follow you up so I can return this to Mari and fill her in on everything?" This backpack couldn't reside in my cabin for any length of time or our cover would be blown.

"Do you have time?"

I nodded. "I have like five minutes." I pulled my shoes on. "I'll hurry."

He shut the trunk and we walked through the camp. It was quiet in the employee section. We reached Maricela's cabin and I stopped.

"Okay . . . good night," he said.

"Yes, good night."

He hesitated for a moment. "Some of your hair is wavy." He reached out and picked up a piece as if I could see it.

"The braids," I reminded him.

"Oh yeah." He dropped the hair and I took a breath, wondering if he was going to give me a hug right here in the middle of employee village.

The door swung open and Maricela stood in the square of light. "What are you guys doing out here?" she asked.

"About to knock," I said, holding up her backpack.

"Well get your cute butts in here and tell me how it went."

Brooks gave Mari a quick wave, then said, "Avery will fill you in. I should probably do the same for Kai and Levi."

"Fine." Maricela took me by the hand and pulled me into her cabin, shutting the door on Brooks. "So?"

"Where is Tia?" I asked.

"Oh, she's working the campfire tonight. Actually, now that I think about it, Kai and Levi are there too." She opened the door,

221

looked both ways, then shut it again. "Wow, Brooks is fast. He'll figure it out when he gets to an empty cabin." She turned to face me. "Tell me everything."

I filled her in on the day and she literally jumped for joy when I told her we made it. "I knew it! That's so amazing! I'm so happy for you!"

"Me too! Thank you for all your help with everything."

"Of course."

"I'd love to stay and celebrate but I really need to make sure I'm back before my parents."

"I get it." She gave me a hug. "I can't wait to watch you perform. In two weeks! That's crazy!"

"I know!"

"And I can't wait to get me some amazing food-truck food at the festival!"

I laughed. "Which one are you more excited about—the performance or the food?"

"It's too close to call. Probably the food." She held her thumb and finger up, a millimeter apart. "But just barely."

"Funny."

"Good night," she said.

"Night." I turned and stepped off the porch. The door shut behind me with a click.

I walked down the path, past a cabin where I could hear its occupants talking, past the EMPLOYEES ONLY sign. The whole day—staring at Brooks as I sang, sleeping beside him in the hall, being scooped up in his arms when we made it, riding on his back through the parking lot—played on repeat in my mind. I stopped and turned, sliding on some gravel. I stared back up the hill to Brooks's cabin. No, I really did need to get back before my parents found out I'd been gone all day. I faced the path again and took one step, two, then a third before my rapidly beating heart kept me from going any farther.

"Oh, screw it."

Chapter 27

I RUSHED BACK UP THE HILL, TRYING NOT TO MAKE ANY noise as I walked past the talkative cabin, then Maricela's. The lights in Brooks's cabin were on, shining through the thin curtains and water-stained window. By the time I stopped on his porch, I was breathless, my heart in my throat. And it wasn't from the walk.

I placed my hand flat on the door. I didn't do things like this. I wasn't the type to make the first move. To grab what I wanted. To go after things that scared me. But maybe today on that stage, I had realized that doing scary things and actually succeeding was the best feeling in the world. I rolled my shoulders once and knocked quietly on the door.

The twenty seconds that followed felt like an eternity. Then the handle turned and the door swung open. Brooks met my eyes with a questioning look. I held his gaze as I walked into the room; then I closed the door, holding the handle behind my back and walking it backward until it clicked into place. As if he wanted to make sure the door was closed himself, he placed his hands against it on either side of my head, his eyes not once leaving mine. I kept hold of the door handle, because I was sure it was the only thing keeping me upright.

Then, ever so slowly, as if he might back away if I moved too fast, I let one hand leave the handle and find his chest. He took in a deep breath and my hand rose with the inhale. His movements were slow, too, deliberate, as he tucked some hair behind my ear, then let his fingers trace my jawline all the way to my chin.

I leaned my head back against the door, my eyes fluttering closed. His fingers glided up my chin to my lips. He traced a line around them and then his warm breath touched my mouth. I drew in air, not from surprise but because once again I couldn't breathe. His hands went to my waist, where they grabbed hold of my flannel. I pushed up on my toes, letting our lips finally meet. His lips were soft.

I pulled him closer, needing him against me. He complied, bringing me into his arms, wrapping me up. With his chest against mine, I could feel the heavy beating of his heart. I let my hands run along his sides, sliding down his ribs. His mouth was warm and perfect. I felt like I could live in this space, this moment, forever.

That is, until he pushed me against the door and the handle dug into my back. I must've gasped because he pulled away. "Did I hurt you?"

"No." I moved away from the door. "Just the handle." I reached out for him but he took both my hands in his and led me to a couple chairs. He sat in one and pointed to the other.

I lowered myself down into it, already dreading whatever he was about to say. If he apologized for that kiss, I might have to pretend to agree and that wasn't at all what I wanted to do. But if we were going to be in a band together, even if only for a couple more weeks, we both needed to be comfortable. Had I made him uncomfortable?

"Did I pressure you into that?" he asked.

"What? No. I'm the one who came to *your* door, remember?"

"I thought maybe you forgot something," he said.

"I did," I said.

"What?"

I tilted my head in the universal *don't be dumb* fashion.

"Oh, right." He reached over and I offered him my hand. He pulled me out of my chair and onto his lap. "You forgot this?"

"Yes." My cheeks went red even though I was the one flirting.

He stretched up and I kissed him, thinking it was going to be a short peck. But then neither of us stopped. His hands went to my back and mine were in his hair, which was so soft and amazing.

I smiled against his mouth, unable to contain the giddiness in my chest any longer.

He pulled away. "What?" he asked with a smile of his own.

"It's been a good day."

"It has," he said.

"Is this how your summers always go?" I asked with a laugh. "Some music, some friends, some sneaking around with guests?"

His brows went down immediately. "You think I make out with all the guests?"

"Not *all* of them," I said, still smiling.

"Avery." He shook his head and I could see the hurt in his eyes and immediately regretted saying it.

"I'm sorry, that's not what I meant." I kissed one of his cheeks and then the other.

"What did you mean, then?"

"I just . . . I don't do things like this."

"And you think I do?"

"I was trying to protect myself a bit, by asking a very passive-aggressive question. I'm sorry."

"You don't need to be passive-aggressive," he said. "Just ask me questions if you have them."

I nodded. "I know. I always have." Which was different for me. I normally wasn't so direct with people.

"Good," he said.

In that moment, I had the sense that he could break my heart in two if I let him. More than anyone had in the past. But I also knew, as he pulled me close again, that I was willing to take that risk.

◎ ◎ ◎

A pounding on Brooks's door had me jumping off his lap and patting my hair down. Brooks stood, straightening his shirt and steadying his breath. I backed up against the wall and he opened the door a crack.

"Have you seen my sister?" Lauren said from beyond the door.

"No," Brooks said. "Why? What's up?"

"Is that a real no?" she asked. "Because my parents have been done at the spa since five and they've been looking for her. I was able to keep them calm at first but every hour they've gotten more worried and now they're on their way to report her missing to Janelle so that she can enlist the help of the employees. So if you really don't know where she is, then maybe you can help me find her."

Brooks cursed under his breath and then met my eyes.

"I'm here, Lauren," I called out.

She pushed past Brooks and into the cabin. "Avery, jeez, where have you been?" She wrapped her arms around me and I realized she must've been worried too.

I hugged her back. "Let's go stop Mom and Dad before they disrupt the entire camp."

Brooks squeezed my hand as I walked by and I threw him a smile over my shoulder.

"Good luck," he said.

"Seriously," Lauren said as we speed-walked down the trail. "Where have you been all day?"

"I—"

"Don't lie to me," she said. "I have a feeling you've already done enough of that."

She was right. I had. But it was for survival. I had barely gotten through the audition today; I couldn't imagine how much worse it might've been with added pressure. "I auditioned with Brooks."

"What?" Her voice went cold. "You went to Roseville today?"

"I was going to tell you, once I figured out if I could do it. I'm sorry."

"Are you? Because I don't think you are!"

I looked around at guests who were walking the path around us in the gray skies of twilight. "Lauren, shhh."

"No, I'm not going to shhh. You knew I wanted to make a documentary about this! You knew that!"

"You told me that it wasn't about that."

She clenched her fists. "You knew I was just saying that so you would do it!"

I did know that. "This isn't about you."

"It isn't about me? I'm the one who went to the first band practice, not you!"

"Lauren, please be quiet," I said.

She held up her hands. "I will now shut up."

I might've been relieved at this announcement but the more we walked, the more she seethed. I could feel it in her angry breaths and her stomping walk and her pointed glare. By the time we entered the lodge, my nerves were shot. And seeing Mom and Dad standing there in a tight circle with Janelle and D didn't help at all.

"I'm here!" I said. "I'm here."

Mom turned first and relief washed over her face. She gathered me in a hug that was quickly joined by my dad, and I immediately felt terrible.

"I'm sorry," I said. "I didn't mean to worry you."

"Where have you been, Avery?"

I thought I'd be done lying after today but there was no way I could tell the truth right there in front of Janelle and D. Not when Brooks's job was on the line. "I went on a hike and got a little lost. I would've left a note but I thought I'd be back before you were done at the spa."

Lauren scoffed from where she stood ten feet away, her arms crossed. D noticed, her gaze going back and forth between Lauren and me.

Janelle clasped her hands together. "I'm glad you're safe, young lady. You should always use the buddy system when going on a hike."

"True," I said. "I wasn't thinking. Sorry for the scare, everyone."

Mom kept hold of my arm as we said our goodbyes and left the lodge. It was darker now and the cicadas were chirping from the bushes and ground cover, highlighting the fact that none of us were talking. I really just wanted this to blow over.

"How was the spa?" I asked when we were halfway back to the cabin and nobody had said a word.

"Oh, honey," Dad said. "It was great. Thank you for sending us."

"Ask her *why* she sent you," Lauren said.

I shot her a look.

"It doesn't feel good to be betrayed, does it?"

I had turned Lauren into an enemy, and I realized now, too late, that had been the wrong call. I should've made her my ally. She had the power to ruin it all and I hoped she wasn't going to use it.

I tried to ignore her. "I'm glad you had fun," I said. "What did you do?"

Mom spoke now. "Let's see, we did this mud bath thing, which was a little gro—"

"Avery went to Roseville today with a guy who works here and tried out for a music festival! That's why she sent you to the stupid spa! She's been lying to you," Lauren spit out in an angry rush of words.

My shoulders slumped. I had just thought she was mad, but she was more than mad, obviously; she was hurt. And now she accomplished her goal of payback, because I was hurt too. I couldn't believe she was doing this to me. Mom and Dad exchanged a look that must've said, *Let's wait until we're back in the cabin* because neither of them responded until the door was unlocked and relocked behind us.

Then Mom asked, "*Where* were you today?"

"Roseville," I said quietly.

"Not on a hike?"

I shook my head.

"Trying out for a music festival?" she asked.

I nodded.

Dad looked at me with a mix of disappointment and anger.

"I'm sorry. I should've told you, but—"

"You absolutely should have told us," Mom said. "Who? Who did you go with? Some stranger? You got in a car with some stranger?"

"No! Of course not. He's a friend. We've known him since we got here. Lauren was making a documentary of his band." I pointed at her, my insides on fire.

"Exactly!" Lauren said, patting her chest. "*I* was making a documentary of his band here at camp and then *she* completely cut me out of it!"

"Well, I'm sorry your fifty viewers are going to miss out on a thrilling documentary."

"*Fifty?* Fifty! Try over six thousand! Glad to know you've actually looked at my channel before, sis."

I flinched. Six thousand? When had that happened? Obviously when I was busy not caring. But my shame at that revelation wasn't enough to overpower my anger. "I guess we're both screwed, then, because we actually made it today."

Lauren's eyes immediately went from hard and angry to shock, then something like regret, letting me know that from the second she'd heard what I'd been doing today, she assumed I had failed. She sputtered a little before saying, "Well, if you had told me—"

"Girls!" Dad said, the first thing he'd said since the revelation. "That's enough! There will obviously be some consequence for you. Your mother and I need to discuss what that will be."

"For just me?"

"Yes, your sister has done nothing wrong."

"I just told you she's been sneaking around making a documentary with employees. That's perfectly fine with you?"

Lauren narrowed her eyes at me.

"We obviously wish you wouldn't have lied, Lauren, but—"

"But?" I asked, my eyes burning and my throat raw. "There's a *but* after that? Her lie is somehow different from mine because hers makes her so creative and full of potential and mine just makes me a liar?"

"Avery, where is this coming from?" Dad asked.

"It came from you, Dad! Straight from your mouth where you were bragging about your amazing daughter." I pointed at Lauren, then moved my hand to my chest. "And just happy your other daughter could obediently walk the path chosen for her. Well, Dad, I guess I'm not obedient after all, so what's left to be proud of, right?"

I was positive I was making this worse as I rushed through the living room, heading for my bedroom, but I couldn't stay there any longer.

"We aren't finished!" Mom yelled after me.

"I am!"

Chapter 28

LAUREN JOINED ME IN OUR ROOM SECONDS LATER. WE were both breathing hard and now glaring at one another.

"I hate you so much right now," she said.

"Ditto," I responded, even though I didn't mean it. In fact, all I wanted to do at this point was fix this.

"Ugh," she groaned, and stomped the three feet to her bed and crawled under the blankets. She pulled them up to her chin and stared at the ceiling.

I quietly changed into a pair of pajama shorts and a tee and climbed in bed as well. My heart was still racing, so I knew I wouldn't be able to go to sleep anytime soon. I clicked off the lamp on the nightstand between us and plunged the room into darkness. Through the wall came the muffled sounds of my parents talking. I wondered what consequences they were conjuring up for me.

My brain frantically tried to figure out how I could still perform at the festival. If I had been thinking more clearly out there, I wouldn't have lost my temper. I would've tried to apologize with the hopes that they'd soften and let me sing in two weeks.

I took in several deep breaths as I stared into the blackness above me.

"You really made it?" Lauren asked, her voice barely above a whisper.

"Yes."

"I . . . That's good."

"Yeah." Several more quiet minutes passed. "You really have six thousand followers?"

"Yes."

"That's impressive."

"Yeah."

At some point after that, without another word between us, I fell asleep.

◎ ◎ ◎

The next morning at the breakfast table was somber. Mom and Dad sat on one side, Lauren and I on the other. The light from the front window of our cabin cast a perfect square of yellow on the untouched fruit and Danishes between us.

Dad placed his clasped hands onto the table and looked at me. "We're not sure what's gotten into you, Avery. This is very unlike you."

"I know," I said. "I shouldn't have lied."

"Well, your mother and I have discussed this," he said. "And we think the proper punishment for you is a week of grounding. And you obviously can't see this boy again."

Panic gripped my chest, but I tried to keep it at bay. We only had two weeks until the festival. I couldn't be grounded for one whole week of that. We had an entire song to write. "Okay," I said. Fighting them right now would be pointless. I had to show them I was sorry first, humble, let everyone calm down. Then maybe I'd be able to change their minds.

"What?" Lauren said. "No! She made the festival. You have to let her sing in it!"

I squeezed my sister's knee. "It's fine, Lauren. They're right, I messed up."

"And if we do catch you together again," Mom said, "we'll report him to Janelle."

I took in a deep, shaky breath. "Okay." I could tell they were done and it made me sad. I'd thought maybe my dad would apologize for what he'd said about me to that couple at the beginning of the summer. That maybe he'd say, *I'm sad that you lied but I'm proud that you sang.* But he didn't.

"For the record," I said, "I think you'd like Brooks. He's a really nice guy. And maybe if you met him, you'd see that." *Really, Avery? You couldn't hold it in for one more second?*

"A really nice guy doesn't need to sneak around with a girl," Mom said.

"I agree," Dad said. "We're beyond disappointed in you, Avery."

I stood abruptly, my chair scraping the tile in a loud whine. Once in my room, I tried to calm my emotions but that seemed to only make them worse, so after three times pacing the small aisle between our beds, I threw myself on my pillow face-first and cried.

Several minutes passed before the door creaked open and then shut. My mattress shifted as someone sat down next to me.

"Avery." It was Lauren.

"Leave me alone, Lauren."

She started scratching my back softly. "I'm so sorry. I was just mad and hurt and I didn't know all this would happen."

I sniffled as more tears came.

"So you actually cry like the rest of us."

"If you record this, I swear . . ."

She laughed a little at my obvious joke but then sniffled herself. "Do you really hate me?"

"No."

"I don't hate you either."

"I know," I said; then I sat up and wiped at my eyes. She wiped hers as well. "You don't think they'll tell Janelle, do you? Brooks needs this place, this job. He has so much guilt inside him and he'll think this is the universe punishing him for having dreams."

Lauren's eyes shot back and forth between mine. "Oh, you're in love with him. I didn't realize that."

"I'm not in love with him. I've known him for like five weeks."

She gave an exaggerated sigh. "Excuse me. You like him very much."

I pressed my right thumb into my left palm. "Yes."

A little smile snuck onto her face. "My sister the no-drama queen likes the unpredictable rocker."

"Your sister has never been so full of dramatic angst."

She laughed. "You'll figure something out, Avery. You always get the parents on your side."

"That's because my side has always been their side! Until now . . ."

"Oh . . . I guess you're right. That sucks. Oh, and by the way, I'm grounded too."

"What? Why?"

"I guess Dad analyzed what you said last night and decided I'd been lying too."

That's what my dad took from what I'd said the night before? The least helpful part? "I'm sorry."

She shrugged. "It's fine."

"Did they tell you what a grounding on vacation consisted of?"

"They said we got the lovely privilege of staying here the rest of the day to think long and hard about our actions. Then for the rest of the week, we get to do every single activity as a family."

"Ugh," I said. So both Lauren and I were on house arrest for twenty-four hours and on guarded watch for a week, and I had no way to tell Brooks what was going on.

"Yeah. They're good at punishments."

"Welcome to my epic adventure."

❀ ❀ ❀

"I can't live like this," I whined, lying in my bed, staring at the ceiling. My sister hadn't been joking when she'd told me our punishment. We had done everything as a family going on forty-eight hours now. I loved my family, but this was way too much.

The day before at the lake, I'd been able to sneak a letter to Maricela for Brooks. The letter spelled out everything that had happened since I last saw him and told him I'd try my hardest to still make the festival, but this time I needed to do it with my parents' permission and I wasn't sure I could get that. *Cross your fingers for me* was how I'd finished the letter, then signed my name. I thought about adding a little heart after my name, but I hesitated and ended up clicking the pen closed, leaving my letter heartless.

"You're being so dramatic," Lauren said from her bed, repeating the words I was sure I'd said to her dozens of times in our lives.

"I know! I'm so bad at being grounded. How do you do this all the time?"

"Wait, is this your first time? How had I not realized that before now?"

"I'm going to die of boredom," I groaned.

She threw her pillow at me and I laughed.

She flipped onto her stomach. "Tell me about the auditions. Were you scared?"

"Terrified."

"So is this it? Your passion? Your life's purpose or whatever it is you've been after all summer?"

I thought about that question as I watched the ceiling fan go around and around above us. "I don't know. Maybe? I barfed afterward, so not sure my body agrees with me."

"Lots of people get nervous stomach."

"Like who?"

"I don't have a list or anything, but I've heard it happens. Maybe it will get better the more you do it."

"Yeah, I definitely need to do it more to see if it's something I'm good at."

"But you obviously did well. I mean, you made it."

"Yeah . . . we did well. And honestly, aside from the barfing, it felt good."

"I'm happy for you."

There was a tap at our bedroom window and fear gripped my heart. I looked at Lauren.

"Don't look at me, lover girl. That's for you."

"Is he *trying* to get fired?" I moved the curtain aside. Brooks stood there, just like I'd both dreaded and hoped for.

"I'll go turn on the shower in the bathroom and if the parents ask, I'll say you're in there. You have twenty minutes. Tops."

Would that work? That would work! "Thank you so much," I said to Lauren, then opened the window. There was a screen that I popped out and let fall to the ground outside. Then with very little grace, I tried to step over the nightstand to the windowsill.

"Don't be dumb," Lauren said. "You have to step on the nightstand first. Here, let me move the lamp."

But I was already climbing and the nightstand was tipping and Lauren let out a squeal as she held me up from behind. Then we both stared at the closed door for a long moment. Nobody came.

"Hurry," she said.

I finished my climb out the window.

She leaned her head out. "Stay close."

I nodded and she moved the curtain back into place. I turned around and faced Brooks.

Chapter 29

"HEY," BROOKS SAID.

"Hi," I said back.

An awkward tension hung in the air. I hadn't talked to him since we'd kissed. Did he regret that or was this tension from the letter? From the fact that I was single-handedly crushing his dreams?

My parents' window was on the complete opposite side of the cabin, so I wasn't too worried, but I pointed to a group of trees about ten feet away from the house and lit pathways. He nodded and we made our way there.

Once protected by the foliage, I nervously played with my hands.

From somewhere nearby, a frog croaked a low deep song over and over. Finally, Brooks said, "Avery, are we good?"

My breath hitched. "I think so. Are you not good?"

"No, I'm good. I was just worried about you after reading the letter."

"I'm so sorry."

He immediately started shaking his head. "No, it's fine. I

understand. I didn't want you to get in trouble over something you were doing for me. That's never what I intended."

I reached out and took his hand. "I know. I hope that by the end of the week they'll have softened a bit."

"What do you think the odds are of them coming around? That you'll get to sing in the festival?"

"I don't know." My eyes found a mushroom growing out of a crack in the tree bark. "It doesn't seem likely right now. But I'm hopeful."

His jaw tightened.

"I know, I know. Hope is a four-letter word."

"I'll try to find it somewhere deep in my black heart."

I smiled. "Did you tell Kai and Levi about making the festival? What did they say?"

"They were surprised. Asked if we needed two more band members."

"They did?"

"Yeah." He bit his lip. "What do you think?"

The request surprised me. "Oh. Is that even a possibility? We're allowed to add them?"

"Yes, the rules are pretty loose about band members, actually."

"Yeah, I mean, I don't care. That's fine with me. You guys are the originals anyway."

"Thanks, Avery. I didn't want to have to tell them no," he said. "So . . . do your parents hate me?"

"What?" He was worried about that? "No, they don't even know you. It's this festival thing, the lying, it's all just an initial impression."

"Aren't those the ones that matter?"

"That's what they say, isn't it? But I honestly don't think so. Initial impressions are stupid. Superficial. If people really cared, they'd want to know more than their first thoughts about a person." I hoped my parents would give Brooks a chance.

"But isn't that the point?" Brooks said. "People *don't* care. Or they're always trying to decide if they're going to care. Hence initial impressions."

I took a tiny step closer. "What was your very first opinion of me in the theater, in that staff shirt?"

His face, which had been nothing but worried since I crawled out the window, softened into a smile. "We are *not* going there."

"So it was bad," I said, putting my hand on his chest.

"No. Not at all. I was excited that you'd be around all summer, let's just say that." He covered my hand with his. "And what was yours of me?"

"I thought you had a magic smile."

"A magic smile?" He offered it to me now.

"Yes, that one. I also thought you were very confident and way too pretty for me."

"It's the hair, isn't it?"

"Trust me, it's the face."

"Well I like your face too."

I smiled and we fell into silence again. His thumb began making small circles over the back of my hand.

I reached out with my free hand and let it travel from his shoulder to his neck.

He closed his eyes. His lashes were dark and long; his mouth was relaxed, making his lips look soft. I inched forward until our noses touched.

"Brooks," I whispered.

"Yes?"

"You're pretty cool."

He chuckled a little and I closed the space between us and kissed him.

He responded, pulling me close. His body felt warm as the air around us became colder. His hands moved from my shoulders, then down my arms and back again.

"When can I see you again?" he asked, pushing his forehead against mine.

"It's probably best we keep our distance until I'm done being grounded."

He let out a small groan but nodded.

Then we both heard a distinct whistle back by the cabin.

"I have to go," I said.

"Wait." He reached into his back pocket and pulled out a piece of paper that had been folded in fourths. "I started on the second song. Think you can look it over and add another verse?"

"Of course." I pushed myself up on my tiptoes and kissed him one last time before I ran back to the window where my sister was waiting. I climbed inside, gripping the paper to my chest, and fell on my bed with a happy sigh.

"So dramatic," Lauren said, replacing the screen and closing the window.

I laughed, then sat up and unfolded the page. The lyrics were written in his messy way—words crossed out, or underlined, or squeezed in as an afterthought—but that only made my smile bigger as I read through them.

> *Sometimes the stars align.*
> *Sometimes the path seems moved for you.*
> *Sometimes it's just in time.*
> *Exactly when hope was almost through.*
> *And sometimes is all I need*
> *And more than I deserved*
> *So I read into every sign*
> *Because sometimes, yes this time, sometimes brought me you.*

I took a sip of air. My boy who normally wrote soul-sucking lyrics wrote a love song? I read over the words again. Did he write *our* love song? Already a second verse about my side of the story was starting to take shape in my head.

> *Sometimes the moon goes dark*
> *And the path ahead unclear.*

"I need a pen," I said, scrambling to the nightstand and searching the top drawer before the words slipped away. "Give me a pen."

"Chill," Lauren said. "Here." She reached into her laptop case and threw one onto my bed. And I began adding my neatly written lyrics beneath Brooks's messy ones.

Chapter 30

THE REST OF THE WEEK WENT BY PAINSTAKINGLY SLOW. Every day we did a different activity with my parents—minigolf and tennis and crafts. We even left camp and went to some hot springs one day. And every night, I worked on the second verse of lyrics or the arguments I'd make to my parents at the end of our grounding about why I should sing in the festival.

By the time the week was up, I felt anxious. I hadn't seen Brooks in days, not even in passing, and began to make up stories in my head that he was somehow discovered and fired.

"Hey," I said to my sister. I was lying in bed and had just read over my festival arguments again.

She looked over the top of her laptop. "What?"

"Do you have some footage of Brooks?"

"What?"

"From practices. I just wondered if you ever got an actual interview with him."

"Are you going through withdrawals? You need a Brooks fix?"

"Yes." I didn't even try to deny it.

She patted the bed next to her and I rolled off my bed and onto hers.

She exited the window she had up and opened another.

"What were you working on?" I asked, pointing at the screen where the other window had been.

"Oh, nothing, just a project. Let's see, Brooks, the unhelpful guitarist." She proceeded to show me several clips of him not answering her questions. His teasing eyes made me happy.

I tapped a video thumbnail. "What's this one?"

She opened the clip. Brooks was sitting on the edge of the stage staring down, as if he didn't love the camera but was willing to talk to his hands.

"Music has gotten me through everything," he said. "It's been my best friend when I felt like I had no one."

My heart ached for him and how alone he'd felt over the years.

Kai's head popped over Brooks's left shoulder and he gave a funny growl, his tongue sticking out.

"Kai," Lauren said off-camera. "You got your turn. Go practice or something."

Kai walked away, but the moment was gone. Brooks moved to a squat and then stood. "I should go practice too."

"Are you going to cut out the part where Kai interrupts for the documentary or keep it in?" I asked.

"What do you mean?" Lauren said, closing that video and scanning the screen, probably to see if there were any others of Brooks. "I'm not doing this documentary anymore."

"Oh, right." How could I have forgotten that?

She held up crossed fingers. "But maybe Mom and Dad will say yes to you singing and then I can do a new one, on you . . . right?"

The arguments I'd been practicing all week with my sister about why my parents should let me sing suddenly sounded nonsensical and unconvincing. And a documentary starring me sounded even more ridiculous. "Do you think that would be interesting?"

A knock on our door was followed by Mom opening it. "You girls wanted to chat?" she said.

The pasta we'd had for dinner seemed to turn over in my stomach.

Lauren and I both stood, somberly. I grabbed the letter I'd written so I could remember everything I needed to say and we joined our parents in the living room. The expressions on their faces didn't look any softer than they had a week ago despite all the quality family time we'd been having.

"Well, girls," Dad said when we sat on the couch. "You are officially free."

"But there's a twist," Lauren said in an operatic voice.

I didn't think her joking was going to help in this moment, so I held up the letter. "Can I read you something?" I asked, looking at Mom, then Dad.

They exchanged their own look but Mom said, "Yes, go ahead."

I cleared my throat. "Mom, Dad . . ."

"Countrymen," Lauren said.

"Lauren, please," I pleaded.

"Wait, just wait," Lauren said. "I have something we should all watch first."

"What?" I said, dumbfounded.

She held up her laptop, which I hadn't realized she'd been hugging to her chest.

"Lauren, do you have to do this right now?" I asked, shaking the letter.

"Believe me, I do."

I sighed and Dad nodded the go-ahead. She put the laptop on the ottoman and forced us all to squeeze onto the couch so we could see better. Then she pushed play.

Some footage of the band came on the screen from one of the nights before Ian got hurt. I wasn't sure Lauren showing my parents the half-finished band documentary would change their minds about me singing, but maybe it would help them get to know the guys better, which was actually a good idea.

The music rang out of the small speakers of her computer.

Just when I thought the video was going to cut to an interview with Kai or Ian, the camera panned over to me, sitting there, listening to the band play. I had the biggest smile on my face as I watched. The video zoomed closer and closer to my face and that look of happiness. When the song was over, the me on the computer screen clasped her hands together in a giddy gesture. I hadn't realized I'd done that at all.

Then the video faded and a phone screen filled the picture. I remembered when Lauren had grabbed my phone earlier in the summer and had recorded a video of her scrolling through one of my playlists. "Do you know how many songs you have on here?" she asked on the video.

"No," I'd said. "A lot."

"More than one person could listen to if they listened to music every day for a thousand years."

"Too bad most of them aren't downloaded." I'd made a face at that. "Can I have my phone back?"

She flipped the camera to her own face and whispered, "Avery loves music. It's a sickness. Someone get this girl help."

That day, I'd been too busy exiting out of the screens she'd opened on *my* phone to actually hear what she'd been saying to *her* phone.

The next cut was to a scene of me lying on my bed and staring at the love song lyrics I'd been working on. I was repeating lines over and over and then mumbling, "No, that's not quite right. What would be better? Hark? No, park . . . missed my . . . mark!" I'd looked over at Lauren. "Dark and mark! It was so obvious."

"Sure was," Lauren had said.

Screen me nodded absentmindedly and scribbled the words on the page.

Another cut and I was sitting on my bed cross-legged, holding a different paper in my hand, practicing what I wanted to say to our parents tonight. I hadn't realized she was recording.

"Mom, Dad, I have been holed up in my room a lot of this week, causing me to have clarity on many issues."

"Did you really use my 'holed up' suggestion?" Lauren asked.

Screen me turned the paper toward her and pointed.

"I thought you'd replace it with some of your fancy words."

"No, I liked it. Now stop interrupting."

She tilted the camera slightly so the view was on her and she rolled her eyes at the camera. "Fine, keep going, then."

Screen Me went on. "I am not arguing the fact that I definitely should've had consequences for my actions."

"And Lauren shouldn't have had any," video Lauren whispered.

"Do you want me to add that?"

"No, everyone already knows it."

"I understand that lying leads to losing your trust. I hope that by being completely honest now, I might gain some of it back."

"They're going to like that part," Lauren said.

"I'm not saying it because I think they're going to like it. I really do believe that," Screen Me said.

"I know, I know," Lauren said. "Continue."

"Several weeks ago, Dad, you mentioned offhand to a perfect stranger how amazing and creative Lauren was and how bright and exciting her future looked. In basically the next breath, you called me laid-back and predictable. Ever since then, I've been on a journey, of sorts, to discover something exciting within me. So when this opportunity to sing for a festival arrived, I felt everything was pushing me to do it."

I glanced over at my dad, who was watching the video intently, and his eyes looked sad.

Screen Me continued. "I hadn't intended to lie when this all started. I genuinely thought that I'd sing and realize I couldn't do this at all, just like all the other things I've been trying for the last several weeks. But then I did . . . and I enjoyed it . . . and it felt too late to come clean."

"Come clean makes it sound worse than it is," Lauren said on the video. "Mom and Dad are easily led. Pick the right words."

Lauren, on the couch next to me, coughed. "I meant to edit that part out," she whispered.

Dad chuckled a little and for the first time since I sat down, a little hope blossomed in my chest. I enjoyed hope.

"And so," Screen Me continued, "I am begging you that I might be able to sing at this festival with someone who has helped me see that I'm not boring and predictable."

Lauren kept recording as I gave a fake bow.

"What do you think?" Screen Me asked.

"I can make it work."

"What does that mean?"

"Nothing. Go shower."

I'd left the room and Lauren pointed the camera at herself. "I mean, no wonder she's everyone's favorite."

The video cut back to band practice. This time I was looking up, thinking. Brooks had his notebook out and everyone onstage was staring at me. "You want me to play your game, but won't teach me all the rules," Screen Me said. It was the lyric I had offered that night. I remembered being nervous about it, feeling self-conscious. Onscreen, as the guys gave positive feedback, the video zoomed in closer and closer to my face. Finally I broke into a smile, which then became a still image and faded to black.

Everyone was silent for at least ten seconds. Then my sister closed the laptop. I looked at her and said, "Wow, Lauren, you are really good at that. No wonder you have six thousand subscribers."

Her cheeks went pink. "Thank you."

Mom stood, gestured toward the bedroom with her head, and Dad followed.

"You are totally going to get to sing at the festival," Lauren said with a happy clap.

I hoped she was right. And if she was, it was all because of her. I leaned over and gave her a crushing hug. "Thank you."

Chapter 31

LAUREN AND I WALKED THROUGH CAMP HAND IN HAND.
Free! No more being grounded, no more worrying about my parents turning in the guys. Mom and Dad agreed that I could sing in the festival and do whatever I needed to do in the next week to prepare for that. And that's where we were headed now, to tell Brooks we needed to resume band practice. We only had one week to get everything perfect!

"Avery!" I heard from behind me. I turned to see Maricela waving.

I pulled Lauren to a halt as Maricela collided with me in a hug.

"I missed you this week. Brooks told me you've been grounded!" she said. "How did they find out?"

"Well. . . ."

"You can tell her," Lauren said. "I was a jealous tattletale."

"No, it's fine. It all worked out."

"So where are you going now?"

"To talk to Brooks." I couldn't wait to see him. It felt like forever.

"You're heading the wrong way," she said.

I pointed up the hill toward the employee cabins. "He's not up there?"

"No . . ." She tilted her head, like I should already know what she was about to say. "He's in the lodge . . . for band practice."

"Oh! Perfect!" I'd told him I would be grounded for a week. It was exactly a week. Maybe he was setting things up for a final sign. When I walked in the door tonight and he saw me, he'd know once and for all that hope wasn't dead.

I swung Lauren and I around and as we walked away, I called back to Maricela, "You're still going to the festival, right?"

"Yes!" she said.

"Avery, you're going to rip my arm out of its socket," Lauren said as we continued down the path. "I know you're excited to see your boyfriend, but you need to calm down."

I loosened my grip on her. "He's not my boyfriend."

"Technicalities."

"By the way, when we get back to internet," I said, "I'm going to watch every single one of your videos."

"That's days' and days' worth. Don't worry, I'll tell you the ones to skip. I might completely delete my seventh-grade year. Eighth grade has a really crappy few months in the middle . . ." She continued to give me a rundown until we reached the lodge.

D was behind the desk, and if she was surprised to see us, she didn't act like it. She just smiled. Almost too big.

I thought maybe it was all in my head until Lauren said under her breath, "That was weird. Since when is she ever happy to see us?"

I just waved; I was too excited to read into anything D did tonight. We reached the doors to the theater and I swung one open.

Music was already playing, drifting down the aisles and between the seats and filling the whole air. I was happy we were adding the drums and bass to the song; it would make it bigger for the bigger venue.

It took me too long to realize there was a voice mixed in with the music as well. A voice I recognized.

Lauren gave a little squeal next to me. "Ian?"

The lit stage displayed the band members perfectly, each in their designated spots: Kai on drums, Levi on bass, Brooks on guitar, and Ian behind the microphone.

A big smile took over Lauren's face. Then she seemed to realize what I'd realized the second I saw him—I'd been replaced—and her smile faded.

I stopped, going still, and watched as Ian leaned into the microphone, perfectly steady on his feet, and sang "Rewriting History," our audition song. He sounded good.

"Let's go find out what's going on," Lauren said.

"Isn't it obvious?"

"But they can't do that to you," she said.

"Ian was in the band first."

I didn't know if we were talking too loud or someone just finally saw us, but the music stopped in a sporadic waning—guitar first, then Ian's voice, and finally the bass and drums.

Kai raised both hands in the air. "Hi!"

We walked forward. I wasn't brave enough to look at Brooks yet; if I did, I wasn't sure what I'd do.

"You're back?" Lauren asked Ian as we walked up the stairs.

He reached a hand up to his forehead, where his stitches had been. There was now a thin, dark pink line. "Not back, back."

As I started to take a relieved breath, he said, "Just back to sing for the festival."

And just like that, any last bit of hope I'd been holding on to vanished. Hope was for suckers.

"What do you mean?" Lauren said, and I grabbed her hand and squeezed.

"It's fine," I said. "This is perfect. Lauren already has great footage of you guys. She can pick up where she left off." After having seen what an amazing job she'd done on the video for the parents, I knew she could make this band documentary something special. And since I hadn't been honest with her, she had nothing of my singing journey. But she had tons of footage of Ian. She deserved this. It had been her idea from the beginning. "Did you bring your phone?" I asked Lauren.

She nodded but was busy studying my face. Probably trying to see if I was sincere. I was.

"Avery." That was Brooks.

I steadied my breathing and turned toward him, putting a smile on. "Hi." He looked so handsome. I'd missed him.

"You're ungrounded?" He was trying to get his guitar off but seemed tangled in the strap somehow. Finally, he shook his arm in frustration and broke free. He set his guitar down and walked closer.

"Yes, we have been released," I said, smiling at Lauren.

"Who knew being forced to hang out with parents all week in an internet-free environment would be such torture?" Lauren said.

"I think everyone knows that," Kai said.

Lauren laughed. "Whatever."

"Can I talk to you for a minute?" Brooks asked me, nodding toward the curtains and back room. Kai's brows shot down.

"Yeah, sure." We walked, and once behind the curtain, Brooks grabbed my hand. In the room, with the door shut, he pulled me into a hug.

"Hi," he said against my neck.

I smiled, then kissed his cheek. "Hi."

When we separated, I noticed we were standing by the box of T-shirts. I pulled one out. "Bear Heads," I said, noting the picture of a poorly drawn bear on the front. "That should be your band name." I pointed to the number on the ear. "Two Thousand Bear Heads. Has this box of shirts really been sitting here since the year 2000?"

He took the T-shirt from me and tossed it back into the box.

"You obviously don't like that idea?" I teased.

"Avery, talk to me. What happened? What are your parents going to do?"

"Don't worry, they aren't going to tell Janelle," I said.

"That's good. But . . ." He looked up and then shoved his hands in his pockets. "What *are* they going to do? Are you even allowed to be here?"

"Yes, they know I'm here."

"Wait . . ." He raked his hand through his hair. "They weren't going to . . . *Were* they going to let you sing?"

Were. He said the word *were.* "My sister made this video that totally won them over. It was pretty great. So . . . yeah . . . they were . . . but Ian's back, so I get it. How did that happen?" My eyes started to sting. I looked up at the chandelier for a moment to keep my emotions in check.

He paced in front of me. "You said the chance that they'd give you permission was low."

"I know. Exactly." I *had* said that.

"And you got so sick after performing last time, I thought you were just doing it for me. I felt guilty. Then Ian called and said he was better and I told him about the festival and how we were screwed . . . again . . . and he said he could come. I thought it must be . . ."

"A sign?" I said. Signs were really starting to get on my nerves.

"Yes."

I found myself nodding.

He groaned. "This is a mess. Ian moved back up here. Janelle is even letting him stay in the cabin with us, which is so unlike her."

"It's obviously meant to be."

"No, I mean, I thought so at first, but no." He looked so worried and torn as he walked back and forth in front of me.

"Brooks, come here." I grabbed his hand as he passed and pulled him close. "It's fine. I'm fine. Ian will do great. He sounded amazing just now. Plus, he has experience. You're right, I'd probably choke in front of hundreds of people at a festival. I could barely handle five. This is obviously how it was supposed to happen."

He put his forehead to my shoulder and didn't deny anything I'd just said. "You think so?"

"Yes," I said, trying to convince both of us.

"I'm sorry."

"Please don't be. I will be perfectly happy in the audience screaming and lip-syncing with those hundreds of people. I'll be the proud girlfriend."

"Was that your way of asking me to be your boyfriend?" For the first time, I could hear the smile in his voice.

My cheeks went red but still I said confidently, "Yes, yes, it was." Because I liked this boy. I liked him a lot.

He wrapped both arms tight around my waist. "Yes. Absolutely."

My cheeks hurt from smiling so big. He leaned down and kissed me while shuffling us toward the couch. I fell back, sitting first, and then he was next to me, our lips hardly separating with the change of elevation.

"I should probably," he said between kisses, "go back out."

"Yes . . ." I could kiss him forever. "Oh!" I pulled back and freed the page of lyrics from my pocket, handing it to him.

"What's this?" he asked.

"The song. I added the second verse."

"Oh." He read over the words and his smile softened to a look of genuine emotion. "Avery . . . I . . . this is so good."

"You like it?" I'd been nervous but his reaction made me happy.

"You should write songs for the rest of your life." He took my face in his hands and kissed me softly. "You are seriously amazing."

I shrugged. "Sometimes."

He smiled at the paper, then stood. "So good." He headed for the door but looked back when I didn't move. "You coming?"

"I'll be out in a sec."

He nodded and then was gone.

I slumped back onto the couch, my hands running back and

forth over the cushions on either side of me. The feel of the material under my fingertips brought back the memories of all the nights I'd spent in here, my voice going hoarse. It was over. This impractical journey was over. This was a good thing, I told my stinging eyes. Maybe the uncertainty I'd been feeling all summer about myself and my future could go away as well.

Chapter 32

THE NEXT DAY I STOOD BY THE PAY PHONE, STARING AT THE handle, my quarters gripped in my fist. For someone who had yet to actually talk to anyone on the pay phone, I felt like I had spent too much time in this spot.

My plan when coming here was to call Shay, invite her to the festival. That had been in the back of my mind since the day before. I needed some closure and I was sure she did too. Whether that was forgiving her or moving on without her, I wanted to give us both that answer before the end of summer.

I took a breath in through my nose and as I exhaled, the phone rang. My first instinct was to pick it up, but I hesitated. I looked to my left, toward the closest cabins, and it rang again. Most employees were on their shift; that's where Brooks was. It was just after ten in the morning. So when it rang a third time, I picked it up.

"Hello," I said.

"Hi, can I speak with Brooks?" It was a woman on the other end, her voice confident and to the point.

"Um, he's not close by. Can I take a message and have him call you back when I see him?"

"Sure, this is his mom, Teresa. Will you let him know I called?"

"Is everything okay?" I said without thinking.

"Who is this?" she asked.

"I'm sorry, this is Avery, his . . ." Had he told his mother about me? I guessed the only people he'd told were his friends here at camp. He'd said he and his mom weren't exactly on the best terms. "Friend."

Maricela appeared around the building and she pointed at herself and mouthed, *"Is it for me?"*

I shook my head. "Brooks. His mom."

"Hi, Teresa!" Maricela yelled out. "Ask her if she's going to the festival!" Did that mean Brooks had told his mom about the festival? Last I'd heard, he thought she'd be too busy to come.

"Who is that?" Teresa asked.

"Maricela. Here, she wants to talk to you."

I handed the phone over.

"Hi!" Maricela said into the phone like they were old friends, which didn't surprise me. Maricela made friends fast and easily. "No, the festival. It's Saturday in Roseville . . . Yes, you should come . . . Oh, he probably just didn't want to inconvenience you."

So Brooks hadn't told her and now Maricela was extending an invite? I wondered how he'd feel about that.

"Yes, I'll tell him you called. Tell Finn I say hey . . . Okay, bye."

She hung up and then turned toward me. "Hi!"

"You know Brooks's mom?"

"Not really, but between last summer and this one, I've answered at least a half dozen phone calls from her or his brother."

"Finn."

"Right."

"What did she say about coming to the festival?" I asked.

"She said that punk didn't invite her. Good thing I did."

I held up my hands. "And you make sure he knows I had nothing to do with that."

"Chicken," she said.

"I already told you once this summer that I definitely am."

"You are not."

An uneasiness settled into my stomach and I wanted it to go away. "Why didn't you tell me?"

"Tell you what?" Maricela asked. "A little context, please."

"That Ian was back. When I saw you last night?"

"I thought you knew! I thought that's why you were going to band practice."

I felt myself nodding or at least attempting to.

"You didn't know . . ."

This time I definitely shook my head.

"Come here. Let's talk." She pulled me to her cabin and inside, where she shut the door.

I sat on the pile of clothes on the extra bed, not bothering to move them.

"So Brooks didn't tell you about Ian?" She sat on the bed opposite me.

"He couldn't. I was grounded. He thought I wasn't going to be able to sing."

"But you got permission?"

"Yes."

"But . . . ?" She circled her hand in the air, encouraging me to continue.

"But Ian is back."

"Wait, Ian's still singing even though you got permission?"

"It's their band, not mine," I said.

"What?" Her voice rose an octave. "That's dumb! You secured the spot at the festival, not Ian."

"I mean, technically. But I only sang because Ian was gone. And now he's back . . . It's better this way."

"How so?"

"I'm not good at stuff like that."

"Stuff like what?" she asked.

I shrugged one shoulder. "Singing onstage."

She narrowed her eyes. "And yet obviously you are since . . . you know . . . you made the festival."

"This is their thing," I said. "I can't take it from them."

"Huh," Maricela said.

"What?"

She held up both her hands. "Nothing. This isn't my life. It's yours. I'm going to trust your decision."

"Thank you," I said. "Now, tell me everything that's been going on with you the last week."

Chapter 33

"HOW IS BAND PRACTICE GOING?" I WAS SITTING ON THE
floor in Brooks's cabin after lunch a couple days later. It was his day
off, so I felt like I wasn't breaking any rules. Plus, I'd brought my
homework. I hadn't worked on it all summer and I was way behind.
"You guys going to be ready in three days?"

He was reading over my government assignment. He looked up
with my question. "I'd forgotten how much we all fight, but yes,
we'll be ready."

"The pros of a two-person band," I said.

He bit his lip, the worry line between his brows back.

Why had I said that? "Sorry, I just meant that fewer people
equals less fighting."

"It really does." He handed me the paper. "I think it's just asking
you to draw out the government branches in an actual tree form."

"Like literally draw a tree?"

"It seems like it."

"I did that in elementary school," I said. "I guess I should've saved my work."

He smiled. Brooks was a little different in his room, more relaxed. His shoes were off, his hair was ruffled, and he was smiling so much easier. I liked seeing him this way.

While I began drawing a tree on a paper, he picked up his guitar, sat down on his bed, and began to play.

"Have I mentioned that you're an amazing guitar player?" I said.

"I'm showing off for you," he said. "So you'll think I'm cool." He was teasing me for how I'd called him cool the other day outside my cabin.

"Be careful or I'll take it back," I said.

He smirked, put his guitar off to the side, and crawled to where I sat.

I help up my hand with a laugh. "Don't, I'm trying to work."

"Don't what?" He rounded my outstretched hand and kissed my neck.

"Homework. Homework needs to get done."

"I thought this was your vacation. Homework shouldn't exist on vacation. Only summer. That means sun and water and relaxing."

"This isn't sun or water or relaxing," I said as he continued to kiss my neck and cheek.

"What?" Faking shock, he hopped to his feet and scooped me up in one swift motion. "This isn't relaxing?"

I let out a scream.

He laughed as he carried me to his bed, where he dropped me onto the mattress. "How about that? Is that more relaxing?"

I smiled up at him and grabbed the front of his T-shirt, pulling him down into a kiss. "Much, much more relaxing." I cuddled up against his side as he joined me on the tiny bed.

"I agree." He ran a light finger down my arm, causing the hairs to stand on end.

"Brooks?"

"Yes?" His blue eyes focused on mine.

"Will you sing the song we wrote? I never got to hear the melody of it."

"What?"

"The second festival song. The love song. I want to hear it."

He smirked. "You've heard me sing. It's not pretty. Maybe *you* should sing it for *me*."

"I don't know it. That's my point."

He sat up and retrieved his guitar from where he had propped it against the wall. I sat up as well, crossing my legs.

He finger-picked a melody.

"That's pretty," I said.

"Yeah? Do you like this chord progression better?" He played one while softly singing along. "Or this one?" He switched it up to a slightly different sound.

"I like the first one," I said.

"Yeah, me too." He paused in his playing. "Do you remember the words?"

"Yes."

"Okay, then sing with me. My voice isn't strong enough to carry it alone."

I nodded and we sang the words he had written. Words I was pretty sure were about this summer and our journey, at least that's what my verse was about. Singing in front of him was so much easier now. I hadn't realized how much until that moment.

He stopped playing before I got to the second verse.

"Did I get the words wrong?" I asked.

"I forgot how much I love your voice."

My breath caught in my chest. "You're sweet."

"Yes, I am." He stretched over his guitar and kissed my cheek.

"Hey, I forgot to ask you if everything was okay at home. What did your mom need?"

"My mom?"

"Did Maricela give you the message?"

He tilted his head as if listening and then jumped up. "Someone is coming."

"Is that a problem?" There was no way it was Janelle. Would D barge into his cabin? She was the only other one I wouldn't want seeing us alone right now. But he seemed nervous, so I slid off the bed and started to gather my homework.

"Leave it," he said, looking around the room.

I was looking, too, because there was really no place to hide. There was a knock at his door, followed by the rattling of the handle. I practically dove under his bed, then rolled once, ending up on my back. He stacked my homework, shoved it in my backpack, and pushed it under the bed with me just as the door creaked open.

Kai's loud voice filled the room. "Hey, I thought you were coming to town with us to eat."

I let out a breath of relief and started to roll back out but stopped when Brooks said, "No, just wanted to look at the notes you guys gave me for the song."

"You're not mad that I don't want to do the mushy love one, right? It's not our style at all."

They weren't singing the love song? Why had Brooks pretended they were a minute ago? A pang of disappointment that surprised me radiated through my chest.

"It's fine," Brooks said. "We're a band. You all outvoted me."

He was mad; I could hear it in his voice.

"Great. You *are* mad," Kai said.

"Yes, I am." That was all he said. He didn't expand.

"What's that all about anyway? The band breaks up for a couple weeks and suddenly you're writing love songs?"

My eyes were staring through the bed's wooden slats, at the underside of the water-stained mattress above me. And that's when I saw something else up there too. Sitting between two of those boards in an intricate web was a big, fat, black spider. I took a sharp breath.

"Is this about that Avery girl?" Kai finished.

"That Avery girl?" Brooks asked in an annoyed voice. "You mean the one you've known all summer and who got us into the festival?"

Please, spider, don't move.

"Whatever, Brooks," Kai said. "Are you in love with her or something? Are you guys together now?"

"No, of course not."

I flinched and my movement or the breath I let out with it made the spider's web shake. Its legs twitched. I bit back a scream.

"Good," Kai said. "Because I haven't forgotten the huge lecture you gave me at the beginning of the summer about getting involved with Lauren. I wouldn't want you to lose your job over a summer fling with a guest. I know how much you need this place."

I was trying to process what was being said while a spider was seconds away from descending on my face.

"Did you just come here to harass me, Kai, or did you need something?" Brooks snapped.

"Thought you might want to hang but I guess not." There were footsteps and then a slamming door.

I slid out from under the bed as fast as humanly possible and then shook my whole body while simultaneously wiping it and saying, "Spider, spider, spider," over and over.

Brooks took me by the shoulders and studied my front, then circled to my back. "You're clear," he said.

I shook out my hair, just in case. "There's a massive spider under there. You might want to kill it later."

"Noted."

I dragged my backpack out and gave it a thorough inspection as well before putting it on my back.

"Are you leaving?"

I was halfway to the door. "Yes."

"Avery, wait. Don't be mad."

"I'm not mad." I was beyond mad.

"Yes, you are. Let me explain."

I turned to face him, arms crossed.

His eyes twinkled. "So that's what your angry face looks like."

"Just talk, Brooks."

"I'm sorry, I'm sorry. Where do I start?"

"You're not singing the song? Why did you pretend like you were? You told me you loved the song."

"I didn't know how to tell you. I wanted to sing it. I think the song is amazing. And the band liked it too; they just didn't think it fit our vibe."

"Wish I would've known that before I wasted hours on it."

"I'm a jerk. I'm sorry, you have every right to be mad. But the song is great. Maybe we can record it together."

Why did that offer feel like it was made out of pity? I didn't need his pity. He was supposed to be my boyfriend. "Why doesn't Kai know about us?" I felt so stupid. Like, once again, I had let a ball hit me in the head. I was obviously way more invested in this relationship than he was. It felt like Trent and Shay all over again.

"I know, that sounds bad, doesn't it?" he said. "But you remember when I talked to him about Lauren. . . . I was super harsh with him. Told him if I found out he was with her, I'd turn him in myself. So I didn't think I could then tell him that I was breaking the same rule I'd told him not to break. I doubt he would've reported me to Janelle, but he can't keep his mouth shut. He would've spread it all around employee village and she would've found out."

I wanted to believe his explanation so bad, but that would make me naïve all over again. "But what about Mari?"

"What about Mari?"

"They like each other and he seemed to be able to keep that a secret from the wider employee population."

Brooks clenched his teeth. So he knew that secret too. He was just hoping I didn't. "I promised I wouldn't tell."

"And you couldn't swear him to the same secrecy?"

"I should've, you're right. I've done this all wrong."

"Have you? Maybe you've done it just right. Sneak me around all summer while you decide if I'm worth the trouble. So what did you decide? That there is no future for us? What was it you said a minute ago? Summer is only for sun and water and relaxing? I'm sure this is starting to feel like none of those," I said.

"You're twisting my words, Avery."

"You didn't answer the question. Was Kai right? Am I just some summer fling?" I was walking toward the door again.

"That's not why you're leaving. You're leaving because you're scared. You're scared that if you let me in, if you really trust me, you're going to get hurt. You always run away when you're scared."

"I didn't run away from trying out for the festival, did I?"

He smiled. "That's because you had me." He reached out like he was going to give me a hug.

I pushed his arm away. "Screw you, Brooks." With those words, words I'd never said before to anyone in my life, I stormed out the door.

Chapter 34

MAYBE MY PARENTS WERE RIGHT—I WASN'T ACTING LIKE myself. What *had* gotten into me? I didn't like feeling this way at all. This fire that was burning in my chest, I wanted to throw a blanket over it and smother it out. I had run nearly all the way back to our cabin from Brooks's. And when I got there, Mom and Dad were leaving.

"Where are you guys going?" I asked.

"Just on a walk," Dad said. "We were told there's a trail that leads to a lookout. Do you want to join us?"

"Yes, I do." I wanted to do anything to get my mind off the fight I'd just had with Brooks. Had I broken up with him? I wasn't sure we could come back from what just happened. Did I want to? I deposited my backpack just inside the door and we headed off through the dusty trails of camp until we came to a dirt path just before the lake.

I didn't tell my parents I'd been on this trail before. On the Fourth of July. I let Dad direct us. Mom pointed out squirrels and butterflies and birds as we walked. When we'd been walking for a while, Dad cleared his throat. "Kid . . . about the video . . . about what I said."

"It's fine, Dad."

"Hear him out, honey," Mom said, putting her arm around me.

I nodded and he continued. "If I ever made you feel like I wasn't proud of you, I didn't mean to. I am so proud of you. We're similar in so many ways, and I'm sure that makes me harder on you. I'm sorry."

"It's okay, Dad. I know you love me."

"Good, because I do. You've been so distant this summer, and now I understand why."

"Yeah, I should've just talked to you. I'm bad with confrontation."

He chuckled. "Me too."

"I'm sorry I've been different this summer. I'm trying to get back to my old self."

We watched some kids holding on to a jump rope and pretending to be a train chug by us.

"How is the singing going?" Mom asked when it was quiet again.

"Oh, Lauren didn't tell you?"

Dad shook his head and so did Mom.

"It's not. Ian, the guy with the head injury," I reminded them, "came back. He's singing now."

"Oh." Mom's mouth turned down with the news.

"That's probably a relief for you," Dad said. "I know how nervous you get."

"Yeah . . ."

"I thought you wanted to do it," Mom said.

275

"I mean . . . I don't know. I enjoyed it. But I wouldn't say I *wanted* to do it. I only did it in the first place to help Brooks." I shrugged. "Now he has his original group."

"Right," Mom said.

"Oh, which reminds me. Even though I'm not singing, can we still go to the festival and watch? Please? Lauren needs to record and it would be really fun, I think."

My parents exchanged a look and then Mom said, "Yes, I'm sure you both will have fun."

"No, I mean all of us."

"You want me and Mom to come to your hip music festival?" Dad asked. "Won't we cramp your style?"

"If you use words like *hip* and *cramp,* possibly, but I'm willing to risk it . . . seeing as how I have zero vibe."

Dad smiled. "Wow, it's been forever since we've been to a music festival."

"Did you go to Woodstock?"

Mom gasped. "Woodstock? How old do you think we are?"

"Joke. It was a joke."

"It better have been," she said.

"So speaking of the festival, I'm thinking about inviting Shay too."

Mom and Dad exchanged another look and this one didn't seem as favorable.

I was confused by that reaction. "You remember my best friend."

Mom swatted at a fly by her hair. "We do . . . It's just . . ."

"What?"

"I overheard you on the phone with her before we left. I thought maybe you two were taking a break."

"You know what happened? Why didn't you say anything?"

"I thought you'd come to me if you needed to. But you seemed to be handling it well."

I looked at Dad to see his expression. To see if he was in the know as well. He seemed to be. "Yeah, we had a major fight and I need to talk to her in person."

Mom nodded. "You've always been a good peacemaker."

"And you've always said that's a good thing."

"It is." She squeezed my hand. "Honey, there aren't enough in the world. But I also want to make sure you're not giving away bits of yourself in an effort to keep the peace."

"I don't think I am."

We were all quiet as we needed our breath to climb the last stretch of hill. And when we reached the top, we stopped and looked out over the lake below. Last time I was up here, fireworks were exploding and I was telling Brooks I'd sing with him. The memory pricked at my eyes.

While staring out at the dark water, Mom said, "Sometimes staying in the box we've made for ourselves is so easy. It's comfortable and familiar in there. And a lot of times, the people around us want us to stay in there, too, because that's how they've always known us: in that box." Mom patted Dad's arm like she might be referring to him in that moment. "But sometimes we start to change, grow, and the box begins to get small and cramped. And yet we fight to stay inside because the walls are high and climbing out seems harder than staying."

I knew what she was saying, didn't need her to interpret it, but I immediately felt my defenses go up. "That was a nice metaphor, Mom."

Dad heard the sarcasm in my words. "She's right, Avery. I've always told you that you and I are so similar. But you are your own person and I don't want you to ever feel like you're stuck."

Mom took hold of my hand. "I love you so much and think you're amazing. I'm not saying you need to do anything differently. But if you aren't feeling like yourself lately, if you're feeling uncomfortable and a bit cramped, maybe it's time to start climbing."

Chapter 35

"UGH." IT WAS HOT IN THE CRAFT ROOM. MAYBE IT WAS ALL these kids. Breathing their hot air. Maybe it was the afternoon sun beating on the large window. Why were we in the craft room anyway? I looked at the crappy friendship bracelet I was halfway done with. It had been over fifty-two hours since my fight with Brooks and my talk with my parents and my mind wouldn't turn off. I'd let this stew for fifty-two hours. The quality of my bracelet was a very good representation of my inner battle.

"What?" Lauren asked.

"Mom's right."

"About one thing in particular or do you just mean that every single thing she utters is fact?"

"I only said I didn't want to sing because I didn't want to make anyone mad." I wanted to sing and that was the problem here. I hadn't been mad that Brooks didn't tell Kai about *us*. Well, I mean, I was sort of mad about that, too, but I understood why. What I didn't understand was why Brooks hadn't stood up for me. Why he hadn't said that *I'd* earned the spot, not Ian or Kai or Levi. Because I had. I'd earned that spot, and Brooks just let the guys take it away from me. Even went as far as to tell me I'd only been able to do it because of him. *That* was what I was mad about. That was what I had every right to be mad about. "I want to sing," I said again with more confidence.

Lauren's mouth dropped open but then she nodded. "It's about time!"

"It's about time what?"

"That you figured that out. I've been waiting."

"I don't want to let myself run away from this. I always run away from scary things, from conflict." Like Brooks. I didn't stick around to talk out our argument, to let him hear my side. To tell him how I really felt about singing. One sign of trouble and I was gone. I needed to fix that too.

"I'm excited!"

"You won't be mad at me about the documentary?"

Lauren sighed a big heavy sigh. "Avery, you were doing so good there! It shouldn't matter if I'm mad, which I'm not. All that matters is that you should sing. You tried out. You made it. Ian didn't make it. Kai and Levi didn't make it. You and Brooks did."

"I'm going to tell them. It's not too late, right? The festival is tomorrow!"

"No! It's not too late. You need to let Brooks know," Lauren said. "The last couple nights at practice he's looked like a sad little puppy dog. Put the poor thing out of his misery."

I wasn't sure me telling him I wanted to sing would make his life any easier, but at least we'd put it all on the table. I smiled, knotted off the end of my bracelet, and tied it to my sister's wrist.

She stared at it, curled her lip, and said, "You did a crappy job on this."

"I know!" I said, standing. "But you're a good sister and I want you to have it."

She laughed and gave me a little push. "Go get your music festival."

○ ○ ○

And that's how I ended up on my way to Brooks's cabin, where I was going to tell him exactly how I felt . . . about everything.

I paused in front of his door and listened for a moment. There was nothing but silence. Odds were that he wasn't there, but I knocked anyway.

When I'd left the lodge, it had been close to five. He was probably finishing up his list for the day and heading to dinner. As my mind calculated the most efficient route to the dining hall, a voice called out to me, "He's not here."

I turned. D stood on the porch of her cabin. "Okay." I pointed down the hill. "I'll just . . ." Crap. How could I explain why I was in employee village standing at Brooks's door?

She locked her cabin and joined me as I walked. "He left camp," she said.

"Oh, okay. W-wait, what? Left where? Did he get in trouble? Did he go home? Is everything okay with his dad?"

She was shaking her head midway through my sputtering questions. "No, not home. He and the guys decided to spend the night in Roseville tonight so they wouldn't have to deal with traffic and stress tomorrow. They left like thirty minutes ago."

"Oh."

"Brooks didn't tell you?"

"We . . . no." That completely derailed my plans. Maybe this wasn't meant to happen. No, I was done letting supposed signs dictate my choices.

"Just let it be, Avery," D said. I hadn't thought she remembered my name. "Ian is back."

So she knew a lot more than any of us thought. She'd probably seen me in the back room practicing with Brooks those two weeks. "Why didn't you turn us in?"

"Because I obviously care about what happens to him. You couldn't care less." Did she *like* Brooks? Is that why she'd hated me all summer?

"This is about his future, not just this summer," I said.

"And you think his future is you?"

"I think his future is music," I said.

"And with the band, he can have both this summer and music."

"So you're saying you're going to tell Janelle if I sing with him?"

She let out a frustrated sigh. "No, I'm just saying that if you really cared about him, you wouldn't."

I really didn't feel like I needed to defend myself to her, but I was going to anyway. "I disagree. This isn't a one-sided relationship.

We've always looked out for each other. I'm taking this shot and I think he'd want me to."

I picked up my pace to get ahead of her. At the end of the path I turned around. "Thanks for not telling on him!" Because I knew she wouldn't. She was probably in love with him. And maybe I was too. But that had nothing to do with this. This was for me.

Chapter 36

"IT WAS LIFE IS BEAUTIFUL, IN VEGAS FIVE YEARS AGO," DAD
said from the driver's seat.

"That was at least seven years ago," Mom said.

"Seven?" Dad said. "No way."

They were arguing over when the last time they'd been to a
music festival was as we drove to Roseville.

"It was," Mom responded. "I remember because Avery was ten
and she told me she was old enough to go."

Lauren, who'd been recording my parents on her phone, panned
it over to me. "Do you remember said incident?" she asked.

"In fact, I do not."

"Didn't happen," Lauren said.

Dad didn't react to Lauren; he just said, "Really? Seven?"

Mom continued to think of several other things that had happened that same year.

Lauren put down her phone and reached over to grab my hand.
She still had the crappy friendship bracelet I'd made tied around her

wrist. "It will work out," she whispered. Apparently, I wasn't hiding my nerves well. I hadn't told my parents what I was doing . . . again. But this time it was because I didn't want to disappoint more people if it didn't happen, not because I didn't think they would support me.

"I want both," I whispered back. "And I'm afraid I'll only get one."

"What do you mean?" she asked.

"I want to sing," I said. "But I also want Brooks."

She pursed her lips. "You think he'll break up with you over this."

"We got in a big fight a few days ago. I think we broke up. Or he thinks we did. I don't know."

"A fight doesn't mean you broke up."

"I know, but I said 'Screw you, Brooks.' Pretty sure there's only one way to take that."

Her eyes went wide and then she started laughing.

"It's not funny," I hissed in a whisper.

"Imagining you saying that is very funny."

"He didn't stand up for me with the band, Lauren. I know I should've fought for myself, but he should've too."

She squeezed my hand, her laughter gone now. "He's a good guy."

"I know, but that doesn't necessarily mean he wants me to sing with the band when he has another option."

I kind of hoped she'd disagree with me but she said, "I know."

◎ ◎ ◎

Energy poured through the late afternoon air as we parked the car and walked across a dirt lot toward the sound of music in the distance. People were everywhere, talking and laughing. Once we hit pavement, the smell of food competed with the music for air space. Food trucks and lights directed the crowd down the path and to a big grass field crowned with a large stage.

"This is bigger than I expected," Lauren said from next to me. She had her phone out and was taking it all in.

"Don't remind me," I said, but she didn't have to. I could see for myself. This was bigger than I had expected too.

"You girls want food?" Dad asked. "I want food."

"No, we want to find a place to sit," Lauren said.

I held up the blanket we'd brought.

"Okay, keep your phones on," Mom said. "We'll text you once we have food."

"Texting," Lauren said as though remembering something from the distant past. "What's that?"

Mom gave Lauren's arm a little shove. "You're such a smart aleck."

"Yes, I am," Lauren said.

We continued walking as our parents went to check out the food offerings. We came to a large board that was propped up against a tree. "Look, it's tonight's lineup."

Lauren let her phone travel down, stopping on each band name. About halfway down I saw a name that made me gasp. *Two Thousand Bear Heads.*

"What?" Lauren asked, panning her phone to me.

"I suggested that name. He used it." A little hope bloomed in my chest with this revelation.

"And how does that make you feel?" Lauren asked.

286

"Good . . . nervous . . . ready."

"You're so ready," Lauren said, then clicked off the phone and tucked it away.

I stood on my tiptoes and looked around, as if that would help me see Brooks in the crowd. The stage was empty and I realized it was canned music coming out of the speakers. "Do you think the bands are backstage?"

"I don't know. I think they probably stay out here until it's close to their time to go on."

My phone buzzed in my pocket and I jumped.

"Was that you?" Lauren asked, patting her pocket like she wasn't sure.

"Yes," I said.

"Are you going to look?"

"Yes." I pulled out my phone, hoping I was going to see a message from Brooks but it was from Shay.

I'm here. Where are you?

My heart skipped a beat and I turned in a circle as if she could see me where I stood.

"Where is he?" Lauren asked.

"No, it's Shay. She's here."

I texted her back, telling her we were past the food trucks. A few minutes later, I heard her calling my name. She was in the grass area, like she'd been here for a while, heading my way.

"Avery!"

I faced her. She was Trent-less and that was a really good first step. "Hi," I said when she reached us.

"Hi," she said in a soft voice. "Thanks for inviting me. I wasn't sure . . ."

"If we were ever going to talk again?" I asked.

"Yeah."

"I wasn't sure either. But I'm happy to see you." And that was true. "Tonight is a new moon. It's a chance to start over."

"Tonight's a new moon?" Lauren asked.

"It is. It's been twenty-nine days since the last one."

"Since when have you started keeping track of the moon cycle?" Lauren asked.

"Since twenty-nine days ago," I said.

Shay smiled at our exchange. "I like new moons," she said.

"Me too," I responded.

Lauren was recording again next to us. "Take a look at the leading lady of Two Thousand Bear Heads."

"What does that mean?" Shay asked.

"I have a lot to fill you in on." I wasn't sure everything was going to be exactly the same between us—that might take a while—but I was happy we were giving ourselves a do-over.

"But that's going to have to wait," Lauren said. "Because here comes Brooks."

Chapter 37

MY HEART SPED UP IN MY CHEST AT THE SIGHT OF BROOKS. It got even faster when he gave me a tentative smile. I returned it.

Kai spoke first. "You're here." He gave Lauren a side hug, then looked at Shay. "I don't know you."

"This is my best friend, Shay, from home," I said.

Brooks, who had been looking at me, shot his eyes over to Shay. Then he gave me a look of concern.

I cleared my throat. "Oh, um, Shay this is Kai, Brooks, Ian, and Levi."

"The band," Shay said. "Nice shirts."

With her words, I glanced down at their shirts. They were the brightly colored tees from the back room at camp with the big bear heads on them. Brooks wore an open flannel over his and Kai a black blazer.

"Matching outfits," I said with a nervous laugh. Seeing Ian all confident and decked out and happy made me feel guilty.

Lauren nudged me with her elbow and I took a deep breath.

"Can we talk?" Brooks said, his eyes on mine, and I swallowed the words that were about to come out.

"Yes," I said. "I mean, no. I mean, in a minute? I have something I need to say first."

Out of the corner of my eye, I saw Lauren hold up her phone. It made me more nervous. Kai in all his charismatic glory gave me a smile. "Speak away, Avery."

I gnawed at my lip. This was supposed to be my moment, the "speak my truth and claim what I earned" moment, but unfortunately even though perspective could change in an instant, I was still me. I still didn't like conflict. And this was hard. Harder than I wanted it to be. I liked Ian. He was a nice guy. But that didn't mean I deserved this less, I reminded myself.

"I told him," Brooks said. "You were right, I should've and now I did. I told all of them."

I turned toward him, confused for a second. "What?" I said the word in the same moment I realized what he was saying. He probably thought I wanted to tell everyone about me and him. "Oh. That's . . . good."

"I'm so confused," Shay said.

"We like each other," Brooks said. "Well, I like her. And I don't normally make public announcements about, well, about anything, but she . . . you . . . make me want to open up. I like you, Avery, and I hope you still like me."

I melted a little. His public declaration was going to derail me because it was so sweet and it made me want to hug him and not make his life complicated with my demands. I fisted my hands. No.

I was going to do this and possibly risk what was standing in front of me all vulnerable and cute.

"I do still like you," I said. "A lot. But that's not what this is about."

"It's not?" he asked.

"Avery, you got this," Lauren whispered from my side.

I smiled at her and mouthed, *"Love you."* Then I took a deep breath, looked at the band, and said, "I should be singing today. I want to sing today."

Ian's perfect smile faded. Brooks's attention went straight to Ian, a worried expression on his face. Levi and Kai began talking to each other but I couldn't quite make out what they were saying.

I pressed forward. "I earned the spot. If I hadn't sung that day, the band wouldn't have made it."

"You haven't practiced with us," Kai said.

"No, *you* haven't practiced with *me*," I said. "I know I can do it. I know these songs. I wrote these songs. And honestly, I think I'll give you the best shot at winning." To Brooks, I added, "One of the judges said we had tons of chemistry."

Brooks had his unreadable face on and I was beginning to think I'd been wrong in the car. I had thought I could only walk away from tonight with one of the things I wanted. But it hadn't occurred to me until this moment that it was possible I could walk away with neither. I couldn't let that fear stop me. "I should sing," I said again, this time only to Brooks.

"She's right," Brooks said, shocking me. "We only made it because of her. I didn't think you wanted to. I thought you were just doing me a favor. That it made you super nervous. But if you want to, you earned it."

Ian was nodding when I turned to him with an apologetic expression. "Avery, yes, this is yours if you want it. I should've talked to you about it."

"No, I didn't own it. But I'm owning it now."

"Can I sing backup?" he asked.

"Of course!" I had one more declaration, though, that I wasn't sure he was going to support. "But we're singing the love song."

Kai groaned. "I won't play if we sing that song. That song doesn't even fit with a full band. It sounds ridiculous."

"You're right," Brooks said, and just when I thought he was going to back up Kai, he finished with, "You can all leave the stage for the second song. I'll play acoustic while Avery sings."

Kai felt betrayed. It was more than obvious by the hurt expression he now held. "You're only saying all that because she's your girlfriend."

"I'd say it either way," Brooks said. "It's the better song."

"Thank you," I whispered.

"Whatever," Kai said, and walked away.

"He's such a baby," Levi said. He held his fist out for me and I bumped it. "Let's rock today and don't worry about Kai; he always comes back. I should know."

I smiled.

The loud screech of feedback rang through the air. A voice came over the speakers. "Welcome, music fans!"

Everyone cheered.

All the nerves and emotions that had been raging through me

during the confrontation seemed to come pouring out, melting my muscles. I needed a place to sit and decompress before we actually had to perform. So I turned and walked away.

"Avery," Brooks called.

I kept walking, not because I didn't want to talk to him, but because when we did, I wanted it to be in some hidden corner away from everyone, away from the speakers. I made it to the row of food trucks just as Brooks fell into step beside me. I cut left, to the back side of the trucks, and finally stopped behind a rattling generator and took a seat on a patch of grass.

He sat down next to me.

"I shouldn't have said *screw you* the other day," I blurted out. "I've never said that to anyone before."

"Wow, I'm the first? I feel so honored."

"It didn't feel as good as I had hoped it would."

He laughed but then his eyes went serious. "I know why you said it and I'm sorry. It all came out wrong. I didn't mean that you couldn't have done this without me. I just meant that I had your back that day when you were scared. You could've done it without me. You're amazing."

"I don't want to do it without you," I said.

"I don't want to do it without you either. I'm so glad you came today. That you're going to sing. The songs didn't sound the same without you."

"Do you think Kai will play the first song with us?"

He rolled his eyes. "Yes. He's fine."

I reached my hand out for his and he was happy to comply. "Thanks for telling the guys about us."

"It was never about not wanting them to know." He shifted closer to me. "You know that, right? I *do* see a future with you. We're practically neighbors. I mean, if you didn't think I'd take that as a sign, you don't know me at all."

I smiled. "Plus, you owe me all your future children. So there's that."

"Well, that's only if we win today," he said.

"Then I guess we better win."

He laughed.

"Should we go practice?" I asked.

He nodded but didn't move.

I stretched up and kissed him.

Chapter 38

WE HEADED BACK TO WHERE WE'D LEFT THE GROUP. MY head was buzzing from pride and my lips were stinging from kissing Brooks.

I reached out and grabbed his hand as we walked. He looked back at me, a smile on his face, and gave my hand a squeeze.

"Hey, you'll still like me even if we don't win today, right?" I asked.

"I'll still like you even if we lose every day for forever."

"That sounds like a lot of losing," I said.

"Avery!" My name rang out above the music. I turned and saw Maricela holding a corn dog in the air while weaving through the crowd. She was flanked by Tia and Clay. When she reached us, she threw her arms around me. "Ian said you're singing! Is that true?"

I nodded.

"I'm so proud of you!"

"That's awesome," Tia said.

"Is that what you asked the moon for?" Clay asked.

I laughed. "I guess, sort of."

"That's a solid wish," he said. "I need to up my moon game next year."

"Have you talked to Kai?" I asked Mari, wondering if he'd cooled off yet. I really did want the full band to play for the first song.

"No, I haven't seen him in a while." She pointed her corn dog at Brooks. "Is your mom here yet? I want to say hi."

"No. Why would she be?"

"Because I invited her," she said in a *duh* voice. "Which I shouldn't have had to do. You should've invited her."

"You really like to stick your nose into everyone's business, don't you?" he said, but his voice didn't sound too angry.

"Yes, I do."

"Well, get ready to be disappointed. Because she won't be here."

"You want to make a friendly wager?" she asked.

I relinked hands with him and squeezed.

"Oh really?" Mari said, pointing between the two of us. "Nobody ever listens to my advice."

"I do," Clay said.

"Oh please," Tia said. "You don't listen to anybody."

Brooks narrowed his eyes at Maricela. "What advice have you been giving?"

"I said you're a hot mess."

"Well, that's true," he responded.

"That's not true," I said. "*Life* is messy. It's better when we try to get through it together."

"Okay, Socrates," Clay said.

Tia elbowed him. "Don't be dumb. She was making a good point. We're all in this together."

"Aw!" Maricela said, and smooshed us into a group hug.

◎ ◎ ◎

I felt different this time as we stood off to the side of the stage, waiting to go on. The screams of hundreds of people were drowning everything out, but also vibrating through me, like the energy was holding me up, urging me on. Levi and Ian were on my left and Brooks was on my right, but Kai was still MIA.

The band onstage finished their song. "Should we borrow their drummer?" I asked as a joke, but Brooks seemed to seriously consider it.

"No," he said after a moment. "We'll be fine."

"Please welcome to the stage Two Thousand Bear Heads!"

More cheering pulsed through the air. I jumped up and down a few times to try and channel my energy, then said, "Let's do this." I walked with purpose up the stairs and to the microphone. I grabbed hold of it with both hands. "Hello, Roseville!"

I smiled as the volume of the crowd rose again. "Our first song for you tonight is called 'Rewriting History.'"

A drumroll rang out and I turned to see Kai sitting on his stool.

"Told you he always comes back," Levi said from my left.

Brooks swung his guitar around to his front and gave me a wink. "You got this."

And I did.

It wasn't as scary as I thought it would be to look out at the sea of faces, especially when I saw some familiar ones that had worked their way closer to the stage—Lauren, Shay, and Maricela.

This time through the song was ten times better than the last. It wasn't because I was perfect, because I wasn't. But I had a whole band backing me up. Kai busted out a drum solo when I missed a cue and Ian chimed in when I forgot a lyric. And I finished out the second verse strong and beamed at the audience when they clapped.

Brooks stepped up beside me and leaned into the microphone. "Isn't she amazing? Avery Young, everyone!"

My smiled stretched even farther.

Brooks jerked his head to the side and the rest of the band filed off the stage while he switched his electric guitar for his acoustic. Then he was beside me at the microphone again. "Our second song tonight is called . . ." He stopped. "Did we ever name this song, Avery?"

"I don't think we did," I said, sharing the mic with him and meeting his eyes. "I've just been calling it the love song . . . because . . . well, because it's about our journey this summer." I stopped and felt my cheeks go red. "I mean, I think that's what it's about. Is your verse about me?"

"Of course my verse is about you," he said. "Is your verse about me?"

"Yes."

At least half the crowd let out a big "Awwww!" and my cheeks got even redder. I hadn't meant to share that discovery with an audience, but either way, my stomach was filled with flapping wings of happiness.

Brooks kissed my cheek to another wave of "Awww!"

"You ready?" he asked.

"Yes."

The melody flowed through his fast-moving fingers as he picked the strings. This time I did look at him, not because I needed to but because I wanted to, and I sang.

"Sometimes the stars align
Sometimes the path seems moved for you
Sometimes it's just in time
Exactly when hope was almost through
And sometimes is all I need
And more than I deserved
So I read into every sign
Because sometimes, yes this time, sometimes brought me you

Sometimes the moon goes dark
And the path ahead unclear
Sometimes I miss my mark
And I'm living in constant fear
But sometimes is all I need
To grow and try and learn
Because sometimes, yes this time, sometimes brought me you"

Brooks played the last note and we held each other's gaze for another three beats. I could hear my blood flowing in my ears, muffling the noise of the applause.

"You're pretty cool," Brooks whispered.

I leaned in and kissed him.

◊ ◊ ◊

"You are amazing!" Shay screamed when I found her, Lauren, and Maricela after our set. "Who even are you?"

I laughed.

"She's Avery Freakin' Young," Maricela said.

"No, seriously," Shay said. "You've only been gone for seven weeks, right?"

"I'm glad you came," I said to Shay.

"Me too."

Lauren hadn't said a word and I thought it was because she was recording, but then I noticed her phone wasn't out. "Did your battery die?" I asked.

She shook her head, her eyes shining.

"Lauren," I said. "Are you okay?"

She pulled me into a hug. "You sounded so good."

I had forgotten she'd never heard me perform.

"I'm so proud of you."

I hugged her back, closing my eyes. "You didn't really think I could do it, did you?"

"No!" she said, but then smiled. "Yes, I did."

"Thank you."

She squeezed me hard before we pulled apart. I looked around, my happiness from seconds ago wavering. "Where are Mom and Dad? Are they mad about me and Brooks?"

"No," Lauren said. "They were just here." She looked around, then pulled out her phone.

As she brought up her text messages, I caught a glimpse of Dad across the way. "We don't need it," I said.

"No?"

I pointed.

"Who's he talking to?" Shay asked.

She was right—he was talking to someone, and at first I was just mildly curious, but as we walked closer, I realized it was Brooks. I picked up my speed but then saw the smile on Brooks's face, and by the time I got to his side, my dad was smiling as well.

"Hi," I said. "Everything okay over here?"

Mom hugged me. "Good job, honey."

"Thank you, Mom."

Dad took me in his arms and kissed the top of my head. "You were so brave."

I smiled against his chest.

"When do you find out if you won?" he asked, and I laughed.

"At the end of the night, sir," Brooks said.

"You got that all on video, right?" Dad asked Lauren.

"Of course. What do you think I am, an amateur?"

As they talked about Lauren's video, I looked over at Brooks.

"I promise to never run away from things I want, even if they scare me."

"Good promise," he said.

I took his hand. "I want you to make it too."

"You think I run away from things that scare me?" he asked.

"Far away," I said. "What is this, like four hundred miles?"

301

He smirked. "Good point." Something over my shoulder caught his eye and his smile slid off his face.

"What is it?"

"Mom?" He moved around me and was soon embracing a dark-haired woman.

"I think he owes me something," said Maricela, who had just joined us. "Did I forget to finish that bet earlier?"

"I think you did."

Brooks turned back toward me and held his hand out.

"Wish me luck," I said to Mari, and she gave me a shove in Brooks's direction.

"Mom, this is my girlfriend, Avery," he said when I was at his side. "Avery, this is my mom, Teresa."

"Avery, nice to meet you. I enjoyed the performance."

"Thank you."

Brooks seemed awkward, a bit uncomfortable, but I had a feeling his mom being here was a huge step in the right direction.

◎ ◎ ◎

I wanted to say it didn't matter if we won the prize or not that night, that we'd won either way. That we'd learned things about ourselves and proven things we couldn't have any other way. But that wasn't true. It *did* matter. And as we sat on the blanket, my back against Brooks's chest watching the other bands, I wanted the win so bad. Not for me this time. The singing had been for me. I wanted the win for Brooks. For his future.

So when they called our band's name at the end of the night

as the grand prize winner, I cried. And as we stood on the stage, hundreds of people clapping and cheering for us, I'd never felt so proud and happy in my life.

Brooks put his arm around me. "You were right," he said. "We couldn't have done this without you."

"We did it together," I said through my tears.

Brooks squeezed my side. "If you don't stop crying, you're going to make me cry," he said.

I wiped under my eyes. "I can't stop."

Kai, who was on my other side, scooped me up in a lung-crushing hug. "If you think you can walk away from this band now, dude, you need to think again."

"Don't crush my girlfriend," Brooks said.

Kai released me and moved on to Levi and Ian.

"Hey, Avery," Brooks said.

"Yeah?" I looked at his smiling face.

"Repeat after me. I am amazing!

"You are amazing," I said.

"No." He wrapped his arms around my waist. "You were supposed to say *I*."

Chapter 39

THE CAMPFIRE WAS GOING STRONG BEHIND THE EMPLOYEE cabins. I had my chair as close as possible to Brooks's chair, a little separated from the group. We watched them throw twigs and sticks into the flames while daring each other to do increasingly dumber things. Lauren was up, and Tia had just dared her to eat a chip that had been on the ground for who knew how long. Days? Lauren was studying it carefully in the fire's glow.

Brooks was playing with my fingers. "I can't believe you're leaving tomorrow."

"I know. How are you going to survive the rest of summer without me?"

"It will be very, very boring."

I slouched farther down in my seat, letting my head lean on the backrest. I stared up at the stars. "But when you get home"—I flopped my head to the side so I could look at him—"we'll see each other?"

"Is every day too much?"

I smiled. "No." I brought his hand to my lips and rested it there. "And you got your megasign. You won the festival."

"*We* won."

"So music is in your future."

"Yes." His eyes seemed as bright as the fire with that thought. "I'm going to buy some studio time and go from there."

"Good plan."

"Will you sing with me? At least for our songs?"

"What's in it for me?" I teased.

He circled his free hand in front of his chest, as if referring to his entire self. "All this BS."

I laughed. "Deal."

Acknowledgments

Every new book I get to put in the world feels like a happy bonus that I am grateful for. Thanks to my readers for making it possible for me to keep writing. This book was important to me. Avery reminds me a bit of myself as a teenager. I was a pleaser. A peacemaker. And while I think this is an admirable quality, I also had to learn that sometimes making someone else happy came at the expense of my feelings or happiness. I had to learn to stand up for myself even when the other person was kind and deserving. Being able to write Avery doing this was very cathartic for me, and I'm grateful for this story and this opportunity.

Thanks a million to Wendy Loggia for pulling out the best in this book and helping me shape it just right. She is a rock star editor and I'm happy to be working with her. And thanks to the whole team at Delacorte Press: designer Cathy Bobak, associate director of copyediting Colleen Fellingham, production manager Tracy Heydweiller, SVP and publisher Beverly Horowitz, president and publisher Barbara Marcus, editorial assistant Alison Romig, managing editor Tamar Schwartz, and copy editor Carrie Andrews. I love this book cover so much (seriously, you should go stare at it for a minute and then come back)! Thanks to the cover designer, Casey Moses! And the talented cover artists, Anne Hard (jacket artist) and Jill DeHaan (custom lettering).

I've been with my agent, Michelle Wolfson, for ten years now!

Ten! I feel like I've known her forever, and am so glad she is part of my life. My writing career and journey wouldn't have been the same without you, Michelle, and I am so grateful to have you!

As always, thanks to my amazingly supportive husband, Jared, and my kids, Skyler, Autumn, Abby, and Donavan, who have always been proud of me. I'm so proud of *them* and the fun, unique, awesome people they've become.

I wrote this story in the midst of a global pandemic (just like many others who had to keep working and caring for others in uncertain times), and my weekly Zoom calls with my girls, my distanced workout sessions with friends, and my walks with my sister got me through. So thank you to: Stephanie Ryan (who is also my very talented bio-photographer sister), Brittney Swift, Emily Freeman, Mandy Hillman, Megan Grant, Candice Kennington, Renee Collins, Jenn Johansson, Bree Despain, Natalie Whipple, Michelle Argyle, Elizabeth Minnick, Misti Hamel, and Claudia Wadsworth.

Like I say in nearly every book, having a big family helps me write families. And I have a big, fun, awesome, loud, loving family. I'm grateful for all of them. My mom, Chris DeWoody and her husband, Mark Thompson. My dad, who passed in 2006 and who I think about and miss often, Donald DeWoody. My brothers and sisters, Heather and Dave Garza, Jared and Rachel DeWoody, Spencer and Zita DeWoody, and Stephanie and Kevin Ryan. My husband's parents, siblings, and spouses: Vance and Karen West, Eric and Michelle West, Sharlynn West, Brian and Rachel Braithwaite, Jim and Angie Stettler, Rick and Emily Hill. I also have thirty nieces and nephews. Plus great-nieces and great-nephews! And I love all these people with all my heart. I feel so lucky to have such a big, close family.

Stay tuned for more books coming your way. And please reach out to me on social media. I love connecting with readers! Thank you again for reading my books!

About the Author

Kasie West is the author of many YA novels, including *The Fill-in Boyfriend, P.S. I Like You, Lucky in Love,* and *Listen to Your Heart.* Her books have been named ALA-YALSA Quick Picks, JLG selections, and ALA-YALSA Best Books for Young Adults. When she's not writing, she's binge-watching television, devouring books, or burying her toes in the sand of the Central Coast. Kasie lives in Fresno, California, with her family.

kasiewest.com

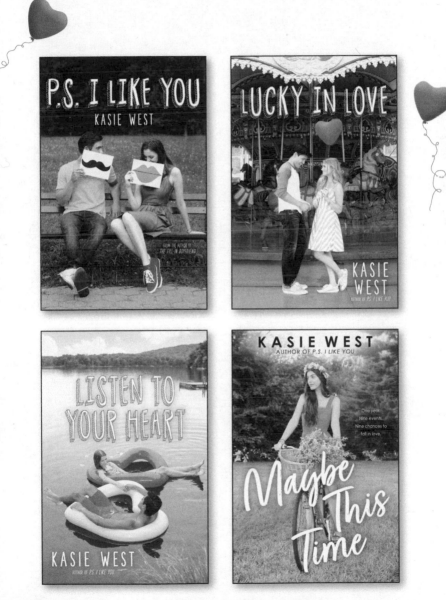